"What will you say to him?" Bethany asked again.

"I might just tell him what's kept me here," he said.

"What's that?"

"I'm Amish. I believe in this life. I want my own *kinner* to have the kind of childhood I did."

That was simple enough, and she highly doubted it would be enough. Micah had left because he didn't believe in their life anymore. He'd been very clear about that.

"And I might tell him that he's left behind a beautiful girl," he added, his voice low. "And that she's beautiful and insightful and . . . that he's dumber than a fence post if he thinks he can do better anywhere else, *Englishers* included."

Bethany blinked back a mist in her eyes. "That's sweet."

"It's the truth," he said. "He beat the rest of us to you, and maybe I'll tell him what it was like for me to watch him move forward with you, what it felt like to see him make you smile the way he did. Maybe he should know how lucky he was to have gotten to you first, because if he'd been a few weeks slower, I would have asked you home from singing myself."

She turned toward Isaiah, her breath lodged in her throat. "Is that true?"

"Yah."

Books by Patricia Johns

THE BISHOP'S DAUGHTER

THURSDAY'S BRIDE

JEB'S WIFE

THE PREACHER'S SON

Published by Kensington Publishing Corp.

The Preacher's Son

PATRICIA JOHNS

ZEBRA BOOKS
KENSINGTON PUBLISHING CORP.
www.kensingtonbooks.com

Chapter One

"Her name is Lovina, and she's twenty years old." Isaiah fixed the bus station ticket agent with an iron stare. "She's short—about this high. Blond hair, blue eyes . . . Amish."

The bus station in Bountiful, Pennsylvania, was located at the far end of Main Street. A fresh busload of *Englisher* tourists had just arrived, and the people came flooding out of the bus, phones held aloft already—although what they figured was worth recording in a small-town bus station, he had no idea.

"That sounds like half the Amish girls we see," the man said with an apologetic shrug. "The name doesn't ring a bell."

"She'd have taken a bus out—I know that." Isaiah didn't have any other information about his sister, only that she was gone. She'd left a note on her neatly made bed that they only found after lunch—two pages, one for them and one meant for Johannes, her steady boyfriend. Lovina said she wasn't coming back, and that she wasn't holding Johannes to sharing this life of shame with her. Their *daet*'s crime and imprisonment was too much for her to handle. He'd been arrested six months ago, gone to trial faster than anyone expected, and two weeks previously, he'd started his three years in prison. It had been horrible for all of them, and Lovina didn't think she had a place with the Amish anymore. The letter, along with the extra note for Johannes, was still in Isaiah's pocket.

It wasn't like Lovina was the only one dealing with that shame—Isaiah had inadvertently helped his *daet*, not knowing that the charity Abe was collecting for was a sham. How *could* he have known? How could he have even guessed? And Lovina thought she had it worse than the rest of them? *She* had the right to leave?

"I'm sorry," the man said with a shake of his head. "There were about three Amish families who left this morning. I think there were a few young women."

"She would have been alone," Isaiah pressed. "I think . . . I'm pretty sure."

But now that he said it, he wasn't positive. Even if she didn't leave with Johannes, she might have left with a friend.

"No one stood out," the man replied. "Sorry."

Isaiah sighed, then tapped the counter. "Thanks anyway."

"Good luck."

Isaiah needed more than luck. He needed divine intervention, but he wasn't sure their family even deserved it at this point. Maybe it was only fair that Lovina left like the others. This winnowing of the faithful was only happening because of Isaiah's father, Abe Yoder. And Isaiah couldn't help but feel somewhat responsible, too. The police had let him off the hook and hadn't pressed charges. But the community wasn't so quick to forgive.

His *daet* had ruined not only the family name, but also Isaiah's personal reputation.

Isaiah turned from the ticket window and stopped short when he spotted Bethany Glick. Her gaze was locked on him reproachfully.

"Have you seen my sister?" Isaiah asked, winding around some plastic seats until he reached her.

"Have you seen my fiancé?" she retorted bitterly.

"Micah?" He felt like the wind had been knocked out of his chest.

"He left," Bethany said. "I thought he would have told you."

"No . . ." His friend had seemed odd the last couple of weeks, but everyone was on edge. "When did he leave? Today?"

"Three days ago," she said, licking her lips. "But yah. He's gone."

Micah leaving—it was unbelievable. But he and Lovina weren't the only ones . . . there had been at least eight other young people who had jumped the fence since Abe's arrest. Isaiah's wasn't the only life being torn apart, and he met Bethany's bitter gaze.

"So . . . the wedding?" he asked hesitantly. It hadn't been formally announced, but Micah had been a close enough friend that Isaiah had known about his engagement to Bethany all the same.

"It would appear that it's off," Bethany said, and her chin trembled as she said it. "Which sister is gone— Lovina or Elizabeth?"

"Lovina." He pulled his sister's letter from his pocket, but he didn't hand it over. Her gaze landed on the paper, then slid off of it again. She'd have received a letter of her own from Micah no doubt.

They stared at each other for a couple of beats, and then Bethany nodded toward the counter where parcels were kept.

"I've got to pick up a package," she said, and she gave him a curt nod of farewell, then turned to leave.

"I didn't know about my *daet*, you know," he called after her. "I was tricked, too."

She didn't answer. Isaiah had told her *daet* the same thing when Abe was first arrested. He'd told anyone who would listen to him—the bishop, the elders, friends, family . . . He hadn't known! But the damage was done.

The *Englisher* tourists stopped to look at him, and Bethany headed for the counter to take care of her business. He gritted his teeth. The last thing he wanted was an audience with cell phones recording him.

His life had been turned upside down even more than anyone else's—and that was a daring claim at a time like this. The Amish who'd been defrauded lost money—and so had he, for that matter. The family farm was repossessed to help pay back the victims, as well as their savings. But Isaiah had lost more than money. He'd lost his *daet*, and their good name.

Across the depot, a female worker hoisted up a large box to the counter, and Bethany hesitated. It would be more than she could comfortably carry—even Isaiah could see that from here. She wanted nothing to do with him, but he couldn't very well leave a woman to carry that alone either. He sighed and headed over.

"That looks heavy," he said.

"I'm fine," Bethany replied.

"Yah?" He stood back. "Okay, then."

Bethany slid the box off the counter and grimaced as she lifted it. Something different glittered in those dark eyes—something sharper than reproach. Was that hatred he saw?

Bethany headed toward the door with slow, careful steps. The box slipped from her grip once, but she caught it and continued on out of the depot without looking in his direction again.

Isaiah scanned the bus depot one last time. Coming here had been wishful to begin with. He'd hoped that something would have held his sister back, given her pause . . . given him time to get to her before she disappeared from their lives for good.

Isaiah pushed out the front door and the fresh, spring air engulfed him. The town of Bountiful was a farming community that had managed to lure some tourist attention because of the Amish who lived in the surrounding area. Many Amish shops lined the streets—a bakery, two craft shops, a gift shop, several eateries, and a fabric shop. Sandwiched between a gift shop and a craft store there was the Glick Book Bindery, a little specialty shop that served people all over Pennsylvania, thanks to a website that was kept up by an *Englisher* company that catered to the Amish's online needs.

Bethany paused a few yards down the sidewalk, hoisting the box once more. It slipped in her hands again, and she set it down, rubbing the small of her back. Isaiah sighed and picked up his pace, catching up with her in a few brisk strides.

"Give it to me," he said irritably.

"Isaiah, I don't need—" she started, but Isaiah bent

down and picked up the box, hefting it up onto one shoulder. He cast her an annoyed look.

"I didn't know, Bethany. And the police questioned me thoroughly. If they had reason to think I was involved, I'd be in jail, too, right now."

"You're still the one who convinced my *daet* that stupid charity was a good thing," she snapped. "I have no idea how my *daet* is ever going to retire now that the money's gone. And to make it worse, my fiancé is gone because of your *daet*. When your father—" Her voice cracked, and she swallowed. "You're asking a little much of me if you want me to be grateful for the use of your muscles. You could have saved yourself the time."

Isaiah adjusted the box on his shoulder. "This might not be the right timing, but Micah asked me to look out for you if anything should happen to him."

"Nothing *happened* to him," she said. "He left."

"Fine. He's gone. I'm here—let me carry the box!" It may have seemed melodramatic at the time when Micah had mentioned it to him, but a promise was a promise, and Isaiah was nothing if not honest.

Isaiah angled his steps across the street toward Glick's Book Bindery. Bethany pulled the door open for him, and as he came into the dim shop, he had to pause to let his eyes adjust a moment.

"Ah, Isaiah." Nathaniel Glick sat in front of a vise that held a book in place. He ran his fingers over the spine and pursed his lips. It wasn't quite a hello.

"Just carrying the box over for you," Isaiah said, sliding it onto the counter. He glanced around the shop—it was only Nathaniel and Bethany here, by the looks of it. And

Isaiah had been looking for work for over a month now and getting nowhere.

"Right. Thank you," Nathaniel replied, putting down the book he was working on and heading over. "I would have fetched it myself, but we've got an order due by tonight. That looks like a full order of leather. I thought this was the half order—"

"You're shorthanded," Isaiah said.

"Yah." Nathaniel pulled a box cutter out of the pocket in his black work apron and sliced the tape on the top. He pulled back the flaps and fingered a piece of leather. "Micah's gone."

Isaiah glanced over at Bethany, and he felt the heat climb his collar. Bethany was watching him, the same pursed lips as her *daet*.

"I know that my *daet*'s crime shook the faith of a lot of young people," Isaiah said. "And I've told you before— like I've been telling everyone else—that I didn't know this was a fraud. I thought it was a plan to help Amish families in time of need. It seemed legitimate, and I'd think you'd understand a son not immediately suspecting his own *daet* of fraud."

Nathaniel nodded slowly. "I do sympathize there, Isaiah."

"You aren't the only ones to have lost someone. Lovina jumped the fence, and we only found her letter after lunch today." Isaiah licked his dry lips. "But I'm not leaving our community. I'm Amish, and I'm going to trust in our community's ability to forgive because I don't have much else to hold on to right now."

"I told you before that I forgave you."

In the strictest Christian sense, of course, Nathaniel

had. How could a man ask Gott for forgiveness if he wouldn't forgive his brother? But what Isaiah needed was something a little more tangible.

"I need work," Isaiah said, his voice low. "As you know, the farm is gone now, and I've been finding some bits of work here and there, but no one really trusts me anymore—"

Nathaniel eyed him speculatively. "And you're staying with your uncle now, right?"

"Yah. My sisters and me. But I've got to contribute, and Uncle Mel already has enough help on the farm with his own sons." Mel had only taken them in because he felt obliged. They weren't exactly welcome. Isaiah was hoping to do more than contribute—he wanted to get a place where he could support his sisters on his own . . . if Lovina ever came back.

"Why should I trust you if no one else does?" Nathaniel asked bluntly.

"If I had been a part of my *daet*'s crime knowingly," Isaiah said quietly, "do you think I'd come ask you for help? I can only face you because I was duped, too."

Isaiah could feel Bethany's presence behind him— her anger like the heat from a woodstove—and his own shame rose to match it. He was here, hat in hand, hoping for a job.

Nathaniel heaved a sigh. "I do need someone to help out here. Bethany and I can't do it all alone, and my sons are off in Indiana at my brother's farm, so . . ." Nathaniel seemed to be thinking out loud.

"I'll work hard," Isaiah said quietly. "I'll do anything you need around here. I'll earn back your trust and respect.

But I need work, and Mel's not keen to have me helping out on the farm."

"Yah, your uncle lost a good amount of money, too," Nathaniel said quietly. "So I can understand his bitterness right now."

"I do, too, but my *daet*'s in prison now, paying for what he did. But I figured we're connected in this. Bethany was the one who told the police about the conversation she overheard—"

"You can't blame me!" Bethany erupted behind him.

"I'm not." Isaiah glanced over his shoulder, the heat creeping up into his cheeks, then he turned back to Nathaniel. "I'm not blaming anyone but my father. I'm just asking for a chance to work." He swallowed. "I need to take care of my sisters. Please."

Nathaniel sucked in a breath, then nodded slowly. "You make a point."

"Daet?" Bethany seemed to want to say more, but she wouldn't. This was her father's decision to make, not hers.

Isaiah licked his lips, watching the older man hopefully.

"I'll try you out," Nathaniel said after a beat of silence. "For a couple of weeks until we get these orders completed. You'll have to learn fast and do as I say. I can't promise more than that."

Isaiah felt a flood of relief. It was something—and who knew? Maybe he'd prove himself indispensable after all.

"I'm grateful," Isaiah said quickly. "Thank you."

"Starting now," Nathaniel said. "It's now or I'll change my mind."

He had that letter to deliver to Johannes, but a few hours wouldn't make much difference anyway.

"Yah. Thank you. I'll start now," Isaiah said.

"Bethany will show you where to put the leather."

Isaiah glanced over his shoulder again, and this time he saw Bethany's full, angry stare directed at him. This was Micah's job . . . Isaiah knew why this stung her, but he didn't have much of an option. A paying job with a family who resented him was better than no job at all.

He'd be grateful for a couple of weeks of employment.

Bethany picked up the box of leather, hoisting it with all her strength, and headed toward the back room where they kept their supplies. Isaiah being here was insulting— even if her *daet* didn't seem to recognize that. Isaiah hardly deserved this job! Isaiah didn't belong here— Micah did. And he wasn't going to slide in and take her fiancé's place on any level.

"I can help—" Isaiah said as she came past him.

"No, I'm fine," she said, even though her muscles were screaming.

"Bethany . . ." There was warning in her *daet*'s tone, and Bethany grimaced. Her *daet would* insist that they forgive in more than just words. But she wasn't ready for that.

"Okay," she said, softening her tone.

Isaiah took the box from her grip, and she led the way through the shop, past the worktables, the book presses with the heavy slabs of metal, around the sewing frame that stood with lines of thread already piercing the spine of a book in progress. She opened the storage room door and stepped in first, letting him follow her.

The back room was lined with aged wooden shelves

that lined every wall except for the one that sported a tall window, letting in the bright afternoon light. The shelves held various styles of end sheets, Davey boards in different sizes, bottles of glue, a roll of muslin, rolls of thick binding thread, leather thongs, and large, leather sheets. . . . There were bottles of dyes, boxes of gold leaf, and various instruments that Bethany had never seen used before, but still had a place on these shelves just in case her father might need them for a specialty project. This was the family business, and the Glicks had been book binders for four generations now.

Bethany gestured to a small, wheeled cart. "You can put the box there."

Isaiah did as she asked, and she turned her back to him, picking up the last sheets of leather and arranging a tipping pile of Davey boards to make room for the new shipment.

"I can't believe Micah left," Isaiah said. "He didn't breathe a word to me."

It wasn't reasonable, but she felt a bit of victory that she was the one Micah had confided in.

"He wanted me to go with him," she replied, her voice tight.

"Where'd he go?" he asked. "Maybe my sister went to the same place."

"It's some Mennonite newcomer housing place in the city. It's for immigrants, but Amish use it, too," she said.

"Oh . . ." Isaiah swallowed. "He's gone English."

It was a shameful thing to do—escape to the easier path—but Micah wasn't the only one who should be ashamed of himself.

Bethany turned to face him. "He left because of *your* father."

"I know. So did my sister. Micah will come back once he's had some space to think."

But Bethany wasn't so sure about that. When Micah left he'd told her a few of his secrets—he'd been questioning their Amish ways for a couple of years already, and he'd been sneaking out to a Mennonite Bible study in town. He'd been slipping in that direction longer than anyone had suspected. When Abe was sentenced it was all the proof Micah needed that their way of life was in no way spiritually superior to other Christians, and he couldn't pretend to believe something he no longer did.

"So, he *told* you he was leaving?" Isaiah asked when she hadn't said anything.

"Yah."

"And you didn't tell anyone to try to stop him?" Isaiah asked. Was that recrimination in his eyes?

"For what?" she asked with a weak shrug. "To keep a man who didn't want to be here?"

Bethany pulled back the flaps on the box and lifted out the first fifteen or twenty leather sheets. Isaiah followed her lead, and together they began to refill the shelf. There were several different shades of brown, some dark green, and a blood red. She liked the red color best, and she paused, running her fingers over it. It was a color that would never bind an Amish book—too fancy.

"He loves you," Isaiah said, his voice low.

So Micah had claimed, too, when he held her so very close and promised her that it wouldn't matter if they did some things before marriage, because his love for her would never waver, and they'd be married in a matter of months anyway. . . .

"Not enough to stay," she said bitterly.

"I know him—" Isaiah started.

"How well?" she snapped. "He was tempted to jump the fence a couple of years ago before we started courting, but it was your *daet*'s preaching that changed his mind. So when your *daet* ended up being a liar and a thief, it changed things for him. So if you knew him so well, why didn't you see this coming?"

"You were just as surprised," he countered.

"Of course I was. But don't go telling me you know what was happening in his heart—none of us knew."

Isaiah took over in emptying the box, his strong arms nudging hers aside as he pulled out another handful of leather.

"What does your *daet* say to all this?" she asked.

"I don't know." His voice was low and rough.

"Does he claim to be innocent?" she demanded. "Did he believe anything that he preached? Because he was powerful when he spoke. He could boom from the front of a service, telling us how ugly *our* sins were, and how desperately *we* needed Gott's mercy . . ."

Isaiah looked over at her, his eyes filled with misery, but he didn't answer. There was something in his expression that made the bitterness in her heart seem unnecessarily cruel.

"Yah, I found his preaching to be rather powerful, too," he said with a weak shrug. "You aren't the only one who was duped by my *daet*, too."

"What does he say for himself?" she pressed.

"I have no idea. I haven't spoken to him."

Bethany hadn't expected that answer, and she eyed him uncertainly. His *daet* was shunned, but . . . he hadn't spoken to him about it at all? Not even before the official shunning?

The bell tinkled over the door in the other room, and Bethany brushed past him and headed back out to where her father was working. An *Englisher* couple came inside, looking around in idle curiosity. They looked middle-aged—a tired-looking man with a receding hairline of gray-tinged hair and his blond wife with fluffy hair and earrings that glimmered beneath it. Jewelry always drew Bethany's gaze—not because she wanted it, but because it was so out of place in Plain society. It seemed garish, almost.

The door opened again and Tessa Weibe, Micah's mother, came into the shop behind them. Tessa didn't look around—she smoothed her hands down her white apron that already had a few dusty streaks on it, and her gaze sought out Bethany. Her stomach dropped—she hadn't spoken to Tessa since Micah left, and that conversation had been an emotional one for both of them.

"Do you really bind books here?" the *Englisher* woman asked with a smile.

"Yah." Bethany's gaze flickered over the *Englisher* woman's shoulder to Tessa. "We do, everything from self-published memoirs to academic theses."

"Now that's neat," the woman said. "How long have you been doing this?"

"We're the fourth generation," she replied.

"And you get enough work to keep you all going?" the woman asked, looking around in that curious way *Englishers* had.

"Yah. We manage." These were all ordinary questions Bethany fielded on a daily basis. The *Englishers* were curious, and they liked the idea of work being done by hand, so long as their hands weren't the ones doing it.

"Can we get a picture with you?" the woman asked, lifting her phone hopefully.

"I'd rather not," Bethany replied. "But you're welcome to look around."

The *Englishers* moved over to get a better look as Nathaniel ran the bone tool over a leather cover, smoothing down any bubbles of air that might be caught beneath it, and packing down the leather tightly into the creases. The woman took a surreptitious photo with her phone, and Bethany ignored it, moving over to where Tessa stood by the door.

"How are you holding up, Bethany?" Tessa asked quietly.

"I'm . . . okay," Bethany said. "You?"

"I'm not okay." Tessa smiled shakily. "Have you heard from Micah yet?"

Bethany shook her head.

"He hasn't called the neighbor to talk to us, or his *daet*'s work at the assembly plant. He knows how to reach us, but—" Tessa's lips quivered. "I thought of all of us, he'd call you. It's been long enough for him to get to a phone."

Bethany shook her head again. "No. And I don't think he will."

"What about the wedding?" Tessa asked. "What about all your plans?"

"He walked away from them," Bethany said, her throat tight.

"Did he say that, in so many words?" Tessa pressed.

"Daniel and I were talking about that after we saw you last, and we wondered if maybe he hinted that you should wait for him . . . He loves you, Bethany. I know he does! And while a boy might not come home for his *mamm*, he will come back for the girl he loves."

"Tessa, I wanted to marry him; I did! I was looking forward to our wedding and starting our life together, but he's gone! I can't bring him back any more than you can!"

The *Englisher* couple turned to look at them in open curiosity, and Bethany realized that she hadn't kept her voice down. She'd been speaking in Pennsylvania Dutch, though, so the *Englishers* wouldn't understand the words.

"Will you wait for him?" Tessa asked, turning her body to afford them a little more privacy.

"He's left me," Bethany said, her voice shaking.

"But he might come back yet," Tessa pressed. "I don't believe he'll stay away completely. I think he's upset, but we raised him well, and I know how he feels about you. I can't imagine him just walking away from everything so easily. I know my son!"

Bethany didn't answer, but her throat grew thick with rising tears.

"Would you wait for him—just a little while?" Tessa pleaded.

"I don't have any suitors banging down the doors," Bethany said. "And I'm heartbroken. I'm not ready to move on."

"So you'll wait—" This point seemed to matter to Tessa, that all their hopes and plans might still be salvaged. And there was a part of Bethany that wished all this could be rewound and go back to the way it was a week ago—when Bethany's thoughts were fixed on her wedding plans, not on how she was supposed to move on from them. But something inside of her hesitated now.

If Micah came back again, would she still want to marry him? Would she want a husband who was capable of abandoning their life so easily? He'd been hiding an awful lot from everyone very successfully. . . .

"No," Bethany said, clearing her throat.

"No?" Tessa whispered.

"He left me," Bethany said. "I can't just hang on a thread, waiting. We aren't married, and he's free."

And as much as it hurt, so was she.

Tessa nodded, pressed her lips together.

"I have to respect that," Tessa said, and she blinked back tears.

"I'm sorry," Bethany whispered, and Tessa nodded and moved toward the door again. The *Englishers* watched them in unabashed curiosity, and Bethany turned back to the door just in time to see it swing shut. She couldn't give Tessa what she wanted—but deep down what Tessa longed for was for Micah to come back. This wedding— it was the carrot to lure her son back again.

Bethany brushed past the *Englishers* and went behind the counter toward the next book waiting to be bound. This was a large order of literary journals being bound for a private library. There were thirty-five years' worth of journals, and she'd only made it through the first five years.

"Are these for sale?" the *Englisher* woman asked, pointing to some leather-bound, blank journals piled next to the cash register. They were made in various sizes.

"Yah, those are for sale," Bethany said. "The prices are on the backs."

Bethany went to the cash register while the *Englisher* woman selected three journals of various sizes and colors.

"My nieces are going to love these," the woman said, pulling out her wallet, and then she glanced over her shoulder toward the door again. "Was that about a man?"

"Pardon me?" Bethany said.

"The woman who came in and was talking to you— that was about a man, wasn't it? It's just that some things are universal, and even though I couldn't understand your language, I understand other women, and that tension looked familiar."

"It . . . was," Bethany admitted hesitantly.

"A boyfriend or a husband?" the woman asked.

Bethany was tempted not to answer, but there was something so sympathetic in the woman's eyes that Bethany sighed. What did it matter at this point? Everyone in her community knew about her heartbreak. "An ex-fiancé. That was his *mamm* . . . his mother."

"Ah, that's hard," the woman said softly. "I won't pry into details—I know how obnoxious that is. But can I just say . . . You don't have to chase down the right man. The right man stands by you—just try and get rid of him! My husband there? He's been by my side for nineteen years, and he proposed three times to get me to marry him. I've fought off cancer twice and had a mastectomy and he's still here."

Bethany smiled faintly. The gentleman in question was still watching Nathaniel work, his attention absorbed in the other direction. Ironically enough, that sentiment, that the right man would be by her side, not in some Mennonite newcomers' facility, was what Bethany was trying to tell Tessa. Micah had left, and that simple fact said everything.

"That's some common wisdom," Bethany said. "I agree wholeheartedly." Bethany rang up the sale and put the journals into a paper bag. "Thank you. You have a good day."

"Hang in there," the woman said, and her husband turned then, and the couple left the store together.

Bethany headed back over to the literary journals awaiting her attention, and she looked up to see Isaiah watching her uncertainly.

"We need to strip the magazine covers off these journals and keep them in order for binding. I've got that started. But next, we trim them down with the paper cutter. That takes some strength." She eyed him uncomfortably. "I'll show you how."

She might not want to work with Isaiah, she might be adrift in her own anger and grief over her fiancé's abandonment, and Isaiah might be the very last man she wanted to rely on, but she'd make use of his farm-honed physique. As much as she hated to admit it, they needed a man's strength to get these orders done, and Isaiah was the man who was here.

Chapter Two

That evening, Isaiah unhitched his buggy and brushed down the horses. The stable was dimly lit, dust motes dancing in the light that came through the narrow windows. The horses shuffled comfortably in their stalls, the sound of teeth grinding oats filling the silence.

After working with Nathaniel at the book bindery, he'd gone by the Miller farm to see Lovina's boyfriend, Johannes. Isaiah had given him the letter—and for a few minutes, he'd watched as a torrent of emotion raged through the young man.

"How could she do this? No . . . No . . . she wouldn't just go. I saw her four days ago—and she wasn't considering this! I know she was upset, but . . ."

"It's my father," Isaiah had tried to explain. "It's because of him."

"Where did she go?"

Johannes knew as much as Isaiah did. And after an hour of comparing their letters, Isaiah left. There was nothing else he could do. Everything had changed—and he didn't even recognize his life anymore.

Not too long ago, Isaiah's life made sense. He'd always

been a serious guy—and he'd gotten baptized right after his Rumspringa, making his permanent choice to be Amish. He was going to be a preacher like his *daet*, and the elders and other preachers were supportive. They weren't anymore, though.

Isaiah felt hollow tonight, and sad. It was just sinking in now as he tended to the horses that Lovina wouldn't be in that house, and for the thousandth time since he'd first seen her letter, he sent up a silent prayer for her safety.

The stable door opened and Seth came inside carrying a bale of hay by two metal hooks.

"You're back," his cousin said, dropping the hay into the corner with a grunt. "I'm guessing you didn't find Lovina?"

"No," Isaiah replied. "You were right. She was long gone. I asked at the bus depot, but no luck. I just came back from the Miller place. They don't know any more than we do."

"I didn't want to be right," Seth said.

"Yeah, well, unless we want to go after her—" He eyed his cousin for a moment, wondering if that were an option. Would Seth help him, or would he be on his own in that? Maybe Johannes would go with him.

"She didn't say where she was headed, though," Seth countered.

"No, she didn't." Isaiah came out of the stall and shut it firmly behind him. "There's a Mennonite group in Pittsburgh that helps out lapsed Amish kids, though. She might have gone there."

"There are about four of them within a hundred miles of us," Seth retorted.

"Micah's gone, too," Isaiah said. "Apparently, he went to one in Pittsburgh."

"Micah's gone?" Seth breathed.

"Yah."

"Are you serious?" Seth shook his head. "I don't believe that!"

"Yah, well, Bethany told me today. He left three days ago."

Micah, Seth, and Isaiah had hung out together since their teens, and the three of them had been best friends. Seth rubbed his hand over his face and let out a sigh.

"How's Bethany taking it?" Seth asked.

"Not well," Isaiah admitted. "She blames my *daet*. So do I, for that matter."

"Remember when all three of us had a thing for Bethany?" Seth asked quietly.

Bethany Glick was beautiful, funny, and she made a great pie. She was the girl they all declared they'd court just as soon as they were done with their Rumspringas, but Micah got there first, and Seth and Isaiah had respected that.

"I thought you're taking Mary Fisher home from singing," Isaiah pointed out, unsure why he was feeling irritable with Seth for that memory.

"I am," Seth said, and he shrugged weakly. "I'm just . . . I can't believe Micah's gone, too."

They both headed toward the stable door together. Seth hung the hay hooks on the wall, and they both took one last look around before opening the door to summer evening sunlight—low and warm.

"So . . . you saw Bethany today?" Seth asked.

"Yah. I got a job with her *daet* at the book bindery," Isaiah replied.

"Yah?" Seth's eyebrows went up.

"The thing is, you and your brothers have the farm covered, and I just seem to be bothering your *daet* by being here, so—"

"That's not true."

"Sure it is."

"You're family, Isaiah," Seth said.

"Yah, and you know how our fathers got along. It doesn't always matter."

Isaiah and Seth arrived at the house and headed up the side stairs that led to the mudroom. As they went inside, he could already smell the cooking and heard the murmuring voices of his younger female cousins and Aunt Rose.

"So, you started work, then?" Seth asked.

"Yah. I worked for a few hours. Maybe next week I'll be able to give your *daet* a bit of money, and that might make us less of a burden." Isaiah pulled off his boots and then headed to the sink and the thick bar of soap. Outside, Isaiah could hear Uncle Mel and his other two cousins making their way toward the house.

When Uncle Mel and his younger sons Bart and Vernon came inside, Isaiah and Seth headed into the kitchen, where the girls were already putting the food onto the table.

"I hope you're hungry," Rose said with a smile.

Isaiah saw his sister, Elizabeth, at the kitchen sink washing dishes, and she looked over her shoulder at him, her expression granite. What had her day been like with the girls here? At least Isaiah had been able to get a job off this farm.

"Any news on Lovina?" Elizabeth asked, her voice rising above her cousins' chatter, and they all fell silent.

"Uh—" Isaiah cleared his throat. "No. I asked around, and I went to see the Millers this evening, but nothing. Johannes had no idea where she might have gone. He's just as stunned as we are."

"She took the bus, I imagine," Collette said. "She'll be long gone."

Collette was eighteen and had only just come off her Rumspringa. She seemed to think herself an expert on life at large.

Elizabeth cast her cousin a flat look. "It's dangerous out there."

"Micah left, too," Seth added.

"The bishop came by to see us today, and he told us about Micah," Collette said.

"Maybe she's with Micah, then," Dawn offered. "Maybe he came to get her."

Dawn was only fifteen, and she had blue eyes and blond hair much like Lovina's. In fact, people who didn't know the family directly often mistook them for sisters instead of cousins.

"Micah's engaged to Bethany, Dawn," Isaiah retorted. "He wasn't running off with my little sister. Micah might be a lot of things, but he's not like *that*."

"I agree with Isaiah," Seth said. "Micah wasn't looking around for another girl."

Isaiah exchanged a look with Seth. How well did either

of them really know Micah, after all? But no one wanted to admit how much one person seemed capable of hiding.

"Lovina isn't like that either," Elizabeth cut in. "She wouldn't run off with an engaged boy."

"Not so engaged now that he's left," Collette said primly.

Isaiah didn't answer that because his younger cousin had a point. Micah had left Bethany high and dry, and he wasn't exactly her fiancé anymore. Elizabeth set a shallow dish of brown noodles on the table, and Dawn came up behind her with a platter of fried chicken.

"But it's not safe out there," Dawn added. "Remember Solomon Lantz? He jumped the fence and he's in jail now!"

From what they'd heard, Solomon had been implicated in a robbery, and he'd been sentenced to a year in jail. Was he in the same prison as Abe? Isaiah had no idea. All any of them knew was that there were dangers out there, and the Amish weren't immune.

"And that's why you stay Amish," Aunt Rose said pointedly.

"Bishop Lapp actually came to see you, Isaiah, but you weren't here," Dawn said quietly.

"Yah?" Isaiah looked between his cousins, then toward his aunt.

"He wanted to see how you and your sisters were doing," Aunt Rose said. "And . . . he had to be told about Lovina."

Of course—Lovina leaving wouldn't be kept a secret from the bishop, but Isaiah deeply wished they'd have a few more days before having the religious officials know the worst.

"Is she going to be shunned, then?" Isaiah asked woodenly.

"No, no, not yet," Rose replied. "Bishop Lapp wants to give her some time. Maybe she'll come home. There are . . . extenuating circumstances."

Funny how the grace could be extended now that Lovina was already gone, but when she was here and the Yoder *kinner* were losing the family farm they'd been raised on, they didn't get much in the way of emotional support from anyone.

Uncle Mel, Vernon, and Bart came into the kitchen, and everyone headed to their places at the table. Elizabeth and Isaiah squeezed in at one end, side by side, elbow to elbow. They all bowed their heads and Uncle Mel said a blessing:

"For this food we are about to eat, make us truly grateful, and form us for Thy work, we pray. Bless our family near and far. Amen."

Isaiah wondered what his *daet* was having for dinner in that *Englisher* prison. Was he safe? Was he hungry? Did he pray? Because for all the anger that Isaiah carried with him about his father's crime, Abe was still his *daet*, and he still remembered his father's contagious laughter and reassuring hand on his shoulder. . . .

"So where were you today, Isaiah?" Mel asked as he picked up the dish of brown noodles.

"I went to see about my sister," Isaiah said. "And then I got a job."

Silence descended around the table, and Isaiah met Seth's mildly amused look.

"Where?" Dawn asked.

"The Glick Book Bindery," Isaiah said.

"You know Bethany's the one who put your *daet* in prison, right?" Collette said pointedly.

"No, his *daet*'s in prison because he's a thief and a liar," Mel said, his voice quiet but carrying. "Bethany Glick only told the truth about what she overheard. That's it."

"A job is a good thing," Aunt Rose said with some forced brightness. "Can you spare him, Mel?"

Ironically enough, Mel had done nothing but complain that he didn't have enough work for an extra man for the last weeks they'd been living there, and now there was a worry about sparing him?

"If he pitches in in the evenings, we should be okay," Uncle Mel said. "We're feeding them, after all."

Elizabeth, who had been dishing herself up some vegetables, startled, then returned the serving spoon without taking anything.

"I'm going to be paying you rent," Isaiah said curtly.

"Nonsense!" Aunt Rose said. "We don't accept rent from family, Isaiah!"

"He's a man who feels the need to contribute around here," Uncle Mel countered. "I'm not going to stop him from pitching in. But we still need help with evening chores."

"Of course," Isaiah replied. What did his uncle expect, that he'd just put his feet up in the evenings? But he wouldn't be goaded either because he and Elizabeth needed a place to stay until Isaiah could get enough money together to get them a place of their own.

"You must be hungry," Aunt Rose said, and she reached across the table to put a big piece of chicken onto Isaiah's plate with a sympathetic smile; then she did the same for Elizabeth, and nudged the dish of vegetables toward her niece again.

Aunt Rose could always be counted on to make up for her husband's sandpaper personality, but this time Isaiah wasn't sure he even blamed his uncle. Isaiah's father had ruined the family at large. That was a lot to forgive.

The Glick family lived on an acreage a few miles from town, and Bethany sat on the edge of her bed, her hope chest open in front of her. This wooden trunk had been carefully crafted by her own *daet*. He'd spent several months on it in the evenings while she was on her Rumspringa. Her *daet* would go out into the work shed, meticulously fitting the edges together—not a single nail used in the entire trunk. Then he carved it and sanded it and polished it until it gleamed.

During her Rumspringa, when she was permitted to have more freedom and see what the *Englisher* life was all about, she came home to find her *daet* in the shop, tirelessly working on her hope chest. On the top of the trunk her father had engraved the words in German: *She is worth more than rubies*. It was referencing Proverbs 31, which talked about the ideal wife.

Of all the verses her father could have chosen, this one surprised her, and it brought a lump to her throat every time she looked at it. Her *daet* prayed for each of his nine *kinner* every night, and when he prayed for Bethany, he prayed for the man she'd one day marry, too. "Gott, may he see what a treasure Bethany is and love her all the days of his life."

We all thought that Micah was an answer to Daet's

prayers. I thought I'd be packing this hope chest for my married home. . . . I was going to keep it at the foot of my bed, and it was going to be a reminder to Micah of just how treasured I was by my family, and he would treasure me, too.

But Micah was gone, and she wasn't exactly a treasure to him now, was she?

He doesn't want me. . . .

The sun was setting outside her bedroom window, low, rosy light flooding into the room and mingling with the golden glow of her kerosene lamp. Bethany pulled out some tea towels that she and her *mamm* had embroidered together—each one with a different Bible verse on it. Underneath those were the pillowcases that Bethany had made herself, embroidering the edges with a simple pattern of cross-stitches. She'd been all of thirteen when she'd made those, but she'd been thinking ahead to her future wedding when she'd made them.

"What are you doing?"

Bethany wiped the tears from her face and looked over to see her younger sister, Lily, in the doorway. Lily was only nine, and she stood there barefoot, her blue dress loose and a little too big.

"I'm having a cry," Bethany said.

Lily came into the room and sank into a chair opposite Bethany. She leaned her elbows on her knees in that tomboyish way she had and looked into the hope chest. She didn't wear a *kapp* yet, or an apron. Her hair hung down in front of her shoulders in honeyed curls.

"Do you miss Micah?" Lily asked.

"Yah." It still felt unreal, like he still might show up at their door to take her to singing. How could he say he loved her so much and then leave?

It was more than his words that worried her, though. His actions, too. He'd taken things further than a boyfriend should, and she'd allowed him because she trusted in their engagement. It only made their promise more secure, he'd told her. For what that was worth now . . .

Her *mamm*'s footsteps came up the stairs, and she tapped on the door, then came inside. Mamm's hair was curly and graying, and it didn't lay flat beneath her white *kapp*. She sank onto the bed next to Bethany and put her arm around her. She smelled of cooking and rising bread.

"I'm so sorry about this, my girl," Mamm said softly.

"Tessa came to see me at the shop today," Bethany said.

"Oh?"

"She wants me to wait for him," Bethany said, her voice choked. "In case he comes back. She wants the wedding to go forward."

"Don't *you*?" Mamm asked. "If this could all just go away . . ."

Bethany shook her head. "He left me, Mamm! And I begged him to stay! If you'd seen the way he looked at me—he just pulled away from me, cutting the threads between us. And I'm supposed to trust him again?"

"If he made a mistake, shouldn't you forgive him?" Mamm asked.

"Should I?" Bethany asked. "His *mamm* . . . if you'd seen her. She's heartbroken. She hoped that he had contacted me, but he hasn't. She's miserable."

"You'll know that kind of love when you have *kinner* of your own," Mamm said. "I went over to see Tessa this morning, and you're right about her heartbreak. She has to hold the home together for the younger *kinner*, of course, and she says all the right things about young men having to choose the righteous path on their own, but you know that when she thinks of Micah, she's remembering when he was little, too. And he was a sweet little boy . . ."

"Yah, yah. So you both say," Bethany replied. "When he was a little boy he used to steal muffins from the neighbors' kitchen window, you know."

Mamm smiled at that. "You've both grown up."

"He wanted to leave before," Bethany added. "He'd been very close to jumping the fence. It was only because of Abe Yoder's preaching that he changed his mind. He said he hated farming, and he wanted to drive a truck, and he wanted to know about the world, and about other people, and . . ."

"And Abe changed his mind, how?" Mamm pressed.

"He preached about our Amish life and how it is the way to salvation, and how temptation might be very appealing in the moment, but it leads to years and years of heartbreak."

"Ironic," Mamm murmured. "Considering the direction Abe went."

"Yah. But now that Abe turned out to be more wicked than the *Englishers*, Micah said he didn't know why he was holding back."

"Maybe he needs to learn the hard way that the *Englisher* life isn't for us," Mamm said sadly.

That was what the entire community was hoping—that the young people would go out and have their hearts broken, and then come home where they belonged.

"And what if he does come back?" Bethany asked bitterly. "What if I wait for him like Tessa wants me to, and we get married after all? What's to hold him here? What's to keep him from changing his mind again?" she asked. "I'd be alone, raising *kinner*. Or worse, alone with no *kinner*, and I couldn't get married again. I'd grow old by myself! Like Goldie Stoltzfus!"

"Who's that?" Lily asked.

"Goldie married an Amish convert," Mamm said. "After they got married they hit some bumps in their marriage, and he went back to his *Englisher* life. She was left alone with their three *kinner*. She moved to be closer to her brother a few years ago."

"I don't want to be like her," Bethany said. "I remember how lonely she was."

"She had her community, though," Mamm said.

"But a community won't keep a woman cozy in her bed!" Bethany shot back.

Mamm gave her a warning look. "Enough of that kind of talk. But I agree—Goldie was to be pitied. And you're a wise girl to be thinking ahead like that. Marriage is for life, and if he goes English in a few years, you'd either have to go with him, and risk your own eternal salvation, or stay and live like . . . Goldie."

Lily sat silently, watching them with round eyes. This was how girls learned about the pitfalls they'd want to avoid for themselves. Still, there would be no discussion of things like the marriage bed or the sorts of ways a woman might be lonely if all she had were her *kinner* and no husband. There were some thoughts that should not be awakened in a girl too early.

"But he loves her," Lily said.

"Oh, Lily, love is more than words, it's actions," Mamm said, reaching over to tenderly tug on one of Lily's loose curls.

The very words that Micah had used when he convinced

her to let him go further than she knew was right in the hayloft: *I can tell you how I love you, but let me show you*. . . . Bethany felt the blood rush to her face. She should have said no.

"I don't think he loves me enough," Bethany said, her voice shaking. "I saw his eyes when he was leaving me, and he felt bad about it, but not bad enough to stay with me. That's not love, it's . . . something else. But not love."

It was lust. But she couldn't say so.

Mamm reached into the trunk and pulled out a stack of neatly stitched white aprons. There were gray aprons, too, ones to be used in the garden and for messy kitchen work, but the white ones were what a woman wore when she was neatly put together.

"You should use these," Mamm said, her voice firming.

"I don't want to," Bethany said.

"Why not?" Mamm asked. "They're yours. We made these together, you and me. Of course you'll get married, Bethany. I know you will, but some of these things will only be good for a little while. A woman puts on some weight as she gets older—"

"How old do you think I'll be before a man wants me?" Bethany demanded.

"I'm not saying *that*," Mamm said, shaking her head. "I'm saying, we've spent the last few months filling this chest, and I don't want our hard work to be hidden away and going yellow because of that foolish boy!"

"How are you supposed to know if boys willl do that?" Lily interjected. "Because we all thought Micah was a good one. Even Daet thought so."

Bethany looked over at her mother, and the older woman shrugged weakly.

"That's the risk of marriage, my dear," Mamm said quietly.

"Then how does anyone get married?" the girl demanded.

"It happens when a woman finds a man she can trust—and she has to pray very earnestly to know that," Mamm said simply. "If she's behaved well, she attracts the right kind of man. When I met your *daet*, I knew I could trust him with my very life. He was solid and honest and good, and he loved me so tenderly that I wasn't afraid at all."

This was the love story they had all looked up to—the one between Mamm and Daet. It led to a lengthy marriage with nine kinner, all but two of whom were married and moved away already. It was the story Bethany had been told over and over again with a reverence that nearly equaled the telling of the Bible stories—but today, Bethany found the story irritating. Mamm, who'd never experienced heartbreak, who married the first boy who took her home from singing, and who followed every rule with grace and ease. What help was that to Bethany right now?

Bethany had been a good girl, too . . . up until her recent stumble . . . but she'd been good! Was it her fault for choosing the wrong man to trust? Because even her *daet* had trusted Micah! Daet was a good judge of character, and he'd heartily approved of their relationship. Micah had been apprenticing at the shop, and he was going to work at the book bindery with his soon-to-be father-in-law.

Whose fault was this, Gott? she prayed. *If Daet didn't seen this coming, and* Mamm *certainly never said anything! I trusted Micah because they trusted him . . . so how come I feel like* Mamm *is blaming me?*

Chapter Three

The next day, Isaiah stood at the vise that held the signature pages together. It was his job to use the saw and gently saw the sewing holes into the folded edges of the paper, creating the holes where a needle and thread would pass through in the next stage of binding. He worked carefully—he didn't want to make a costly mistake. He was grateful for this job, and there was something about the meticulous work that created these smooth, leather books that appealed to him.

"That's good," Nathaniel said, looking over his shoulder. "Make sure you stay level, though, or the holes will be too deep on one end."

Isaiah adjusted his grip on the handsaw.

"Yah. Better." Nathaniel left again, and Isaiah felt a wave of satisfaction. He'd been intimidated by the work at first. Farmwork was less particular—more heavy lifting and less tiny detail work. Animals required a certain sensitivity so that he could stay on top of their health and well-being, but it wasn't the same sort of skill. Still, he was finding his pace, and even though this was his second day, he was contributing to the workload.

He hadn't slept well last night. He'd been worried about Lovina, about Micah, about all the others who'd left their community over the last several weeks. Had they found one another in the city? Was there a little group of Bountiful Amish young people who were helping one another stay afloat out there?

If it wasn't for his sister, he'd hope that they hadn't found each other so that they'd be forced to come home again. But having Lovina away from home like this changed his perspective just a little. . . . There were dangers to be considered, and last night when his cousins were snoring in their beds and he'd lain awake on his mattress on the floor, he'd seriously considered going after Lovina and seeing if he could find her himself.

But the bishop had advised against it, and going against the bishop's direction would lead to discipline. His sister wasn't the first Amish young person to jump the fence, nor would she be the last. Taking the advice of his elders was smart . . . and the right thing to do. The elders wanted her back, too. And there was a right way and a wrong way to go about this. His sister's desertion wasn't any more important than Micah's or any of the other young people who'd left, and part of being Amish was acknowledging this.

Two yards away, Bethany was working at the sewing frame—a wooden structure that held the pages together with threads running through to allow her to properly sew the signature pages together to form the spine of a book. She was bent over her work, her lips pressed together in concentration.

Bethany was beautiful—more so than any other girl, and it wasn't just her pink lips or her big, brown eyes, or the color in her cheeks. There was something intangible about her that had always tugged at him.

Isaiah wasn't the kind of man Bethany would attach herself to now, though, even without Micah in the picture. If Isaiah was going to get the community's respect back again, if he was going to be the kind of man a good, solidly Amish girl would turn to, he'd have to work for it and prove that he was an upright, proper man. And that kind of proof took time.

That proof would also require obedience when the bishop said to give Lovina a chance to come home on her own.

"I promised your mother I'd pick up her fabric order," Nathaniel said, tightening the clamp on a book press. "I'll be back in a few minutes, Bethany."

"Yah, Daet," she replied.

Nathaniel puttered about for a moment or two, picking up his keys and wallet before he headed for the door. It was close to lunchtime, and Isaiah was already hungry. But Bethany didn't show any sign of slowing in her work, and he wasn't about to slow down first.

Nathaniel pulled open the front door, then stood back to allow Mary Fisher inside. Isaiah froze for a second. Mary Fisher—the girl Seth had been sweet on for the last few months, and who had finally agreed to let him drive her home from singing. Her family would be expecting more than just dating at this age, too. You didn't ask a twenty-two-year-old girl home from singing for nothing.

"Hello," Mary said, smiling at Nathaniel, who held the door for her.

"Ah, Mary. Nice to see you. How is your *daet*?" Nathaniel asked.

"Good! His foot is healing."

"Glad to hear it. Tell him I'll come by to help him out tonight with some chores," Nathaniel said.

"Yah, thank you. He'll be glad to hear it."

Nathaniel carried on out of the shop, and the door shut behind him, leaving Mary on the welcome mat. Mary was slim and tall, with work-reddened hands and a pleasant smile.

Bethany tied off the thread she was working with and snipped it with the large pair of shears that sat on the table next to her, then she moved toward the counter to greet her friend.

"How are you doing?" Mary asked. "I can't imagine how you must feel. . . . I know you weren't announcing it yet, but we all saw the celery your *mamm* planted, and it isn't like Lily is old enough for an engagement."

Mary laughed at her own little joke, and when Isaiah looked up, he saw Bethany's spine straighten.

"I'm doing as well as anyone would expect, I suppose," Bethany said.

"Did he tell you why he left?" Mary asked, lowering her voice a little. "I mean . . . was it Abe Yoder? Or did you have a fight with him? Did *you* break it off?"

"No, we didn't fight!" Bethany snapped. "And as for his reasons for leaving, I think that's private."

"Even now?" her friend asked. "I mean, he's gone. If he's gone English, that's it. None of us will ever see him again, least of all you."

"I don't want to talk about it," Bethany replied. "I know it's very juicy gossip at the moment—"

"I'm not gossiping," Mary replied, looking offended. "I've come to you, not gone behind your back."

Isaiah put his attention back into his work. This wasn't exactly his business, but all the same he was curious about the girl his cousin had set his sights on.

"Yah, I know. I'm not calling you names." Bethany softened her tone. "It's a hard time right now, Mary. I'm sure you understand."

"So the wedding is off, then?" Mary pressed.

"Yah. It's off."

Isaiah loosened the clamp holding the folios he'd been working with and he removed them and set them on the table next to Bethany's workspace. He picked up the next group and tapped them together until they were flush.

"Are you coming to the wiener roast tomorrow at the bishop's farm?" Mary asked.

Right—the young people's gathering was happening at the bishop's farm, and Isaiah had briefly considered going. It would be a start in getting back into socializing again. He'd been avoiding the young people's gatherings ever since his *daet*'s trouble.

"I don't know . . ." Bethany said. "I don't think so."

"You should," Mary said. "People aren't talking about you. Just come."

"Yes, they are," Bethany said with a short laugh. "How could they not be?"

"Well . . . then who cares if they are?" Mary amended. "It might be good for you to come along and just be single for a while, you know. Not everything is about getting married. Friendships matter, too, and you've been very preoccupied with Micah."

"I was . . . preoccupied?" Bethany shook her head. "I was supposed to be! We were courting!"

"Not anymore . . ." The words hung in the air, the

implication thick, and Isaiah darted a look at the girl. Mary looked . . . victorious. Was that what was underneath this friendly visit, a chance to gloat at another girl's misery?

"Look, Bethany, your value doesn't lie in whether or not you're engaged, or married, or single, or . . . anything. You should just go with friends," Mary said earnestly. "It will be good for you. Don't stay home being sad. Come out. Show Lily that a boy can't end her happiness that easily. You know?"

"Maybe you're right. I'm sure my parents would agree with you. Is your *daet* driving you?" Bethany asked hesitantly. "Do you want to go together?"

"Oh, Seth Yoder is driving me tonight," Mary said demurely. "So I can't."

Yah, this had been a chance to gloat, and it made Isaiah's heart speed up. That piece of information right there had been Mary's entire reason for coming by—she had Seth driving her home from singing, and she'd come to rub it in. Bethany didn't deserve this—especially not from a flippant little thing like Mary Fisher. And maybe it would be a good thing for Isaiah to show his face again with the people his age . . . if he dared.

Bethany took an instinctive step backward, and Isaiah raised his voice and said, "I was planning on driving Bethany to the wiener roast tonight."

Both girls turned toward him, equally surprised.

"What?" Bethany said.

"Yah." Isaiah ambled toward them and shot Mary a smile. "I was hoping to drive her myself, I just hadn't gotten around to asking her yet." He glanced down at Bethany to catch her gaze hardening into something close to anger. Had he gone too far?

"Are you going with him?" Mary asked, her tone losing some of that earlier victorious timbre.

"Let me drive you," Isaiah said, and he met Bethany's gaze, smiling somewhat sheepishly. "She has a point about getting out. And I'm a friend . . . aren't I?"

They were more tenuously connected than through friendship, but that shouldn't matter for this purpose. It would spare Bethany from being the object of questionable pity, the one girl who was cast aside when the celery crop intended for her wedding soup was already planted and growing.

"Maybe," Bethany said, and she shrugged. "I'll see how I'm feeling. But maybe. I really need to get back to work, Mary. You understand."

"Oh, of course." Mary nodded. "I'll see you at the wiener roast. Maybe."

Mary gave Isaiah a cautious look, and he wondered if she was only now realizing that she'd behaved badly in front of Seth's cousin. She headed out the door, the bell overhead tinkling merrily at her exit.

Bethany cast Isaiah an annoyed look. "That wasn't necessary."

"Then you could have turned me down," he replied with a grin. "It still would have given Mary something to choke on."

"So I wasn't imagining that?" she asked, squinting toward the door.

"No, she was gloating," he replied.

"Hmm." She headed toward her worktable again, then looked back at him. "I'm not going to that wiener roast. You can go without me and let Mary rub *that* in your face."

"I don't care what Mary thinks," he replied. "Besides, they've got more interesting things to rub in my face than whether or not Bethany Glick finds me insufferable."

Bethany smiled faintly at that, and he was gratified, even if it was at his own expense. She turned toward her work again, and he watched her as she pulled up her stool and started cutting the last book free from the sewing frame.

"She had a point about you going out and having some fun," he said.

"I have the right to be sad," she said.

"Yah, you do." Maybe he'd been wrong to push her anyway.

"I'm not going," she said more firmly.

"Okay."

He might not want to admit it, but he didn't want to go to the young people's event alone either. She wasn't the only one being gossiped about and having someone with him—having *her* with him—might have been a comfort. But he had to keep showing his face, enduring the looks and the whispers, because this was his community and he had to find a way back in.

Bethany looked toward the door and sucked in a deep breath. Had Mary really come to see Bethany to brag over having a boy to drive her home from singing? And Seth Yoder—one of Micah's friends, and Isaiah's cousin. In a community their size, everything was a little close.

That had been cruel on Mary's part. Bethany knew that she had harbored a crush on Micah, but to be happy that he left Bountiful completely, just so that Bethany couldn't have him? Was that what this was about? Or just a thoughtless girl who needed to crow about her good fortune and didn't care what Bethany was going through?

Isaiah lined up the handsaw and swiped it across the folded edges of the folios. He bent down to get a good view of the cut. He was getting good at this—he seemed to have the touch, at least. And while that was a good thing for the shop, and for Daet, Bethany found it irritating right now. Micah should not be so readily replaced.

Bethany looked at the clock on the wall. It was time for lunch, and while her stomach was clamped in a knot, she could use the break. She hadn't brought a packed lunch today. She was going to get a meal from the bakery— Eileen's beef stew was something quite amazing, and her bread was always fluffier than either Mamm or Bethany could manage at home. Besides, Bethany needed something to look forward to today—a bit of comfort.

"I'm going for lunch," Bethany said.

Isaiah looked up at the clock, and she wondered if he meant to stay.

"Daet doesn't expect anyone to work through lunch," she said. He wasn't going to endear himself around here by working harder than anyone else. At least not to her.

"Let me just finish this, and then I'll eat," he said.

Bethany nodded and headed for the door. She didn't need his pity either. She flicked the sign in the window to "Closed" and headed out into the street. It wasn't like Isaiah could mind the shop on his own anyway.

Bethany looked up the street and saw Mary Fisher just entering the bakery. She heaved a sigh. Whatever—Mary might be gloating a little bit, but she was still a friend. She headed in that direction, too.

Bountiful Baked Goods was an Amish-run establishment, and their specialty breads were shipped to some nearby grocery stores, too. There was a lineup of people waiting for their orders when Bethany came inside the fragrant shop. The walls were lined with shelves, all filled with loaves of bread, buns, muffins, strudels . . . The shop was full at this time of day with English and Amish alike, and Mary was at the back of the line to give her order, another Amish girl, Emma Hochstetler, standing with her.

As Bethany approached the end of the line, Emma's voice carried back to her.

"Isaiah Yoder?" Emma was saying. "Working with the Glicks, after all that?"

Mary was about to answer, but as she turned toward Emma, she caught sight of Bethany out of the corner of her eye and her face immediately colored. Emma turned, then, and Bethany had the urge to turn and run. She wouldn't, though. She might be the topic of gossip, but she was no coward.

"Hello," Bethany said, stepping into line behind them.

"I didn't know you were coming for lunch. I would have waited for you," Mary said, just a little too brightly.

"Yah." Bethany eyed her friend. How much did Mary talk about her behind her back these days? Was there anyone who didn't?

"Do you really trust him?" Emma asked Bethany, lowering her voice. "I'm sure you heard us talking, and I'm sorry about that. But Isaiah Yoder was helping his *daet* to convince people to invest in that charity scam, you know."

"Yah, I know."

"He almost convinced my brother," Emma said. "And my uncle, too, for that matter. We must have had some protection from above, because they decided against it, but I heard even the bishop put some money into it."

"Yah, I heard the same," Mary said, as if that settled the rumor into a fact.

"My *daet* gave him work," Bethany said. "It isn't up to me. You know that."

"So you don't trust him," Emma pressed.

"No," Bethany said with a weak shrug. "I don't."

But her reasons were more complicated than his involvement in his *daet*'s crime. It went deeper than that. Isaiah seemed to want something more from them that she wasn't willing to give—absolution, maybe. Or some legitimization in their community. Her *daet* should have sent him away.

"Abe Yoder's farm is sold now," Mary said. "Seth told me about it."

"Who bought it?" Bethany asked.

"Englishers."

Of course. With the farmland being eaten up, it was harder and harder for the Amish to get into farming, or stay in farming. To have a good Amish farm turn English was disheartening.

"It's been in the Yoder family for three generations," Mary added. "Seth says it's a huge blow to all of them to have it taken over like that. They had to sell it to try to pay back some of the victims."

So there was some hope that her *daet* might get some of his money back—that was something.

"It sold for cheap, too," Mary added. "In fact, I heard that the Bachmanns from over in the Highbright community tried to buy it, but the *Englishers* got there first, which is a tragedy. We could have had a new Amish family in the community instead of losing one."

"Isaiah and Elizabeth aren't gone exactly," Bethany said.

"Or Lovina," Emma added.

"No, Lovina left yesterday!" Mary launched herself into the telling of the story, which was surprisingly accurate.

"Did Isaiah mention anything?" Emma asked, turning toward Bethany.

But Bethany didn't feel quite right about this gossip. Whatever Isaiah might have said in the last day was said with some expectation of privacy. And while she didn't like having him in their shop, she found herself hesitant to say anything more.

"Next—" Eileen's niece's voice rose over the chatting voices in the shop. Mary stepped forward to give her order.

"There's people from three different Amish communities that got defrauded," Emma went on. "So I don't know how they'll figure out who gets their money back and who doesn't."

"So Isaiah and his sisters—what did they get to keep?" Bethany asked.

"Nothing." Emma shook her head. "From what I understand, the *Englisher* police took away everything— land, money, anything that could be sold to pay back the victims."

"It's not the police," Mary said, stepping to the side. "It's the government, I think."

"It doesn't matter who—it gets taken away," Emma said. "Hold on, I have to order."

Bethany waited while Emma placed her order and paid,

and then she stepped up, too. She ordered the beef stew with extra bread on the side, and then stepped over with Mary and Emma to wait for her order to be ready.

"They've got nothing," Emma said, lowering her voice. "I heard that Jeb Miller Senior, down at the dry goods store, forgave Elizabeth Yoder's tab because there was no way she could pay it. And Mel Yoder said he wasn't covering his brother's tabs, so Jeb didn't have much choice. He just forgave the whole thing."

To have nothing at all . . . that was a frightening thought. It was that very thing that made people willing to contribute to a fund that would help fellow Amish in dire straits. Isaiah had come to them for a job—how desperate was he?

Bethany's order came up, and she accepted the plastic bag from the Amish girl behind the counter. The food smelled savory and wonderful, but Bethany's appetite had slipped.

"I have to get back to the shop," Bethany said.

"Are you coming to the wiener roast tomorrow?" Emma asked. "Mary's being driven home by Seth Yoder, and Daniel Riener is going to drive me. But don't let that stop you. You should come—we're losing too many people."

"Isaiah Yoder asked to drive her home," Mary said, raising her eyebrows and waiting for the information to land.

"You don't say . . ." Emma breathed. "And what did you tell him?"

"I'll come," Bethany said. "And I'll find a way home again."

"Good," Emma said, leaning over to give her a hug.

"I'm really sorry about Micah. I can't imagine how you must feel."

That was all that Mary would have needed to say, and she noticed Mary's cheeks flush.

"Thank you," Bethany said. "I'll see you both later."

Bethany went out of the bakery, her heart pounding. The noon sunlight was welcomingly warm, but she felt like she was swimming through a fog. How long until Bethany was no longer the subject of gossip? But she might as well ask how long it would be for Isaiah, because their difficult times both had the same root—Abe Yoder.

She headed down the street once more. So many of their own had left for an *Englisher* life, and now it seemed so strange that life could simply carry on with gossip and wiener roasts. But life didn't stop, no matter how much Bethany might need to catch her breath.

When Bethany got back to the shop Isaiah wasn't at his workstation, but she could see him at the back hunched over a little table. He looked up as she came in.

"You're back," he said.

"Yah. I thought I'd eat here."

"There's room." He pulled a couple of apples closer to him, and she realized that his lunch was paltry—a few small apples, some carrots, and what looked like half a peanut butter sandwich. Her stomach sank—he wasn't even eating.

"Who packed your lunch?" she asked as she came to the other side of the table and sat down.

"Oh." He laughed uncomfortably. "It was a busy morning."

That wasn't much of an answer, but it looked like Isaiah

needed this job more than she'd realized, especially if the gossip was true.

"I got too much food," Bethany said. "Eileen always gives more than one person can eat. And I'm not really hungry anyway. Do you want some?"

"I'm fine." Isaiah shook his head, but his gaze flickered down to the bowl of stew. She and her *daet* always kept some extra cutlery at the shop for eating their homemade lunches, and she grabbed two spoons, passing him one.

"I'm serious. Help me finish this," she said.

"You sure?" he asked, accepting the spoon.

"Yah."

He took a chunk of beef and popped it into his mouth. The man was hungry—that much was obvious—and she nudged one of the servings of bread toward him. His gaze caught hers, and a smile tugged up one side of his mouth. She dropped her gaze to her own food, unwilling to be tugged in by Isaiah's well-known charm. He and his *daet* had that irrepressible charm in common, and while she didn't like the idea of him going hungry, she wasn't willing to let her defenses down either.

"How is Elizabeth doing?" Bethany asked.

"She still doesn't believe Daet did it," Isaiah replied.

"Not after all the evidence?" Bethany said.

Isaiah chewed slowly, then swallowed. "The bishop talked to her. The elders, too. Even I sat her down and told her straight that Daet had done something terrible, but she just won't accept it. She says the *Englishers* framed him."

"I heard him discussing it with those *Englishers*," Bethany said. "Does she think I was part of framing him?"

"No . . . it's more of a belief in Daet as her father," he replied. "She adored our father and he treated her like . . .

well, he treated us all like the favorite. But of all of us, I honestly thought it would hit Elizabeth hardest. She's the most stubborn of us all—you can't bend her. I didn't expect Lovina to be the one to jump the fence."

Bethany could understand a girl's loyalty to her *daet*, and she thought of her hope chest, lovingly carved by her *daet*'s own hand. Did she blame Elizabeth for not believing her father was capable of criminal activity? Bethany would never believe it of her own father either.

"I can understand you not jumping to the conclusion that your *daet* was stealing, but—" Bethany put down her spoon—"but you must have seen some hint that things weren't right."

"Daet was busy," he said. "He was always out visiting people, or preaching at gatherings. I didn't see that much of him."

"You never saw him with *Englishers*?" she asked.

"Sometimes. He talked to tourists. They liked him. He was open and friendly with everyone."

"You know what I mean."

"Did I see him skulking about with shady-looking *Englishers*?" he asked, irritation edging his tone. "No! My *daet* preached—it's what he did. He preached the Word of Gott, and he did it well. I wanted to be like him. I never saw anything that would suggest he was involved in this kind of business."

But a shadow crossed his face and he fell silent. He passed her back the last piece of untouched bread.

"People all think I knew," he said.

"Yah, I suppose they do," she agreed.

"Do you?" he asked.

Bethany shrugged. "It's crossed my mind."

"What will convince you otherwise?" he asked.

Bethany swallowed hard and met his tortured gaze. She didn't know. Abe's confusing behavior had turned everything upside down. Who could they trust if they couldn't trust Abe Yoder?

"I'm the same man I was six months ago," Isaiah said. "I'm no different."

"Yah, you are different," she said. "This is going to change you, whether you want it to or not."

"It won't change my principles," he countered. "I'm the same man."

Isaiah cleared away his garbage and headed back to his workspace. Bethany watched him go. She'd offended him—she could tell.

"Are you going to the wiener roast still?" Bethany asked, raising her voice.

"I'm going."

"Even with everyone talking?"

"I said I'm going!" He turned back to face her, his dark eyes flashing. "I've got something to prove—I wasn't involved in my *daet*'s crime! And this is still my community. So I'm going to be there, even if they talk."

They'd be talking about her, too, for that matter, and his determination to face it was oddly encouraging. "I might need a ride."

"You want to be seen with me?" he asked incredulously. "You sure about that?"

"I don't want to hide from my community either," she said. "And maybe you're right about just facing it."

Isaiah gave her a curt nod and turned back to his work. "Yah, okay. I'll pick you up tomorrow evening, then. Around seven."

They both had something to prove—that they weren't broken and they weren't changed. Except they were both a little broken from all this. The whole community was in denial about that. Nothing would ever be quite the same again.

Chapter Four

Isaiah flicked the reins and the horses sped up a little bit as they plodded in the direction of the Glick acreage. The evening was warm and the sun was low in the sky, still a couple of hours away from sunset. His sister sat next to him, her back rigid.

"She's the one who had Daet put away, you know," Elizabeth said curtly. "And you're taking her home from singing?"

"I'm also taking her to singing, and it isn't exactly like that," Isaiah replied.

"That's how it looks," Elizabeth replied. Taking a girl home from singing was the start of courting—a demonstration of intention. Normally, at least. These weren't normal circumstances.

"Trust me, Bethany isn't seeing it like that. And she's the one that matters for that," he replied. "Besides, it wasn't Bethany who put Daet away. She just said what she heard. That's it. The court decided the rest."

"Daet didn't do it," Elizabeth said, her voice shaking. "And if you'd read his letters, you'd know that! I got a letter from him today."

Isaiah looked away. He didn't want to know what his father had said. Obviously, he was still reassuring Elizabeth of his innocence, which was exactly what Elizabeth wanted to hear—that Abe had been duped, too. But with the weight of evidence against him, even Isaiah no longer believed that.

"Just be practical, Lizzie," Isaiah pleaded. "Bountiful is our home. Daet is shunned and in prison. If you want to stay Amish—and you do, don't you?"

"Yah. Of course."

"Well, if you want to stay Amish, this is our community and we'd best make our peace within it. Without Daet."

"He's our father." Her voice shook.

"He's a thief!" Isaiah sucked in a breath, trying to cap his rising anger. This wasn't a new discussion between himself and his sister. No matter how many people told her that Daet had committed a crime, her loyalty was to him.

"Do you even know what he said in that letter today?" Elizabeth pressed.

"I don't care. He's shunned, and we aren't supposed to be reading his letters, are we?"

"You should care. It was about you."

Isaiah's fingers went cold and he jerked his head to look at her. "What about me?"

"Daet *was* tricked. He only figured out they were stealing from everyone once he'd already helped them collect from a few different families. And when he confronted them, they said if he didn't keep going along with it and helping them, they'd tell the police that you were involved."

"Me?" Isaiah swallowed. "I helped him, but I didn't

know. And the police questioned me about it—three times, you might remember. They believed me."

"They might not have, if they didn't have Daet to take the punishment," Elizabeth replied.

"Why didn't he tell the authorities the truth, then?" he demanded.

"To protect you!" she said. "He's *our father*. And you're his son. And he's suffering in that jail. It's a terrible place."

Isaiah's mind ground over this new information, and he turned his attention back to the road. Had his father chosen to damn himself to spare him? And if that was the case, why not tell Isaiah about it? Granted, toward the end Abe had been insisting that he didn't need any extra help, that the charity was doing just fine and that he need not worry about it anymore. . . . That had seemed strange at the time. So maybe there was truth to this story.

"Daet didn't have to continue robbing people!" Isaiah said. "He could have gone to the police himself, for one. If he didn't want to do that, he could have made a terrible argument for the fund so no one would invest in it. He didn't have to go on to defraud fifty other families like that," he said. With or without Isaiah.

"Yah. Maybe," she agreed. "But our *daet* isn't the monster they all make him out to be either. And if he can't count on his own *kinner* to love him still—"

"I didn't say I stopped loving him!" Isaiah snapped. "He's shunned!"

Love wasn't so easy to turn off. A son didn't just stop loving his own father. He didn't stop worrying about him, praying for his safety . . . But he might be forced to accept a shunning. And that shunning might be a guilty relief.

"That's why I'm not telling anyone but you about the

letter." She looked over at him, and Isaiah thought he saw rebellion in his sister's clear gaze, and that chilled his blood.

"We're either Amish or we're not," he warned her.

"He's my father. Part of our Amish faith is rooted in family, isn't it?"

"You aren't thinking of going English, are you?" Isaiah asked, his voice low.

"No."

"Because Lovina left, and—"

"I'm Amish," she said curtly. "But that doesn't stop me from thinking things through."

They fell silent, and the horses plodded onward. There was a lot of gray area out there with the *Englishers*, and all that gray, uncharted territory was exactly what the Amish strove to avoid. There was right and there was wrong. There was the Ordnung to guide them when they weren't sure, and there was a community to support them when they needed it. The Amish life was not an easy one, and his *daet* hadn't needed to continue on with those *Englisher* fraudsters. He should have done the right thing, no matter how painful, and trusted Gott to protect Isaiah, like Abraham with his son, Isaac. *That* was part of their faith, too.

And yet a shiver ran down his spine at the thought of being the one in prison right now, the one whose life was in the balance. Innocent or not, he could have been the one sitting alone in a cell, and that gave him pause.

They arrived at the Glicks' place a few minutes later, and when Isaiah guided the horses into the drive he spotted Bethany standing outside, waiting for them.

"Let's not make this harder on us than it needs to be,"

Isaiah said to his sister, his voice low. "This is still our community."

Elizabeth didn't answer, and he'd have to trust that she could see that they still needed their neighbors.

Isaiah reined in the horses, and Elizabeth scooted over on the seat to make room for Bethany.

"Hi," Bethany said as she hoisted herself up. "Thanks for picking me up."

"Yah, no problem," Isaiah said, and he turned the buggy around, then headed back up the drive. He could see Nathaniel and Barbara Glick in the window, their expressions sober. Nathaniel had given him a job, and for that he was grateful, but no one had told him yet if Barbara was supportive of that choice or not, and seeing her face as they drove past didn't put his mind at rest. Nathaniel would make the decisions as the man of the home, but that didn't mean the women were in agreement.

Isaiah would drive the buggy back the way they'd come, pass Uncle Mel's farm, and head a couple of miles farther up the road to the bishop's farm, and he was already mentally navigating. Elizabeth sat between them, silent, and Bethany seemed to sense the tension because she stayed quiet, too. All he could see of Bethany were her hands on her knees.

If Isaiah and his sister were going to keep a place in this community, Isaiah was going to have to break through a few of these tensions, and Elizabeth's conviction that their *daet* was morally innocent wasn't helping.

"It will be good to see everyone," Isaiah said, mostly as a way of making conversation.

"Yah, very good," Bethany said quietly.

"Will it?" Elizabeth said, breaking her silence.

"Elizabeth, other people have reason to be angry, you know," Isaiah countered.

"As do we," she said, casting him an irritated look.

"It's okay," Bethany said. "It's complicated."

Isaiah nudged his sister in the ribs with his elbow and she didn't answer that, much to his relief. They needed a place—even a new place—in this community, and bitterness wasn't going to make it an easy transition.

There were already several buggies parked in the side field when they arrived at Bishop Lapp's farm. The gray buggies sat in neat lines in the lush green grass, the horses grazing beyond. He used to enjoy looking at their own fields—the stretch of green, the meander of fence posts separating pasture from crops. He tore away his gaze— he'd likely never again experience that peace of farm ownership, the confidence of owning the dirt under his boots for as far as his eye could see. . . . He wasn't jealous— just sad for his own loss.

Isaiah let the girls off on the drive before he guided the horses toward the field to unhitch. He glanced toward them as they walked toward the house—Elizabeth and Bethany with about three feet between them and both of their backs rigid.

Was he crazy to be trying to find a place in his own community, or would they be wiser to move on to another Amish center and attempt to start fresh? Except their community wasn't the only one targeted, and they'd only meet with more families who had lost their money to the fraud. If they couldn't find forgiveness here, he doubted they'd find it elsewhere either.

Isaiah unhitched the horses and sent them out to graze with the others, then headed over toward the bonfire that the young men were already attempting to start. A few girls sat around, watching them work, and as he approached, he saw his sister sitting off to the side. The other girls had angled their legs away from Elizabeth, and there was something about his sister's posture that stabbed at his heart. Johannes sat a couple of feet away from her, looking equally isolated.

Johannes was a tall man, bulky and muscular, and tonight his expression was empty.

"Are you doing okay?" Isaiah asked.

"Not really." Johannes cleared his throat.

"Did you remember anything more?" Isaiah asked. "Anything that she might have said to give us a hint about where she went?"

"If I had, I'd be on my way to find her," Johannes said, his voice thick.

"I'm sorry all the same," Isaiah said. "She'll come back. I'm sure of it."

"I hope so." But there was a catch in Johannes' voice. "But if your father comes back and she doesn't, I'm not going to let him forget it."

"He won't need the reminder," Isaiah said quietly.

Johannes looked miserably in the other direction.

"We should go home," Elizabeth whispered from his other side.

"No, we stay," he said firmly. "This first time will be hard. It'll get better. Johannes is here, too. We can weather this."

Elizabeth blinked back her tears and brushed a finger under her eye. She leaned forward to look at Johannes, then sighed.

"Lovina didn't know how much he cared, did she?"

"Maybe not." And maybe she was just too wrapped up in her own pain to think of the pain she'd cause the ones who loved her.

The fire started to crackle, and Isaiah looked over as the younger boys pushed dry sticks into the pile of brush and crumpled paper. A waft of smoke swept past him, making his eyes sting, and Isaiah pushed himself to his feet.

"I'm glad you came, Isaiah," a deep voice reverberated just behind him, and Isaiah turned to see Bishop Lapp standing there with his arms crossed over his chest. "I wasn't sure you would."

"This is still our community," Isaiah said.

"Hello, Elizabeth," the bishop said with a smile. "And Johannes. I'm glad you made it, too."

Johannes looked up and nodded. "Yah. I'm trying."

"Can we talk, Isaiah?" the older man asked, putting a hand on his shoulder.

Isaiah glanced around, then stood up, and he and the bishop both stepped a few paces away from the rest of the group. Isaiah glanced back—the young men had the fire started now and they were adding small, dry twigs and sticks. One of the boys called Johannes to help carry more wood, and he pushed himself to his feet, heading over to give a hand.

Johannes would be okay. He'd be heartbroken, but he'd still be a part of the community—just one more person who lost something because of Abe. It was Abe's *kinner* who wouldn't be so quickly accepted back into things.

"How are you all holding up?" the bishop asked.

"We're—" Isaiah shrugged. "We're surviving. Johannes looks pretty wrecked right now."

"Do you know where your sister went?" The bishop stroked his hand over his graying beard. "I heard that some went to Pittsburgh."

"I don't know," Isaiah replied. "She's young—I don't think she'd even have much of a plan. I'm just hoping she's with someone she knows."

"Because I suspect she went to visit your *daet* at the prison," the bishop said quietly. "And with him being shunned, she couldn't go with permission, could she?"

"What makes you think so?" Isaiah asked.

"My wife suggested it as a possibility," the bishop replied. "That's why I don't want to be too rash. A feeling doesn't last forever. Emotions are like a field of wheat, bending beneath the wind. And given enough sun, that grain will ripen and mature."

"You think she just needs time?" Isaiah asked. "Are you sure?"

"She's an adult, Isaiah. She's twenty years old. If she wants to leave us, it is within her rights. I just pray that she'll come back, and until then, I shall turn a blind eye and pray for it. She belongs at home. I wanted to make sure you knew my approach."

"Can I go after her?" Isaiah asked.

"And do what?" he asked. "Drag her home? She knows where we are and she knows why she left. She left a man behind who is a shell without her. She has plenty to return for. Give it time, Isaiah. I know this is hard—there are more young people than your sister who've left over this debacle with your *daet*. And there have been plenty who have left before this. I've seen this before. We all have. And trust me when I tell you that stomping off after an upset young person has never been fruitful."

"I know . . ."

There were stories about young people who left. The reasons they came back where plentiful, but they all revolved around lessons learned in personal ways out there in the world. Those lessons couldn't be forced.

"And Isaiah—"

Isaiah looked up at the older man. "Yah?"

"I'm glad you came tonight," he said, patting his arm.

The bishop might be the only one. But then Isaiah's gaze moved back to the group by the fire, and he saw Bethany sitting on the same bench as the other girls, but she didn't look like she was joining in on their conversation. Her gaze was directed into the orange flames, her pale skin reflecting the flicker of light and shadow.

"Thanks," Isaiah said.

Lovina did belong at home—protected and provided for. She belonged at bonfires like this one, and in a warm kitchen with her family. She belonged with Johannes, and she should be here at home, getting past the rough patches with the rest of them and finding a new balance with her friends. Running away was never the answer.

The bishop had a softness to his strength after all, and Isaiah felt a welling of hope. Maybe the bishop was right, and Lovina had gone to see their father. Because shunned or not, Amish or not, Abe *was* their *daet*.

He'd just have to join the bishop and pray for her return.

It felt strange to be at a youth event without Micah. For the last two years Bethany had been by his side, and if she wasn't sitting next to him, a proper six inches between them, she'd been able to look over her shoulder and see where he stood with the other young men. Tonight, she caught herself looking over her shoulder a few times, and every time she did, she spotted Isaiah, his solemn gaze locked on her.

Isaiah was a different type of man from Micah. Isaiah was taller, for one, and his shoulders were broader. His dark gaze didn't just pass over her but pinned her to the spot. His expression didn't betray any feelings, except for that odd intensity. Whatever Isaiah was, he was more than Micah—in personality, in intensity, in size. And feeling his gaze on her made her pulse speed up, so that she would look away lest anyone else notice that the pink in her cheeks wasn't from the heat of the fire.

Bethany didn't sit next to Isaiah during the hymn sing around the fire, but she did sit across from him on a wooden bench next to Emma and Mary, and through the flickering flames of the lowering bonfire, she could see his rugged face and the sadness in his dark eyes.

She'd also noticed that the other young men didn't sit next to him either. Seth sat a few feet away, but there was a visible distance. It was just Isaiah and Elizabeth, sitting there in silence while everyone else sang the hymns around them.

Gott, take care of Micah, she prayed in her heart. *Wherever he is.*

Because even though he'd left her and broken her heart, she couldn't bring herself to hate him. He'd have enough consequences for his rash decision of living out there among the *Englishers*, and at least she hadn't married him. That was a blessing among the thorns.

The night got chillier than Bethany had expected, and she leaned in toward the fire, the warmth welcome. When the evening drew to a close the boys who had already arranged to drive a girl home came to find them, and they paired off, walking together back to the buggies, a proper space between them. Seth came up to where Mary sat, and she gathered up her shawl and Bible, then blushed as she fell into step beside him. Daniel didn't seem quite so smooth in the process, and he stood back a few paces, his cheeks flaming while he waited on Emma.

"See you," Emma said to Bethany.

Emma and Daniel walked away, Daniel with his hands balled up into fists at his sides, as if he didn't know what else to do with them. The last time Bethany was at a youth event, she and Micah had left together . . . walking close enough that her dress brushed against his pants, and they would brazenly hold hands.

The thought embarrassed her now. She'd been stupid.

Isaiah and Elizabeth approached Bethany together. This wasn't the same kind of event—this wasn't a date, and his offer of a ride wasn't part of courting.

"I'm ready," Bethany said. "Thanks for the ride."

"Yah, of course," Isaiah said.

Bethany shot Elizabeth a tentative smile, but it wasn't returned, and Bethany felt her stomach sink. She hadn't been thinking of facing Abe Yoder's *kinner* when she testified for the case. The bishop had agreed that she should simply tell the truth without swearing on anything, and the court had accepted that. She'd been more concerned with her own *daet*'s financial stress, about the other families that had been defrauded. And maybe she'd assumed that Abe's *kinner* would leave the community with their tails between their legs. They hadn't.

The three of them headed to the field where the buggies were parked together, and while Isaiah hitched up the horses, Bethany and Elizabeth waited.

"I'm probably not a friend anymore, am I?" Bethany asked softly.

Elizabeth cast her an unfathomable look. "What if it were your *daet* in prison?"

"My *daet* didn't commit a crime!" Bethany said.

"We could have dealt with it within our community," Elizabeth replied. "We don't use the *Englisher* systems. We deal with sin among ourselves."

"It involved *Englishers*, too," Bethany said. "What else was I supposed to do? The police were questioning me. Was I supposed to lie?"

"Keep quiet," Elizabeth snapped. "You could have just kept your mouth shut and allowed the elders to do their job."

It was the elders who'd approached her about speaking for the *Englisher* court. She was being summoned, so it wasn't like she had much of a choice, but they'd made it clear that the community was behind her. She should have thought ahead to this day, when she'd have to face Abe's daughter.

Isaiah finished with the horses, and he shot his sister a warning look. "Enough, Elizabeth. Now isn't the time."

Bethany hitched up her shoulders against an internal chill, then climbed up into the buggy first. Elizabeth followed, and Isaiah headed around to the other side to get into the driver's seat. From her vantage point, Bethany could see the soft glow of the bonfire's embers, and as Isaiah settled in next to her, she could smell the smoke on his warm arm pressed up against hers.

"Hya. Let's go," he said, and the horses started forward.

The way to Bethany's home went past Mel Yoder's farm, and Elizabeth nodded toward it.

"You could let me off here," she said.

"You sure?" her brother asked her.

"Yah. I'm tired. Let me off, Isaiah. Good night, Bethany."

"Good night," Bethany said feebly.

Isaiah pulled up by the drive and Elizabeth got down. They stayed there, motionless, while Elizabeth walked down the drive, her footsteps crunching in the quiet night. Bethany hadn't moved away from Isaiah's side, and he didn't seem to notice. His arm was pressed lightly against hers, the reins held loosely in his broad hand. He smelled good—like campfire and something slightly musky. And maybe it was that she was used to being driven home by Micah, or just the strange sense of comfort his large frame lent her, but she found herself loath to slide away.

Isaiah waited until the side door opened, spilling light out onto the porch before he flicked the reins again and they carried on. There was the scent of rain on the breeze, and clouds scudded across the sky, blocking the moon and leaving only a few pinpricks of stars. The buggy's head-lamps cut through the night, illuminating the glossy backs of the horses.

"I'm sorry about my sister," he said. "She's pretty upset still."

Bethany didn't answer—there was nothing to say. If Elizabeth carried this grudge for the rest of her life, Bethany couldn't even say she'd blame her. But she did scoot away from Isaiah's warmth, giving a proper distance between them again.

"So how was it?" he asked her as the horses reached their stride once more.

"The evening?" she asked. "I could ask the same of you. You looked miserable."

"It'll take time," he said. "I'm willing to put in the time to get back to normal again. How was it for you?"

"It was . . . strange," she admitted. "A little lonely."

"Yah. For me, too."

"Funny we'd have that in common," she said and smiled faintly. He looked over at her and returned her smile.

"Yah."

"Nothing's going to be the same again, is it?" she asked.

Isaiah reached over and put his warm hand over her, giving her fingers a gentle squeeze, then he pulled his hand back again. "Micah wasn't who you thought. I daresay none of us are who we think. We can see how people behave, doing things the proper way, but we can't see what's going on inside, you know?"

"I suppose," she agreed.

"I remember when Micah, Seth, and I used to talk about the girls we thought were pretty."

Bethany looked over at him, heat coming to her cheeks. "Like Mary Fisher, no doubt."

"Like you," he said. He didn't look at her, but a smile quirked up the corners of his lips.

"Me?" She dropped her gaze. "I'm not one of the girls the boys flirt with."

"Maybe I was too scared to flirt," he said. "I might be able to speak in public, but that's in front of an audience. I've never been good with flirting—one-on-one."

"I never knew you thought that," she said hesitantly.

"Well, Micah asked you home from singing first, and it didn't much matter how I felt at that point, did it?"

"How did you feel?" she whispered.

"Rather jealous." He shrugged. "But you two fell in love with each other, and . . . I backed off."

So, he'd been thinking of taking her home from singing once upon a time? Had he meant this to be a date after all? A breeze swept through the tops of the trees, ruffling leaves and cooling the air around them even farther so, that goose bumps stood up on her arms. The clouds had been moving steadily, and in the darkness she hadn't noticed how menacing they'd become until the wind whipped around her, making her shiver.

"He *said* he loved me, at least," she said.

"He did love you." Isaiah sounded so certain, and she shot him a curious look.

"He left, Isaiah. You don't plan to marry a girl and then walk away because you love her so dearly. I'm many things but not a fool."

Or maybe she was, because she'd fully believed Micah's words up until very recently.

"I think he wanted to be the good Amish husband—

your good Amish husband," Isaiah said. "But somehow he couldn't fit in. I don't think it means he didn't love you."

"You're smooth," she said bitterly. A whole lot like Micah had been, and he'd known exactly what to say to make her trust him completely.

"Am I?" Isaiah asked.

"So I shouldn't be hurt? Offended? Angry?"

He lifted his shoulders. "He . . . um . . . I told you the other day at the bus station, he asked me to look out for you if anything should happen to him. This was a few months ago, before my *daet* was arrested and all of that, so maybe he changed his mind since. I don't know. But back then, when he thought about the future, he was already thinking about making sure you'd be okay if the worst should happen."

"The worst has happened!" she shot back. "And if that was love—it wasn't near enough."

A few drops of rain started to fall, spattering against the pavement and one landing on her hand. They were just approaching a tree's overhanging branches as the sky opened up and a deluge of rain came pounding down. Isaiah reined the horses under the limbs of the tree and they waited there, watching the rain pummel the pavement.

"Come here," he said, reaching over and nudging her knees toward him.

"What?" she said.

"Come on, you're cold," he said.

Bethany scooted closer as another damp lick of wind swept around them. His warm body felt good next to her bare arms, and she permitted herself to lean toward him ever so slightly—just for the warmth.

"How come you didn't start courting a girl?" she asked softly.

Because Isaiah was certainly handsome enough. He had broad shoulders, a muscular physique, strong hands. She sucked in a breath, refusing to let herself go further. Surely there were enough Amish girls who'd jump at the chance to be driven home by him.

"I was . . . distracted," he said.

"By what?"

"I was still trying to figure out who I'd be. It's not fair to drag a girl into your life before you can tell her for certain what that life will look like. That's a recipe for misery, I'd say."

"That's probably wise," she admitted. "I thought you'd inherit your *daet*'s farm."

"I would have. But I wanted to preach like him, too, and that's a demanding life. Lots of travel. Besides—" She saw the color touch his cheeks. "It's probably for the best. I don't have much left to offer a girl, do I?"

Isaiah looked over at her, and his dark gaze met hers, then dropped down to her lips. Her breath caught, and he turned toward her, his arm moving to the back of the seat.

"I'm not a flirt, Bethany," he said quietly.

"You say that," she said, forcing out a breathless laugh. "But you flirted with me all the time. Micah hated it."

"I tried not to," he said, and she felt his fingertips brush just between her shoulder blades. "My friendship with Micah meant a lot to me, and I wasn't about to be inappropriate around his fiancée. And he obviously trusted me." A smile tickled one side of his lips. "But yah, I liked you."

The rain grew lighter, pattering on the top of the buggy, and the horses shuffled their hooves on the pavement. She felt his fingers on her back again, this time lingering just a little bit longer, and she had to hold herself back from leaning into his touch. There was something almost pleading about the way his touch moved over her back, and this time the goose bumps weren't because of the rain.

His gaze moved down to her lips again, and some of whatever had been holding him back seemed to dissipate, because he leaned closer, his lips parting just slightly, but before he could close the distance between them, a car's headlights blasted into them, making them both blink, and the engine roared as it swept by.

Bethany straightened, shame rising up inside her. What was she thinking? Was a bit of sincere sympathy worth this much to her?

Because she wasn't that kind of girl either. She'd given more of herself than she should have to Micah, all because of moments like this one, when the musky male scent seemed to sweep away her proper inhibitions. And she'd learned the hardest way possible not to let herself feel too much. A warm moment in a rainstorm meant nothing. And an engagement without those vows had meant just as little.

Gott, I won't do it again . . . I won't make that same mistake!

"It's late. We should get you home," Isaiah said as if he'd come to a similar conclusion, and he picked up the reins again and gave them a flick. He glanced at her, apology shining in his dark eyes.

Bethany sucked in a shaky breath and fixed her attention on the smooth backs of the horses. This strange, simmering attraction between them didn't change who

Isaiah was. Love hadn't been enough to keep Micah in Bountiful, and Isaiah wasn't much different in that respect. After his *daet*'s arrest everything was different.

Isaiah was more than dangerous if he could make her feel like this so quickly . . . But no. It was just a strange night—that was all. And this had to stop. Isaiah wasn't a man she could trust. What she needed was to get some space to herself so she could think . . . and pray.

Chapter Five

The next morning, Bethany helped her *mamm* to clear the table while her *daet* finished up the chores outside. The kitchen smelled of the pancakes and fried potatoes they'd had for breakfast, and outside the kitchen window Lily headed toward the chicken coop, the egg bucket bouncing against her leg.

Bethany ran some soapy water in the sink, carried the thick, ceramic dishes from the table, and stacked them on the counter. Her *mamm* wiped the tabletop clean, swiping the crumbs into her hand as she worked.

Outside the window her sister disappeared into the coop and Bethany could make out her *daet* coming out of the stable with a wheelbarrow full of soiled hay. The clank of the barrow as he emptied it came softly through the morning air.

Bethany had had disturbing dreams the night before. In them, she was walking down the sidewalk in town, and everyone kept staring at her, and she hadn't known why. One of the silent accusers was Micah, and whenever she tried to stop to talk to him, he'd shake his head in disgust and move away. Then she'd see Emma and Mary, and they'd be whispering behind their hands, their eyes following her pointedly. Even the *Englishers* had been staring—not taking pictures like usual but staring. It had been one of those unsettling dreams where she woke up early but hadn't been able to shake the irrational discomfort. . . . It felt a lot like guilt.

And maybe Bethany did feel guilty, because it was only a few days since Micah had left and she was already sitting out on rainy nights with another man. What did this say about her? Was she the wrong sort of girl after all, the kind her *mamm* and *daet* had warned her brothers against when they'd been young enough to court?

She could still remember their advice to her brothers: *There is a kind of girl you'll want to marry and a kind of girl who will only bring heartbreak and shame. . . .*

It might explain her dreams last night—the guilt. Because a couple of weeks ago she'd been utterly certain about who she trusted and who she didn't, who was good and who was bad. And now those certainties were all jumbled and even she didn't land in the same place she used to think she did. She wasn't quite so "good" and "proper" after all. There was no fiancé to hold up as her security now.

She knew that Gott had forgiven her for her mistakes, but she hadn't fully forgiven herself.

"You look tired lately," Mamm said. "I know this has been hard on you, my girl, but you've got to sleep."

"I do sleep," Bethany said. It sounded like being contrary, but the simple fact was she'd been sleeping solidly all night long and still waking up tired.

"Ada thinks she's pregnant again," Mamm said. "Did I tell you that?"

Ada was one of Bethany's older sisters, and she already had four kinner of her own, the eldest of whom was six years old, so she was busy as it was.

"Again?" Bethany shook her head. "I know that *kinner* are a blessing, but so is the spacing between them."

"I don't think you get to judge that, my dear," Mamm said with a wry smile. "*Kinner* are a blessing, period, and a woman doesn't always have precise control over these things. When you marry, *kinner* come along! So you'd best be ready for them."

"When will she know for sure?" Bethany asked.

"She'll get a test," Mamm replied.

"At the drugstore, right?" Bethany asked. "How do they work?"

"Don't worry about that," Mamm said with a wave of her hand. "I'll tell you all about those once you're married. No need to know too early. But Ada will get one, and then she can confirm it, but she's been pregnant often enough to know her own body by now."

Another baby . . . Ada's youngest wasn't even a year old yet, but what wife and *mamm* didn't pray for more babies?

But only a couple of weeks ago Ada had been complaining about being tired all the time, about sleeping so heavily that Chris had to wake her up to start her morning chores, and that was sounding rather familiar right now. . . .

Bethany swallowed. That time of the month was now three weeks in the past for Bethany, and this was the second one she'd missed. She'd tried to ignore it, thinking that perhaps it was just a weird happening, and when her period next came she could put her mind at ease.

Please, Gott, she prayed in her heart. *Let me not be pregnant. . . . I've learned my lesson and I'll never make that mistake again. Ever! I'll be a proper Amish girl every step of the way if You'll only make it so that I'm not pregnant.*

Bethany had three older sisters, all of whom were married with *kinner*, and she'd heard them talking about their earliest symptoms often enough. Exhaustion, irritability, general puffiness . . . All of which could mean absolutely nothing. She knew that. How many times had women quoted those same symptoms, hopeful for the happy news that she'd finally have a baby of her own, just to have it mean nothing at all? Another of her sisters, Hadassah, had had a lot of trouble conceiving a first child. Pregnancy didn't come as easily for everyone.

Gott, if only You'd bless me with Hadassah's difficulty.

Because over the last few days her worries had grown. A married woman might find a new pregnancy to be difficult for any number of reasons, but an unmarried woman?

Her heart sped up, and she took a deep breath to try to calm her nerves.

If Micah were here, they'd just speed up the wedding—easily solved. But with her fiancé gone? There would be no easy solution to fix the problem.

Gott, please help me.

Bethany went to work with her father at the regular time, and when Isaiah showed up ten minutes after them, she refused to meet his gaze. Whatever had happened the night before could not be repeated—that much she knew for certain.

"Bethany, why don't you show Isaiah how to sew bindings?" Daet said.

"He can just keep cutting edges," Bethany replied. "I can sew."

"Yah, but the more he knows, the more help he is around here," Daet replied. "Show him, please."

That was a command, despite her father's gentle voice. She nodded at Isaiah and headed toward the sewing frame. He joined her, glancing over his shoulder toward her father, and then said quietly, "I'm sorry if I made things uncomfortable last night."

"It's fine," she said.

"Yah? You don't seem fine."

"Not everything is about you, Isaiah." The words came out sharper than she'd intended, and she saw them land, saw him recoil slightly.

"Yah. Okay." He dropped his gaze. "Maybe you could just show me how to do this, then."

She felt bad for the words now, but there was no taking them back, and it wasn't like she could tell him what was really on her mind. Yah, it involved how he'd made her feel, but her guilt went far deeper than that. When a girl was told the virtues of marrying the first boy who took her home from singing . . . what happened when he left? What happened when the first boy she was serious with wasn't going to be her last, too?

The beautiful, pure, Godly marriage she'd imagined for herself was just that—fantasy. And the real life she was facing didn't feel quite so perfect, especially when she was planning a trip to the drugstore to put her mind at ease.

She could deal with her guilt and her regrets . . . so long as she wasn't pregnant.

Bethany's chance came when Daet needed her to pick up some postage stamps for him, and she grabbed her purse and hurried out. The post office was next door to the drugstore, and she bought the stamps her father had requested, then went into the drugstore, her heart pattering nervously in her chest.

She ambled down the aisles, her gaze flowing over first aid supplies, hot-water bottles, cold and flu medication . . . It wasn't a very big shop, and it was run by an *Englisher* pharmacist and her husband. They were quite young—in their early thirties—and they were always rather affectionate with each other, even when customers were around. It was a source of humor to the more relaxed Amish people in the community and an annoyance to the Amish who were more pious. This morning the husband stood behind the till at the front of the store, chatting with a middle-aged *Englisher* man he seemed to know, and the female pharmacist was nowhere to be seen.

Bethany headed down one aisle after another, holding several items she had snatched off the shelf at random that she had no intent of purchasing—foot powder, shampoo, and a little sewing kit—and moving steadily toward the family planning aisle of the shop.

Bethany glanced over her shoulder to see a mirror angled in her direction, likely to dissuade thieves, and she felt the heat move up to her cheeks. Could she bring herself to bring a pregnancy test to the front of the shop and pay for it with that *Englisher* man?

No, there was no way. The other option would be to attempt to pay for it at the back of the shop where the pharmacist did her work, but she wasn't sure she could look her in the face either. There would be judgment regardless, and what if they talked about the Amish girl who came to buy a pregnancy test? She'd heard of some girls leaving the money on the shelf from which she took the test, but that felt risky, too, with that mirror.

Bethany moved into the family planning aisle, her gaze skipping over the various boxes and bottles, her cheeks growing hotter and hotter. The men's voices from the front droned on, and she heard the bell over the door tinkle as someone else came inside the store, making Bethany's heartbeat speed up.

"Can I help you?" The pharmacist came into the aisle, a solemn but friendly look on her face.

Bethany looked around herself hurriedly, wondering who else had seen her.

"It's okay," the woman said softly. "Do you have any questions?"

"No, I'm fine," Bethany said, her voice strangled. In truth, she had a hundred questions, none of which she dared to ask.

At the front of the store the men continued their conversation, and the pharmacist glanced in that direction. "Did you want to pay at the back when you're ready?"

"Yah." Bethany nodded hurriedly. "Thank you."

She turned back to the wall of products, and it was like they all ran together. She didn't know what a pregnancy test even looked like! Her older sisters had talked about taking them, but they hadn't given any details as to how the process worked.

"What do you need to find?" the pharmacist asked.

"A pregnancy test," Bethany said, and the words came out louder than she'd intended.

"Here." The woman plucked a box off a shelf and inclined her head toward the back of the store. "Come on. It's more private back there."

Bethany followed her, and after a short but effective description of how she was to take the test, Bethany paid.

"Do you need help?" the woman asked softly.

"Taking it?" Bethany asked uncertainly.

"No, I mean . . . You're young and I'm presuming not married yet, am I right?"

Bethany didn't answer.

"Are you in any danger if that test comes back positive?"

Danger . . . Bethany wasn't sure what the woman was imagining, but no, no one was going to beat her or anything if she was pregnant. But it would end her life as she knew it, and nothing would be the same again. Everyone who knew and loved her would be disappointed. She'd be unmarriageable if it got out. But her physical safety wasn't in question.

"I'm okay," Bethany said.

"If you need help—any kind—you tell me," the woman said. "There are people who can help, options—"

Yah, like the *Englisher* police who questioned her so compassionately and then arrived at Service Sunday to arrest one of their preachers. The *Englishers'* "help" was often more traumatic than useful. The Amish took care of their own problems—including this kind.

"I don't need help. I'm fine," Bethany repeated and, clutching a white paper bag against her chest, she bolted from the store and emerged back out into the summer sunlight.

What she needed was a private bathroom. She couldn't possibly go back to the shop, even though they had a bathroom there. Where would she throw away the test and the box once she was done with them?

There was a burger place farther up the road—the one very un-Amish establishment where most of the Amish teens went to eat. But there was also a public washroom there. Bethany headed up the road, ignoring the staring *Englishers* who took pictures of just about any Amish person they saw. Her dreams from last night came flooding back, except the accusations today weren't coming from her Amish community, they were coming from inside her own heart.

Bethany had heard the stories of the women who fell pregnant before marriage, and for some, the result was downright tragic—babies given up for adoption, women who never would get married now that they had a child.

Please, Gott. Let it be a false alarm, she prayed fervently with every step. *I've learned my lesson. I don't need any more consequences to befall me to make me learn. I'll be good from now on, I promise. Please, Gott.*

Fifteen minutes later, she came back out of the burger place, the white paper bag crumpled and left under a pile of paper towels in the women's bathroom. Her heart hammered hard in her chest and she sucked in a breath of that deep-fried air, her stomach turning.

The test was easier to take than she'd thought, and the answer came quickly. No more wondering necessarily.

Bethany was pregnant.

* * *

"You need to smooth the bone tool over the leather like this," Nathaniel said. "And move quickly. The glue is already drying. This part is harder than it looks because you have to be able to tuck the leather into these creases here—see?"

Nathaniel ran the tool down the crease of the book along the spine and the book began to take shape.

"Then you're adding more glue here along the spine, and smooth—see?"

Nathaniel turned the book, cradling it in his palm. "Just so—brush on the glue, and then lay down the leather—" Nathaniel put the book into Isaiah's hand. "Now you keep going. Brush on the glue—not too much—yes, brush it. . . ."

Binding books took special skill, and Isaiah was slowly picking up the tips and tricks he needed to know to be an honest contribution. It was satisfying work—something he hadn't expected to enjoy this much. But going from pieces of leather and unbound paper to a neatly bound leather tome left him feeling like he'd created something quite magnificent.

"Bethany told me that you won't be able to retire," Isaiah said, his voice low.

"Well, she shouldn't have told you that," Nathaniel replied. "It is private family business."

"I didn't know that it wasn't a legitimate charitable investment," Isaiah said. "I believed my *daet*."

"As you would," Nathaniel agreed.

"I'm sorry—deeply sorry," Isaiah said. "I know I've said it before, but—"

Nathaniel put a hand on his shoulder. "You'll be wiser now, no doubt."

"Yah." Isaiah swallowed. "I will."

"Good. So will I, for that matter." Nathaniel looked at him meaningfully, then turned back to the book in his hand. "Now, smooth the leather around the cords there—it makes for an attractive spine. Tuck it down hard—use some muscle now. You aren't going to hurt it. Yah, like that . . ."

It wasn't a full-out acceptance of his apology, but Nathaniel was working with him, and for Amish men that meant something. When the bell above the door tinkled Isaiah didn't even look up from his work until he heard Nathaniel greeting the bishop.

"Bishop Lapp! Good morning."

The bishop stood back and talked with Nathaniel in lower tones than Isaiah could make out, and Isaiah finished smoothing the leather over the thick cardboard cover pieces. Then he picked up the razor-sharp knife and cut slices at the corners so he could fold them down. By the time he'd finished, he found both the bishop and Nathaniel watching him.

"Could I have a word?" the bishop asked. "This won't take long."

"Yah." Isaiah put down the bone tool and Nathaniel stepped up to check his work.

"Go on. If this is good, I'll have you practice on some blank journals when you get back," Nathaniel said.

Isaiah wiped his hands on the canvas apron around his waist, and then untied it and left it on his work stool. He followed the bishop outside the shop and around the corner to a little stretch of green grass and relative privacy.

Through a side window, Isaiah could see Nathaniel turning the book over in his hands.

"Is there a problem, Bishop?" Isaiah asked.

"Yah, but not a new one," the older man replied quietly. "I've just come from a meeting with the elders."

"Oh?" Isaiah felt his stomach tighten.

"We have a problem in our community with our young people leaving. Another young man almost made the decision to leave, but his father was able to talk him out of it. Hopefully, it worked, but we can't just turn a blind eye to what is happening here."

"How does this include me?" Isaiah asked.

"The young man said that he'd lost his faith in the Amish way of life. If a preacher he'd respected so deeply could take advantage of his own community, what gave us the moral high ground over the *Englishers*?" The bishop looked at Isaiah expectantly.

"Are you asking me?" Isaiah asked.

"Yah, I'm asking you."

"I . . . don't know," Isaiah replied honestly. "I'm in the same position. Except I know what I *want* our community to be—all those things we were taught as *kinner*. I want people I can count on, Gott's guidance in our corporate decisions . . . I want our unique and Gott-centered way of life to be preserved in all its beauty so that when I marry and have *kinner* of my own, they can experience the same things in their own lives—it won't be a thing of the past, like with the *Englishers*. Time won't have erased it. I won't have to say that when I was young it was different."

The bishop nodded slowly. "Are you willing to do your best to make our community the ideal we strive for, Isaiah?"

"Yah, Bishop! Of course!"

"What would you say to preaching?"

Isaiah frowned slightly. "I thought it was agreed that I shouldn't. Have you changed your mind?"

"I'm talking about arranging a young people's gathering and having you speak."

"What would I say?" he asked.

"What you just said to me—why *you're* staying, even after your *daet* let you down so severely."

Isaiah swallowed, his mind spinning. Could he do it—stand up in front of his peers and preach as if he had any wisdom tucked away that they didn't? Because he didn't even know who he was anymore!

"I can't do it," Isaiah said, his voice dull.

"Because you aren't convinced you'll stay?" the bishop asked.

"No, because I'm no preacher. I wanted to be like my *daet*, and I don't have him to imitate anymore. I don't think Gott wants me to preach. Not anymore."

The bishop was quiet for a moment, and he chewed the side of his cheek in thought, then he sighed.

"We're losing the young people, Isaiah. These would be your friends, but for us older folks, these are our *kinner*. And when you have a child, you pray with all your heart that you can do better than some of the other people before you have done, that you can show this child that the Amish life is Gott's will, and that it holds true and abiding happiness that they won't find over the fence." The older man raised his gaze to meet Isaiah's. "So when I say that we're losing young people, this is an emergency. We have to do something, and because it was your *daet* who broke their faith, I was hoping that you might be able to help give them a reason to stay."

Could he? Or would it just be words? An insincere sermon wasn't going to do any good, and he wasn't going to be able to sound as confident as he'd have to. He could do more damage with his own slipping sense of identity.

"I can't fix what he broke!" Isaiah said earnestly.

"And maybe I'm being too demanding here," the bishop conceded. "I'm asking you to help me keep the young people in our community, but I haven't stopped to ask you what you need to stay. You've always been mature and thoughtful, and I tend to treat you as older than your years. I'm sorry for that."

"It's all right," Isaiah said with a shake of his head.

"So, in this process of finding your footing again, what do *you* need, Isaiah?"

"The one thing I need to make my own peace here is to understand why my *daet* did it."

The bishop frowned. "Does it matter so much why?"

"Yah, it does. Because this is my father. He raised me, told me what was right and wrong, disciplined me when I messed up. He taught me to drive a buggy, how to care for horses, how to read the Bible! And that man went against everything he believed and stole from our friends and neighbors. So yah, I need to understand it."

"Sin is sin," the bishop replied. "The righteous can't understand why the wicked do what they do."

"But not every man who goes so wrong is my father." Isaiah's voice caught.

They fell silent for a few beats, and the sound of the cars on the street mingling with horse hooves from the Amish buggies floated over them.

"I don't think I can give you any answers," the bishop said, at last. "But your *daet* might. I'll have to talk to the elders, but maybe in this unique situation, we might need to adjust how we deal with it."

"What does that mean?" Isaiah asked.

"The Ordnung tells us that when someone sins and refuses to repent, the answer is to shun," the bishop replied. "The worry is that by allowing that person access to the community, it will only make things worse—spread the sinful disease. But it isn't working, is it? The disease is spreading regardless."

"So you'll reverse the shunning?" Isaiah asked.

Did he even want that? There was a certain amount of comfort in knowing that he couldn't talk to his father, that he didn't have to face him. And yet it seemed that any kind of healing was going to come from just that.

"I can't promise a reversal," Bishop Lapp said. "What are we without the Ordnung? The Ordnung gives us that protection from the outside, and it keeps us unique and separate. I'll speak with the elders and see what their feelings are on the matter. And of course we'll all pray about it. But I appreciate your candor, Isaiah."

Isaiah's gaze moved toward that slim side window, and he saw that Bethany had returned, too. She stood at her workspace, and he could only make out half of her face, but she looked pale to him.

"How do I find my place here, Bishop?" he asked quietly. "What advice do you have for me?"

"You'll need to be straight—very straight. You'll have to do things the Amish way, accept the Ordnung, and prove to the community that you're not what they think," the bishop replied.

"Yah . . ."

"My advice isn't all misery," the bishop added with a faint smile. "You should get married to a good girl—someone from a good family."

"A good family wouldn't have me, Bishop."

"Maybe a woman who's gotten a little older," the bishop suggested. "Maybe a woman who isn't so traditionally . . . attractive."

Someone desperate enough to take him. He understood the implication. Isaiah felt his heart sink. He didn't want to make do with a wife he didn't love. And yet he wanted to belong. Maybe he couldn't have it all—maybe that wasn't possible anymore.

"Isaiah, joining a good family by marrying a good woman would go a long way to helping people see you differently," the bishop said quietly. "A woman whose honesty and faithfulness are beyond reproach. If you had a father-in-law speaking on your behalf, it would help."

And maybe the bishop was right, because Isaiah could think of three women off the top of his head who had been passed over in the marriage market for various reasons. They didn't excite him at all, but if he was to find a life here, it would be good to do it with a wife by his side. Maybe he didn't need love or passion. Maybe respect could be enough.

"I need to get back to work, if that's okay," Isaiah said.

"Yah, of course. I'll see you." The bishop reached out and patted his arm. "And son, I'm glad you're still here. I am."

Bountiful was losing its young people and Isaiah wasn't convinced he could give them a reason strong enough to stay if they'd already lost their faith in the Amish life. Once upon a time in one of his father's sermons, Abe had said, *If you believe, then you believe, and nothing anyone can do will change it. But if you don't believe, if you're only Amish because your family is Amish, then all the best intentions of the entire community won't keep you in the fold. Work out your own salvation with fear and trembling, my friends.*

Was there truth in those words? Or was everything his father had given him flawed? That was the problem Isaiah faced. He didn't know how much of his father's teaching he should accept now.

The bishop headed back to the sidewalk and gave Isaiah a nod in farewell, and Isaiah went back into the book bindery shop. The scent of paper and leather mingled with that unique smell of glue in the air, the clank of a book press mingling with Nathaniel's low voice as he talked to his daughter.

Even if Isaiah had no answers right now, at least he had employment.

"You're back!" Nathaniel said. "Your work looked good. I'm going to start you on some blank journals for practice."

It was confirmation that he'd done one small job well. If he could continue long enough with one right step after another, the community might finally be appeased.

Chapter Six

That night, after supper, Isaiah helped Seth fix a fence in the far pasture. It was an old fence—wooden planks instead of proper barbed wire—and Isaiah put a boot against a post and yarded the rotted plank off the post. The posts would need to be replaced, but they'd last one more winter with barbed wire.

The wire cutters required some muscle to snap the wire from the large spindle on the back of the wagon, and as the men worked together, the sun slipped steadily down behind the horizon, the sky flooding with pink and gold.

"Hold that," Seth said, and Isaiah grabbed the wire, a barb piercing his glove and scratching his hand, but he held it firm until Seth had stapled it into place.

"So, how is Bethany?" Seth asked as they followed the wire down to the next post.

"She's all right," Isaiah replied. "Her *daet* is showing me the ropes—I bound six blank journals today alone, and they're up for sale. Such a weird feeling to see them on the shelf with a price tag on the back."

"He's training you," Seth said, straightening.

"Yah. I have to know how to do the job."

"Well, I mean I'm sure he could have had you doing some smaller thing over and over again, but he's teaching you the trade."

Isaiah used the wire cutters to snip off the end of the barbed wire, then straightened as well. "Yah, I suppose so."

"Do you like it?" Seth asked.

"I do."

"I wonder if he'd make you an apprentice."

The thought hadn't occurred to Isaiah yet, and he rolled the idea over in his mind. "I'd need to prove I was going to be worth the effort."

"Yah, I suppose," Seth agreed.

"But if I could prove that much, maybe he would."

It was either finding a different trade in town or becoming a farmhand, but he wouldn't be getting any land unless he bought it himself. Farmland was passed down in families because it was too expensive to simply buy enough farmable land and make it profitable. Seth and his brothers would inherit this farm—or pieces of it. Isaiah could work for his cousins as a regular farmhand, but he'd never own this land. His chance of farm ownership had been confiscated by the government.

"So, how was it driving Mary home from singing?" Isaiah asked, changing the subject. "Have you seen her since?"

"No, but I'll take her home again next time," Seth replied, and his cheeks colored a little.

"So you like her, then?" Isaiah asked.

"Yah. She's a nice girl. She likes to cook and sew. She says she'll make me a pie."

Isaiah smiled at that. "That's nice."

Seth's smile slipped. "It was Micah who told me that

she liked me. She'd told him, and he passed along the message that if I were to ask her home from singing, she'd be inclined to accept." Seth dug the toe of his boot into the scrub grass.

"Yah, I know."

Seth picked up the wire and headed back toward the wagon, then flung it up on the wooden bed.

"What's out there that's better than here?" Seth asked, turning around again.

"Nothing!" Isaiah shook his head. "Freedom, I guess. But at what cost? Just because everything is possible out there doesn't make it smart."

"Lovina, too," Seth added. "She left, and if it was so bad out there, you'd think she'd be back already."

"Maybe it takes some time to figure it out," Isaiah suggested.

"Or maybe it isn't so bad as they say," Seth replied.

Was Seth thinking of leaving, too? Because of his *daet*, or because of something else?

"You aren't saying—" Isaiah started.

"Of course not," Seth cut him off. "I'll take a nice girl home from singing and I'll make my life here. It's just we've been told since we were *kinner* that the kind of people who leave the Amish life are deeply sinful to begin with, rebellious and refusing to be happy with honest, hard work. But the people who left this time around were our friends and family, and they weren't any more sinful than you or me, Isaiah."

Isaiah slung his bag over his shoulder. The wind was warm, but a few cumulus clouds hung heavy around the horizon, backlit with gold and fire. With the direction of the wind, it both made for a beautiful sunset and promised rain overnight.

"What does it mean if they don't come home again?" Seth asked.

Isaiah tossed his bag of tools up onto the wagon bed and then hoisted himself up onto the seat. His cousin followed, then picked up the reins.

"I don't know," Isaiah admitted. "But this *is* home, isn't it?"

Seth didn't answer, but he flicked the reins and the horses started off, leaning against the weight of the wagon as it started to roll through the long, waving grass.

Home was supposed to be a community. It was supposed to be history and future together in one place. It was supposed to be salvation. Bountiful was home, but staying here might be less an instinct and more of a stubborn choice.

Because, as Seth had intimated, there were other options out there.

The next morning Nathaniel, Bethany, and Isaiah worked hard on the binding orders, and Isaiah found that he could now work efficiently with only a little help once in a while when he needed it. Of course, the literary journals were a very basic binding—nothing terribly complicated—but at least he was a part of the team and able to fully contribute as the stack of bound journals got taller. Nathaniel worked with the gold foil, heating it and pressing it into the covers and spine to leave the name and date of each journal for easier reference.

Bethany worked in silence, and she still looked pale.

"Bethany, you're off a half inch," Nathaniel said, coming to the vise where she was cutting the sewing holes into the folios.

"No, I'm—" Bethany sighed. "I'm sorry, Daet. I can fix this."

"You don't look well," Nathaniel said, reaching out to touch her forehead. "You don't seem hot, but you've seemed off since yesterday."

"I'm fine, Daet. I'll fix this," she repeated.

Nathaniel headed back toward his worktable, but before Isaiah turned back to his own task, Bethany put a hand over her mouth and ran to a garbage can and vomited. She stood over it for a moment, then wiped her mouth and tied the bag.

"She needs to go home," Nathaniel said, more firmly this time.

Bethany disappeared into the back room where the water turned on. When she emerged again there was more color in her face.

"You're going home, Bethany," Nathaniel said, raising his voice.

"Daet, we're very busy," Bethany said. "You need me here."

"I need you well!" Nathaniel replied. "Don't be silly, Bethany. Isaiah, would you be willing to drive her back home right now? Then come back and we'll work together and stay late until today's work is done."

"Yah. Not a problem," Isaiah said quickly.

"Daet, trust me when I say—" Bethany began.

"Bethany, you just threw up your lunch," Nathaniel retorted. "If you won't go home for your own health, at least think of mine."

Isaiah put his work aside and took off his canvas apron. He waited for Bethany to gather her things, and then gave Nathaniel a silent nod and headed out to the stable out back to hitch up the horses. It didn't take him long, and when he pulled the buggy around the front he scooted over and offered Bethany a hand to get up.

"I'm fine," she said irritably.

"You look sick to me," he retorted. "Come on."

He reached out again, and this time she took his hand and let him help pull her up. Her hand felt nice in his, but he released her once she was up in the buggy, and when she was settled he flicked the reins and the horses started.

A car slowed down and let them into traffic, and Isaiah kept his attention on the road as he navigated through town. The streets could be busy, and he didn't want to risk an accident. Bethany sat silently next to him, and when he glanced at her, she didn't look sick now exactly—although who could argue with her sickness in the shop?

"I'll help your *daet* finish up tonight," he said. "You don't have to worry about that."

"I know."

"Are you upset with me?" he asked, looking over at her uncertainly.

"For settling in so well?" she asked with a sidelong look. "I don't know. Maybe it's hard to see Micah replaced this easily."

"This looks easy?" he asked.

"You're picking it up pretty fast," she said.

"Why do I feel like you require an apology for that?" He shot her a teasing smile, but she didn't smile in return and he sighed. "You've been really quiet since yesterday, and I thought maybe it was because of the last time I drove you."

He didn't want to say it directly—because he'd almost kissed her. He hadn't actually done it, so he'd hoped that they wouldn't need to mention it, but if she was upset about it, that wouldn't be so easy.

Bethany smiled faintly. "I have other things to worry about besides you, you know."

"So you keep telling me," he said, but he was reassured by her smile.

Isaiah reined the horses in at a stop sign, and then flicked the reins again, easing forward as they got farther from the downtown core and closer to the broad expanse of sunbaked farmland ahead of them.

"But it does . . . factor in," she added. "I don't know what you think of me, but I'm not the kind of girl who bounces from an engagement into another man's buggy."

"I know that," he said, glancing over at her. "Look—if we have some chemistry, you and me—"

"Chemistry?" she demanded. "What does that even mean?"

"It's how the *Englishers* describe a connection, an attraction . . ." And right now, it felt indelicate to be using an *Englisher* phrase. He shouldn't have.

"It counts for very little, you know," she said.

She might be right, but something had certainly changed since he'd been in a buggy with her last. They'd been friends—confiding—and maybe they'd been tempted to go a little further, but Bethany seemed decidedly different today.

"Bethany, I don't know what you think of me either," he replied pointedly. "But I'm not looking to fool around.

I need an honest life—I need to show Bountiful that I can be trusted. I have a lot at stake here."

"Then what *was* that in the buggy the other night?" she asked.

"I . . . have liked you for a really long time," he said. "I didn't mean to upset you."

"I'm not looking for a boyfriend," she said, and she looked the other way.

"Okay. Understood."

Her words stung, because when he'd told her that he needed an honest life, he was trying to tell her that if he made a move, he wasn't going to embarrass her, or dump her. He was looking to do things right. He'd taken her home from singing, hadn't he?

Regardless, he'd offended her, and he felt a wave of regret for that. Whatever had been tugging them together out there in the storm had been mutual, he was sure of it, but this wasn't about a man and a woman who were attracted to each other. It was a whole lot more complicated than that.

And now he felt stupid. Who was he to follow those kinds of instincts with anyone right now? He had nothing to offer—not a farm, not a future, and certainly not a good name! What had he even been thinking?

As they drove out of town, he could feel his nerves relaxing. This was where he felt at home, under the big, blue Pennsylvanian sky with the patchwork fields rolling out around him. Clouds tumbled overhead, leaving shadows in the fields below.

"Are we friends, at least?" he asked after a few beats of silence.

"I suppose," she replied, but when she looked in his direction again, her expression had softened.

"That's something." He shot her a conciliatory smile. "I don't have a lot of those right now. I can't be toying with that."

"Why was the bishop here?" she asked.

"He wanted me to preach," Isaiah replied.

"What?"

"I said no," Isaiah said. "But he was hoping I could help close the gate, as it were, and keep the young people in our community. Apparently, there was another young man who wanted to leave."

"Who?"

"He didn't say. Apparently, he didn't go, though."

Bethany nodded. "That's good. I wonder who it was."

"I don't know, but even talking to my cousin yesterday, people are thinking differently. This scandal with my *daet*, it changed things for everyone. We're supposed to keep things the same, protect our community's standards, but I'm not sure it's possible to keep everything exactly the same, Ordnung or not."

"Is your cousin wanting to leave?" Bethany asked, her voice low.

"No . . . I don't think so, but what do I know? It's just that when so many people you've known incredibly well leave, you can't just write them off as sinful anymore, can you?"

Bethany fell silent, and Isaiah sucked in a deep breath. He couldn't talk all this out with Seth either. Bethany, ironically enough, despite all her reasons to resent him, had turned out to be his biggest confidant.

Maybe that Bethany was the closest to him at the

moment said more about how cut off he was from his own community . . .

"I don't know who I am here anymore, Bethany," he said. "I was so certain up until a few months ago. I could have told you exactly what my life was going to look like."

"Yah, me too," she agreed.

"I have a lot to prove," he said quietly. "And it isn't going to be easy. I've got to prove to everyone here that I'm not like my *daet*, even though I look like him and I speak like him, too."

"How will you do it?" she asked.

Isaiah shrugged. "I'll do things the Amish way," he said. "No shortcuts. I'll work hard, I'll follow the Ordnung, and I'll keep myself out of preaching."

"Even though the bishop is asking you to preach?" she said.

"What do I have to tell people?" he asked, shaking his head. "I don't have the answers for anyone. If this has taught me anything, it's that a good Amish life isn't as simple as I used to think. I'm not going to take responsibility for guiding anyone else's spiritual life."

"No, it isn't simple," she said quietly.

There was something in her voice that gave Isaiah pause, and he glanced over at her. Her dark gaze flickered in his direction, her expression filled with sadness, and if he wasn't completely crazy, she looked a bit scared, too.

"I didn't mean to complicate anything," he said uncertainly. "I'm just talking. I don't mean to dump my stuff on you."

"Like you said, life is complicated—especially a good life. It doesn't take much to throw it off track, does it?"

Isaiah guided the horses around the corner onto a dirt

road, then he looked over at her again once they were bouncing along the gravel. "Beth, is there anything I can do to help?"

"I don't think so." She smiled faintly, but it didn't reach her eyes.

He wished there were—because seeing her like this awakened the male, protective side of him. He wanted to fight something, conquer something, fix it.

She wasn't going to make it quite that easy, though, was she?

Bethany watched the familiar landscape slip by— telephone poles with the sloping wires, the long grass that grew up in the ditches beside the road, and the clusters of buttercups that gathered around the fence posts. A cloud slid between them and the sun, and the bright afternoon light dimmed.

Her family's acreage was just ahead, and her stomach clenched into a knot. She'd have to explain to her *mamm* why *daet* had sent her home, and Bethany had to wonder how obvious an early pregnancy was to a practiced eye. Because she wasn't sick—she'd been completely honest about that with her *daet*. She was worried, yes, and feeling more tired than usual, and apparently a little nauseated, but she wasn't sick.

Gott, can I hide this? How long will I have to figure this out?

"Service Sunday is this week," Isaiah said. "And it's being hosted at my uncle's farm."

That was right—the time she always looked forward to, when she could see her friends and catch up with everyone . . . This Sunday was going to be special—not anymore, now that Micah was gone, of course. The reminder made her throat feel tight with unshed tears.

"Are you okay?" Isaiah's voice softened.

"Our banns were going to be announced . . ." she said, and then she swallowed. "And Micah was going to be baptized so we could finally get married."

When the banns were announced the engaged couple ordinarily stayed home at the girl's parents' home, and she cooked him a special meal, and they had time alone together, seeing what marriage might feel like in a few weeks' time . . . But they would have been there—actually witnessing their banns—but only because of Micah's baptism. Time was of the essence for that.

"He kept putting off his baptism, didn't he?" Isaiah said.

"Yah. He did. It was frustrating." She'd wanted everything organized and ready for their wedding day—and she hadn't liked leaving something so important to the last minute.

"Is that why you've been upset?" he asked. "Part of it, at least?"

"Yah," she admitted. Micah was the father, after all.

"This is going to sound less sympathetic than I mean it," he said slowly. "But it's better that he left before the banns, you know? It would have been harder afterward."

He had a point, and she shrugged faintly. "It would have been better not to ask me to marry him at all if he couldn't stand by it."

Maybe Bethany should have seen his passive resistance in his constantly putting off his baptism. Now she knew why, at least. If she'd recognized the warnings, she could have let him go, found someone else. If she'd done that, she wouldn't be in trouble right now. Maybe she could have found some solid Amish farmer she could have planned a life with instead of keeping herself to the one man who'd abandon her.

He turned in at the drive that led toward her home, those familiar overhanging branches that brought back memories of tree climbing with her siblings and cousins.

Micah was going to have the young men who stood with him all wear green shirts, and her friends were going to wear green dresses. Micah had been working on the eck, too. The eck was a backdrop for during the wedding dinner, and it was the groom's responsibility to build it. Theirs was to include a cabinet, and it was going to display some kitchen items that his *mamm* was going to give them, items passed down for several generations.

She sucked in a breath. All that tradition, all those expectations, and Micah had left it all behind. It still felt unreal somehow.

"I wouldn't have left you . . ." Isaiah said so quietly that she hardly heard him.

"What?" she whispered.

They were approaching the house now, and he reined in the horses just a little bit early.

"If you were marrying me, I wouldn't have left you like that," he said, turning toward her. That intense gaze of his moved over her face, and she saw a tremble of emotion in his eyes that she'd never noticed before. "If I'd asked you home from singing first, and if you'd happened to fall in love with me, I would have been at that wedding, and I wouldn't have toyed around with my baptism either. I'm just saying . . ."

What was he trying to say? She swallowed hard, and the side door opened, Lily's face appearing.

"Why are you home so early, Bethany?" the girl called from the step.

She looked back over at Isaiah, but he'd looked away again, those dark, expressive eyes hidden from her once more. Had he meant what he'd just said?

"Bethany?" Lily called, coming down the steps. There would be no avoiding her sister.

"My stomach was off," Bethany said, and she got down from the buggy, grabbing her lunch bag and the shawl that she'd worn that morning when it was still chilly out. She looked up at Isaiah, and he gave her a nod.

"Feel better," Isaiah said, his voice low and gentle. "I hope you're back at the shop tomorrow."

"Yah." She smiled faintly. "Thank you for the ride. And . . . the talk."

His cheeks pinked slightly at that, and she couldn't help but smile. Was he thinking about what he'd just said? Had he meant to say it, or had it just popped out?

Isaiah got the buggy turned around and headed back up the drive, and as she watched the back of the buggy, she couldn't help but think that it didn't matter. The depth in his eyes, the intensity of that stare that could make her skin rise in goose bumps . . . Even if Isaiah had asked her home from singing first, it wouldn't have changed the outcome of her single state right now.

Because when his father was arrested for fraud, and Isaiah had been the one to convince her own *daet* to invest in that scheme, she couldn't have gone through with it. She would have called off the wedding herself.

There would have been heartbreak anyway.

Lily waited for her as she came inside the kitchen. Mamm stood at the counter kneading some dough.

"What brings you home?" she repeated Lily's question.

"I had an upset stomach," Bethany said. "I think it's the heat. I told Daet that I was fine, but he insisted that Isaiah drive me back."

A lie. It had just rolled off her tongue, and it made her conscience ache, but what she needed right now was some privacy, not prying questions.

"Upset stomach?" her mother said with a frown. "I hope it isn't the flu."

"I'm fine," she said. "Let me wash my hands and help you."

"No, no," Mamm replied. "The last thing we need is the whole family infected. You should go lay down. Lily, you get the washing and hang it out to dry."

Bethany felt mildly guilty going upstairs to lay down while there was work to be done, letting her sister and her *mamm* shoulder the brunt of it. She could easily pitch in, but not without some explanation.

"All right," she said uncertainly. "But I could help with laundry."

"You've been pale for a few days now. And if Daet sent you home at a time like this, when he's that busy, you're sick!" Mamm replied. "Upstairs!"

Bethany headed up the stairs, and she found that her stomach was a little queasy. She made her way up the staircase and headed for her bedroom. She shut the door behind her and stood next to her bed for a moment, looking at herself in the mirror. She smoothed her hand over her apron, flattening the fabric. Her stomach was still as taut as it ever was. How long would it take for her waist to thicken? How long before her sisters noticed?

She sank onto the edge of her bed and exhaled a slow sigh. Somehow, even with all this happening, she couldn't help but think about Isaiah. She'd never thought of him in romantic terms before, but the way he'd looked at her when he'd said that he wouldn't have done what Micah did . . . It brought up goose bumps on her arms.

She had been angry about that night in the rain because she hadn't wanted to feel all those things that had sprung up between them—it reminded her too much of the things she used to feel with Micah. What good had that been?

But thoughts of Micah brought the heaviness back into her heart and she licked her lips, her gaze moving toward the window. If Micah were still at home where he belonged, the pregnancy would be a problem easily solved with a quick wedding. Everyone would guess why their marriage was happening so fast, she knew that, but they'd find it forgivable.

I'm sorry I lied to my mamm, she prayed. *And I'm sick of untruths. I'm going to tell Micah—he needs to know.*

Bethany went to her chest of drawers and opened the top drawer, pulling out a piece of paper with an address written on it. Micah had given it to her before he left— for if she changed her mind and wanted to join him. She'd been insulted at the time, but maybe it was providential that she had a way of reaching him after all.

Bethany got out a clean piece of paper and a pen from her closet, picked up a book to use as a lap desk, and sank back onto her bed again. She leaned against the headboard and started to write:

Dear Micah,

   I'm pregnant.

It just seemed prudent to begin with the most important information first.

   I only found out a few days ago, but obviously the child is ours. If you were here, we'd get married right away and start our family. But you aren't here—you've gone English and I'm on my own. I haven't told anyone yet, but I thought you should know.

   I don't know if this means you'll come back, or if you'll send me money, or if you'll ignore this altogether. Knowing you as I do, I don't think you'll ignore it, but I also never dreamed that you'd go English, so what do I know?

   I'm furious with you. Maybe this isn't the right time to tell you this, but I'm enraged. You said you loved me, Micah! You promised we'd get married and live happily for the rest of our lives, and as soon as your faith trembled, you left our life, our wedding plans, and ME behind. For what? I can't imagine what you have out there that's better than what Bountiful offers us. Freedom? To do what? I hope all those Englisher *gadgets and vehicles fill your heart, because I can't see why that life is better than one with me.*

   I think you're weak. Did you know that Isaiah hasn't left? He's facing all this, and it was his own daet *who did it. He was part of it, and he isn't leaving. He did tell me that you asked him to look*

out for me, but what is that even worth when you
aren't coming back?

She wasn't sure why she was bringing Isaiah into this.
It wouldn't do anything to soothe Micah's feelings; he'd
always been a little nervous about her spending too much
time with his friends. And now she knew why—Isaiah had
harbored feelings. Well, then, let him feel jealousy. He
deserved to feel a lot more than that!

They were supposed to announce our banns this
weekend at service, and instead of looking forward
to our future, I have to figure out how to tell my
parents that I'm pregnant. Can I even keep this
baby, or will I have to give it up to another family?
I don't know.
　　If you care about me at all anymore, you won't
breathe a word of this to anyone Amish. If I can
find a way to find a husband still, I need to be able
to do that, and it won't happen if anyone knows
about this child.
　　But I thought you should know. You'll be a daet,
after all, whether you ever see this child or not.

Bethany

The words had flown onto the paper with the force of
her emotion, and she wondered if she should wait, write
a different version that was less emotional. . . . But why?
What would it even matter if Micah saw her rage and
her desperation? Maybe he should, because he'd made
promises to her that he wasn't keeping.
　　She folded the page, then went back to her closet and

got an envelope. She wrote letters to some cousins in Indiana from time to time, so she had all the supplies to mail a letter. She carefully copied out the address Micah had given her and put a stamp in the corner. She stared down at the envelope, and for the first time since she'd discovered her condition, she felt like she was doing something.

Bethany wanted to pray, but every time she tried to open her heart to Gott lately, she couldn't seem to find the words, and she'd stopped after a sentence, feeling strangely empty. She used to find comfort in pouring out her heart to Gott, and that comfort seemed very distant now. And there was no point in promising Gott anything in return for taking away the consequences of her actions. Now, standing with that letter in her hands, the only words that came to her were fierce: *Please, oh, please, don't make me give up my baby!*

Because even though her stomach was as flat as ever, and even though she was more afraid now than she'd ever been in her life, the knowledge that a baby had begun inside her had ignited a tender flame of love. Boy or girl, she loved this little one already.

Chapter Seven

Service Sunday was hot and still. Not a breeze touched the leaves on the trees as Isaiah and his cousins set up benches in the emptied hay barn. Isaiah and Seth swung the upper doors wide open in hope that some wind might pick up and grant them some temporary relief, but so far there was none.

Sweat beaded on Isaiah's forehead and trickled down his spine as he worked. It was Mel Yoder's family's responsibility this week to set up for the worship service and then clean up afterward. They wouldn't have to do it again for a few months, but the Sunday a family hosted was always frantic. In the house the women had cleaned everything from top to bottom, and they were still bustling about in preparation.

Isaiah hoisted another bench, wielding the weight of it easily enough as he slowly swung its awkward length around to put it in place. He paused at the open sliding door, hoping for a whiff of breeze when he spotted a buggy already parked in the field—the first to arrive. He squinted, trying to make out who it was, and when the man turned around, he recognized Daniel Weibe, Micah's father. Micah's younger siblings stood in their Sunday best, waiting on their parents, and Tessa pulled down a basket—her contribution to the afternoon meal, it would seem.

This was going to be harder than he thought, facing everyone.

"The Weibes are here, huh?" Seth said, pausing at his side.

"Yah, looks like."

Isaiah and his cousin stood in the doorway, looking out at the family, both of them smothered in their own thoughts.

"Did they invest in that scam?" Seth asked, his voice low.

"I think so . . ."

There weren't many who hadn't. The *Englishers* and his *daet* had made over a million dollars combined in that scam . . . and it seemed that the *Englishers* had hidden their assets better than Abe had.

"Did they put money in because of you?" Seth asked hesitantly.

"Not this time," Isaiah replied. "Daet and Daniel were good friends, so . . ."

Daniel Weibe had trusted Abe, just like everyone else. Isaiah turned back to grab a last bench, but his younger cousins had gotten there first. It was easier to pour himself into physical labor than it was to stand here worrying about how he was supposed to fit back into a community that hardly wanted him anymore, but there wasn't much left to be done.

How was Isaiah going to do this? The bishop seemed inclined to help him settle back in, but that was because he was looking at the bigger picture, trying to stem the flow of young people who seemed to be leaving at a disastrous rate. If no one had left because of this, would the bishop be so eager to help in his plight? He wasn't sure.

Bart and Vernon came out the door, pulling off their hats and heading for the pump. Vernon had some bits of hay stuck in his hair, and Bart's shirt was streaked with dust and dirt. Isaiah watched as the younger boys heaved on the handle and pushed their faces under the water. They were young enough that their biggest worries were the chores they'd have to do, and Isaiah found himself feeling a little envious of their innocence.

But wasn't this what they were holding the community together for? For the younger generations who'd grow up learning to work hard, protected from the world's bigger problems? It was for the *kinner* he'd hopefully have one day, too. A good Amish life was a secure way to grow up.

Daniel Weibe came striding across the field toward them, and Seth shot Isaiah a nervous look.

"He looks . . . serious," Seth said.

"Yah, he does." But Isaiah wasn't going to wait here like a boy about to be scolded in front of his cousins; he headed out of the barn to meet the older man.

Vernon stopped his washing at the pump and straightened, watching as Isaiah headed past him.

"Hurry up, Vernon," Seth said behind him. "We have to get changed for service, and people are starting to arrive, so get moving."

It only made Isaiah the more aware of his own sweaty shirt. Daniel stopped a few yards away and Isaiah closed the distance, then held out his hand to shake. Daniel hesitated a beat before shaking his hand, and Isaiah felt his stomach tighten.

"Good morning," Isaiah said.

"Good morning." Daniel glanced over his shoulder, and Isaiah saw Daniel's wife, Tessa, looking at them. She dropped her gaze and started toward the house. "I was hoping to speak with you before anyone else got here, actually."

"Okay," Isaiah said, and he cleared his throat.

"As you know, Micah's gone."

"Yah, I was told," Isaiah said, and he shrugged apologetically. "I would have come by to see you, but I didn't think I'd be welcome."

There was a beat of silence, which was confirmation enough that Isaiah had been right there.

"From what we understand, he'd been questioning our Amish ways a lot," Daniel said. "And when your *daet*, who he respected so deeply, turned to *Englisher* crime, he couldn't line it all up in his head anymore."

"That's what Bethany told me, too," Isaiah replied.

"I was talking to the bishop the other day, and he pointed out that having you here might be a blessing, because for whatever reason, you were able to make your peace with this mess and stay."

"I'm not at peace," Isaiah said.

"But you're here, and that's more than we can say about Micah," Daniel countered. The older man's eyes misted, and he blinked a few times, looking away. "You know how much our son means to us."

"Yah, of course," Isaiah said miserably.

"He told us that he'd asked you to look out for Bethany," Daniel said.

"When did he tell you that?" Isaiah asked, his breath catching in his chest.

"When he gave us the address, just before he left," Daniel replied.

So just before he'd left Bountiful, he'd mentioned Isaiah's promise? Maybe that promise wasn't so far in the past, after all.

"Nathaniel says you've been helping their family out at the shop," Daniel said, and he cleared his throat. "And that's good of you."

Isaiah didn't answer. It wasn't for Bethany that he'd taken that job—it was in spite of her. Did no one else see how badly he needed work?

"The thing is," the older man went on, "if Micah was still thinking about Bethany and who would look out for her while he was gone, it stands to reason that he was considering a return."

"I can see the logic there," Isaiah agreed.

"It certainly gives us hope," Daniel said. "And we were hoping you would help us."

Just like the bishop—

"How?" Isaiah asked with a sigh. "What am I supposed to do?"

"We have an address he gave us where we could reach him," Daniel said. "And we've already written to him, but we only said what we'd told him before he left—showing him from the Bible how the Amish life is Gott's will for all of us, and how if he leaves, he's sacrificing his own salvation. And if it didn't convince him then, I doubt it will convince him now because, apparently, he's gone Mennonite."

"And the Mennonites tell them differently," Isaiah said. "Yah."

Isaiah nodded. "What would I tell him?"

"Why you're here."

"It's very likely the same set of verses you sent him," Isaiah replied.

Daniel shook his head. "No, not your theological reasons—there has to be more than that. You grew up with him. Maybe if you remind him of the good times you had, or tell him the kind of life you're looking forward to here—"

"Daniel, right now, I'm looking forward to a life of being distrusted and held at arm's length," Isaiah retorted.

Daniel's expression softened. "Do this for us, convince him to come home, and you'll be like family again."

"And if I can't convince him?" Isaiah asked, meeting Daniel's uncomfortable gaze. Because he highly doubted that he could. If a girl like Bethany couldn't give Micah reason to stay in Bountiful, boyhood memories wouldn't be enough either. And maybe there was a small, selfish part of Isaiah that hoped Micah would stay away, and he felt a stab of guilt at the very thought. He'd trade his best friend's salvation for a remote chance with Micah's fiancée? He didn't even have anything he could offer her! What did that make him?

"Just try." Daniel pulled a piece of paper from his pocket and handed it over. "Write to him. Please. Even if you tell him how much Bethany misses him . . . This wedding could still go forward! I'm sure of it!"

Another couple of buggies turned into the drive, and Isaiah took the paper from Daniel's hand and nodded.

"I'll do my best," he said, his voice tight.

"Thank you. I know you will."

And that was the hard part—because Isaiah had just given his word, he *would* do his best to bring his friend home. Whatever feelings had been brewing between him and Bethany had to stop. He couldn't let himself fall for her—not in earnest.

As Isaiah turned toward the house, he spotted a fourth buggy arriving, and this one he recognized immediately because it was driven by Nathaniel Glick, his wife at his side, and Bethany on the other side of her mother. Bethany looked slim and she didn't seem to see him yet, but there was something about her face, even from this distance, that made his heart give a little jump in his chest.

He shouldn't be doing this—letting himself feel anything for her. She was single, but only until Micah came home. And Isaiah couldn't exactly argue that he was better for Bethany right now than Micah was because he had nothing to offer her. And Micah had trusted him.

Daniel was trusting him.

This wasn't about Isaiah's feelings, it was about the man Bethany had already chosen. She deserved the chance to decide if she still wanted him.

Isaiah headed inside and went upstairs to wash himself and get into his Sunday best. His shirt and pants were washed and ironed, hanging in his closet, and his cousins were already in their bedroom getting dressed. Bart and Vernon were tussling over a pair of suspenders, and Seth stoically ignored them, inspecting himself in the mirror as he plucked at his shirt.

"You look fine," Isaiah said as he came into the room and grabbed his clothes from the closet.

Seth's cheeks colored and he turned from the mirror. "Are the Fishers here yet?"

"I didn't see them," Isaiah said, and then he grinned. "Waiting on Mary, are you?"

"Just wanted to say hello," Seth said. "Whatever."

"There's no shame in that." Isaiah chuckled. "I was just teasing."

He pulled on his pants, then grabbed his shirt. He stood by the window—the only spot in the bedroom that was free of extra bodies right now—doing up the buttons as he scanned the field where the families were parking their buggies. He could say he was looking for the bishop's family for his cousin, but he wasn't—then he saw her.

Bethany was walking arm in arm with Mary Fisher, away from the buggies and in the direction of the barn, where the service would be held. She wore a plum-colored dress with a crisp white apron. Her hair was neatly pulled under her *kapp*, and he caught himself watching the way her dress fell over her hips. He couldn't make out if she was smiling from the angle of his vantage point, and as if she could feel his gaze on her, she lifted her eyes and looked directly at him. There was no smile, but it was like her entire, heartbroken soul was visible in that stare, and he froze. She held his gaze for a moment, then carried on out of sight.

"Yah, Mary Fisher is here," Isaiah said. "I just saw her."

Who knew? Maybe if Isaiah told Micah the truth, that he was falling for his fiancée, common jealousy would be enough to bring the man back for his wedding.

Sometimes it wasn't about theological reasoning or childhood memories. Sometimes it was about not wanting another guy to make a move on the girl Isaiah knew his friend loved—the most basic human drive.

Even if Isaiah knew for a fact that Micah didn't love her nearly enough.

* * *

Bethany's heart sped up at the sight of Isaiah in the second-floor window. She hadn't realized he was even there until she'd looked up, and then her breath caught. His shirt was open, his bare chest visible for just a moment as his fingers moved, doing up the buttons. There were no suspenders or hat yet—he was still getting dressed, it seemed. It was just the man, his gaze locked on her with a strange, vulnerable intensity.

"Are you coming to the strawberry social?" Mary asked.

Bethany dragged her attention back to her friend. "What?"

"The strawberry social. The Sutters said their first strawberries are ripe, and the youth were going to pick a bunch, and we'll have whipped cream and some games. It'll be fun." Mary smiled. "Come on . . . you should come."

"Is Seth taking you?" Bethany asked.

"I don't know yet." Mary dropped her gaze. "I'll mention it to him. Maybe he will."

"How did the drive home go last time?" Bethany asked.

"Oh . . . fine." Mary cast Bethany a coy glance. "He kissed me."

"Already!"

"Oh, don't be dramatic," Mary said, but she did blush. "You were engaged. You know how it goes on a ride home."

"Are you engaged?" Bethany asked, lowering her voice.

"No, of course not. We just . . . get along well. And he's handsome, isn't he? I mean, Micah might have been better-looking, but Seth holds his own."

"Yah, he's . . . fine," Bethany said.

Could she really judge, though? She'd almost kissed Isaiah that same night, and that hadn't been a date. What did that say about *her*?

"Look," Mary said, dropping all coyness, and turning Bethany to face her. "We're not exactly spring chickens, Bethany. Younger girls than us are lined up to get married this fall, and I don't have three years to slowly reel a man in. I want to get married and have babies, so if this moves a little bit faster, I'd think you, of all people, would understand."

"Because I'm old?" Bethany asked bitterly.

"Oh, stop," Mary said with a roll of her eyes. "Because you're as old as I am. And yah, we know the rules and the boys are supposed to lead in these things, but time is ticking here. I'm wanting a proposal, and I need to show him that we've got the chemistry to make a marriage enjoyable for both of us."

Bethany had never heard her friend so frank before. She looked at Mary, who'd suddenly changed from a coy girl to a frank woman with strange wisdom. Mary knew what she wanted and she was going after it, but in their Amish society, women were supposed to wait to be chosen. Maybe it all came down to making the boy feel like he'd been the one to make the choice. . . .

"Fair enough," Bethany replied.

"You might consider who you'd be willing to marry, too, Bethany," Mary said, and she turned to the front again and resumed her walk. Bethany took two quick steps to catch up.

"I was engaged until very recently," Bethany said. "I

don't think I'm in the place to throw myself into another man's buggy."

"I don't see why not," Mary replied. "You're single. Micah's gone. A buggy is where these negotiations take place, not on your parents' sofa with your *daet* in the other room."

But the detail no one else knew was that Bethany was pregnant with Micah's baby. And that had happened all too easily when she'd been utterly certain she'd be getting married this fall. Some things were dangerous to rush.

"Unless you're waiting on Micah to come back," Mary said.

And up until that point, Bethany's answer to that had been no. Micah hadn't thought she was enough to stay Amish for, and Mary thought that tying herself to the man for life was a good idea? Marriage was long, and Bethany had watched her older sisters' marriages. There were bumps, and she'd seen them crying in Mamm's kitchen often enough while Mamm told each one the very same thing: *Marriage is long, and you'll figure each other out. Assume the best in him now, because you don't have any other option. Now, go home to your husband.*

If Bethany wasn't enough to keep Micah in the Amish life he'd been raised to, what would happen when there were bumps, when they fought, when they frustrated each other? When she found herself in her mother's kitchen, what idealistic time would she look back on to bring back that romantic spark? Because making a man come back for a baby wasn't quite enough either.

"Are you waiting on him?" Mary pressed.

"Maybe," Bethany said, and as the word came out, her stomach sank. Because under any other circumstances, she would let her heart heal and move on, because she'd been raised to believe that she should be treasured by the man she married. But she no longer had any other options.

"Mary!" someone called, and Bethany and she both turned to see Seth jogging up behind them. Isaiah followed, walking at a slower pace, but also coming in their direction.

"Oh, hi, Seth." Mary smiled, and when Seth reached them she sidled closer. "It's nice to come to your farm this Sunday. Everything looks good."

"Yah, we've been busy," Seth replied. "You look nice."

"Oh, you're just saying that," Mary said, and she and Seth moved away a little bit just as Isaiah caught up.

Isaiah was properly dressed now, wearing his black Sunday hat and his shirt buttoned all the way to the top. He gave her a wry smile.

"I should have closed the curtains," he said.

"Probably." She couldn't help but laugh softly. "I think I'm the only one who noticed."

"Here's hoping." But his dark gaze didn't move from her face.

"Should we head toward the service?" she asked. Seth and Mary were already ambling slowly in that direction.

"Sure."

Bethany fell into step beside Isaiah as they followed Seth and Mary, giving them a good distance to ensure some privacy for the new couple.

"So, what does he think of Mary?" Bethany asked.

"Are you checking up for your friend?" Isaiah asked.

"Maybe I am." She smiled faintly. "She's a nice girl."

"He's not the type to toy with a girl. If he likes her, it's for the right reasons," he said, but there was something in his tone that gave her pause.

"But you don't like her, do you?" Bethany asked, glancing at him from the corner of her eye.

"I don't like the way she treated you," he replied.

"I think she really likes Seth," Bethany countered.

"Yah, he's pretty enamored, too," Isaiah replied with a sigh. "There's a lid for every pot, right?"

She felt her good humor slip. Was there? Not every Amish person got married, and just because a couple did take those vows didn't necessarily mean they were an ideal match either.

"I . . . uh . . ." Isaiah stopped walking, then reached out and grabbed her hand, tugging her into the shade of a tree. She followed him, and when he stopped she tugged her hand free.

"What?" she asked.

"I talked to Daniel Weibe this morning," he said.

Her almost-father-in-law. She'd liked Daniel—he was the kind of man she had hoped that his son would mature into one day.

"What did he want?" she asked.

"He wants me to write to Micah and try to convince him to come home," Isaiah replied, and while he wasn't touching her, his dark gaze locked her down as if he were still holding her hand, holding her in place.

"Oh . . . Are you going to do it?"

"Yah."

He was going to try to bring Micah home . . . So what had those moments been between them? What about just now, when he'd grabbed her hand as if he had a right to it?

"What will you say to him?" she asked hesitantly.

"I wanted to ask you . . . what you thought I should say," he said.

She shook her head. "You can't put this onto me."

"Do you want me to tell him that you miss him?" he asked, his voice low.

Bethany swallowed. The words hung in the air between them, and Isaiah seemed to be holding his breath.

"It might be what he needs to hear," he added. "His parents want him home, and I think we can both agree that he belongs here with his community, not out with the Mennonites."

So she was the bait? Except she understood. There were more important things than a romance that hadn't worked. Micah's future—Micah's salvation—mattered more.

"I've already written him a letter of my own," Bethany confessed. "I've said everything I want to say for myself."

Isaiah licked his lips and dropped his gaze. "Did you ask him to come back?"

"Yah." She couldn't lie. "I did. Sort of. It was a bit emotional. I can't even quite remember what I wrote now. I think I was mostly angry with him, but I was asking him to come back to Bountiful."

"Can you think of anything I should say?" he asked. "Because I promised I'd do my best."

"I don't know," she replied. "Some Bible verses?"

He shot her a rueful smile. "You don't really want him back, do you?"

She felt the heat hit her face. "If he doesn't come back for what I wrote, I don't want him."

Isaiah nodded. "All right. That's fair."

They moved toward the barn again, walking slowly. Seth and Mary had stopped at the pump, and various people were moving into the seating area. It would be time to start soon, and Bethany would need to go sit with her mother and sisters. There would be her nieces and nephews to help wrangle during the lengthy service.

"What will you say to him?" Bethany asked again.

"I might just tell him what's kept me here," he said.

"What's that?"

"I'm Amish. I believe in this life. I want my own *kinner* to have the kind of childhood I did."

That was simple enough, and she highly doubted it would be enough. Micah had left because he didn't believe in their life anymore. He'd been very clear about that.

"And I might tell him that he's left behind a beautiful girl," he added, his voice low. "And that she's interesting and insightful and . . . that he's dumber than a fence post if he thinks he can do better anywhere else, *Englishers* included."

Bethany blinked back a mist in her eyes. "That's sweet."

"It's the truth," he said. "He beat the rest of us to you, and maybe I'll tell him what it was like for me to watch him move forward with you, what it felt like to see him make you smile the way he did. Maybe he should know how lucky he was to have gotten to you first, because if he'd been a few weeks slower, I would have asked you home from singing myself."

She turned toward Isaiah, her breath lodged in her throat. "Is that true?"

"Yah." He licked his lips, and this time when his gaze met hers, she felt the moment deepen around them. "But you should have chosen him."

"Why?" she breathed.

"He's inheriting a farm. I've got nothing."

It didn't feel like nothing right now, looking up into those dark eyes, his strong body hovering close, making her feel as if there weren't their entire community here, he might close the gap between them.

"Bethany, let's go in," Mary called, and Bethany tore her gaze away from him, her face heating.

"Yah," she said feebly, and when she looked over at Isaiah again she saw sadness etched in his features.

She'd never known how Isaiah had felt all those years, and now that she did it was far too late. If he'd help her to bring Micah home again, it might be enough to save her from her own rash mistakes. And then she'd dutifully marry the father of her baby and she'd never allow herself to look at Isaiah like that again.

Isaiah moved off toward the men's side of the seating area, and Seth looked back toward Mary, a smile curving up his lips.

"I think I'll marry him," Mary murmured.

"I hope you do," Bethany said quietly.

Someone deserved their happiness, and Bethany couldn't blame anyone but herself for the ruining of her own. Well, maybe she could blame Micah, but it wouldn't do any good.

Then Isaiah glanced back, and Bethany's heart stuttered to a stop in her chest. He was going to try to bring Micah back, but he had no idea why she was willing to accept him . . .

How long could she keep this secret?

Chapter Eight

Late Sunday night, after the rest of the family had gone to bed, Isaiah got up from his mattress on the floor, pulled on a pair of pants, and crept back downstairs. He could hear his cousins' soft snoring, the creak of some springs in another bedroom. In a house as full of people as this one, the nighttime hours were the only chance a man could get a little bit of privacy.

Isaiah had spent a nice afternoon with Bethany, Mary, and Seth. They'd walked, talked, eaten lunch together in the shade of the barn. And the longer he spent with Bethany, the more he felt like Daniel and Tessa's accusing eyes were on him.

If Isaiah wanted to be Amish, he'd have to be Amish in every sense. It wasn't about just where he was born, it was who he chose to be. Isaiah had promised Daniel that he'd write a letter, and he was going to do just as he'd said he would.

Isaiah fumbled in the dark looking for matches and finally found them in the third drawer he checked. He grimaced as he slowly closed it, trying to be as quiet as possible. Then he struck a match, lit the lantern, and sat down at the kitchen table with a piece of paper.

He stared at the blank page for a moment or two.

Gott, I don't think this letter will be sincere, he prayed. Isaiah knew what the right thing to do was . . . he just didn't want to do it. But that was part of the Amish life, doing the right thing even when it was hard. It was called the narrow path, and the broad, easy highway led straight to hell. So the hard way was much preferable, and he'd best get it over with. This letter would be short and sweet.

Isaiah hunched over the paper and started to write in his own looping handwriting.

Micah,

> *You asked me to look out for Bethany if anything should happen to you, and I'm trying to do that. But she needs you, not me. She said she wrote you herself, so I won't say anything on her behalf—just that I don't know how you walked away from her.*
>
> *Don't you remember how you, Seth, and I used to moon after Bethany when we were young? You got her—don't squander that.*
>
> *You're my friend and nothing will change that. Everyone wants you home. Your* daet *asked me to write to you and tell you how I've managed to stay. I guess it comes down to this—I want to belong in a community where people do what's right, even if it hurts. So I'm trying to be that man. I'm keeping my word to the community here, and to you. I said I'd look out for Bethany, and I'm doing that.*

Come home.

Isaiah

Maybe the letter was more sincere than he thought. It was all completely honest—no exaggeration of feeling. He wouldn't give long, beleaguered reasons for Micah to come back. Micah would have to decide he wanted the same thing Isaiah did—that trustworthy community of good people. And if the *Englishers* were good enough for Micah, pages of articulate argument weren't going to change it.

But Isaiah had promised his friend he'd look out for Bethany, and that didn't include moving in on her and trying to be more to her than a friend. If Micah came back, he'd find Isaiah staying true to his word, even if it hurt. How could any of them ask Micah to come back to a community that was anything less than completely trustworthy? Anything less and he might as well stay Mennonite, with all the modern conveniences, because the Amish were people who believed in hard work and uncompromising ethics.

Isaiah folded up the letter, addressed an envelope, then licked a stamp. He pushed his feet into his shoes and, as quietly as possible, crept outside into the night.

He'd put this letter in the mailbox now, to be collected first thing by the mail truck that rumbled past just after dawn. He'd put it out now, before he had time to second-guess himself. It was the right thing to do—he could feel it in his bones. But it also meant that Bethany was off-limits—completely.

* * *

Monday evening, after a long day at work, Isaiah returned home tired and somewhat irritable. Bethany seemed more closed off than usual and he hadn't pressed the issue, thinking that maybe it was a blessing in disguise. He was obviously too attached to her as it was.

But when he got back to his uncle's farm he found that even the smallest things were getting to him—his younger cousins' roughhousing, his uncle's silent, disapproving stares, his aunt's way of clucking her tongue at her daughters when they were about to make a mistake in the kitchen. . . .

Most of it wasn't a big deal, and he knew that, but it was hard to come back to a house where he didn't feel comfortable after a long day at work. He felt like an unwanted guest. He'd hoped that by sending that letter to Micah, he could free up his emotions, but it hadn't exactly worked that way. No matter how much he prayed that Gott would wipe his heart clean of whatever it was he was feeling for Bethany, Gott wasn't answering.

Even when he "put his foot in the Jordan" by mailing that letter, it hadn't helped! Isaiah was doing the right thing, taking a step of faith and trusting Gott to do the rest—just like his *daet* should have done—so why wasn't Gott answering?

Even Gott felt far away right now. And so did Bethany.

After dinner Isaiah helped his sister with the dishes, and they were just wiping the last of them when there was a knock at the door. Uncle Mel went to answer it, and it was Bishop Lapp.

"Good evening, Bishop," Aunt Rose said with a smile. "Come in! Can I get you some pie?"

"As hard as it is to pass up a piece of your perfect pie,

Rose, I only meant to stop in on my way home," Bishop Lapp said with a smile. "I wanted a word with your nephew, if you wouldn't mind."

His cousins looked over at him in curiosity, and Uncle Mel sent him a flat stare. When the bishop popped by it was an honor or a reprimand. Isaiah handed his towel to his sister and went over to the door.

"Step outside?" the bishop asked.

Isaiah's heart sped up at that. Had people been watching him at Service Sunday? Was there gossip? Had he not hidden his feelings as well as he'd hoped?

"Yah, sure," Isaiah said.

They stepped onto the porch, and Isaiah pulled the door shut behind him for some privacy, although someone would overhear something, he was sure. That was just the nature of a large family.

"I spoke with the elders on Sunday," the bishop said quietly. "We all agreed that this is a unique situation, and that by simply cutting you off from your father, we aren't making it possible for you to make a life here."

"I can obey," Isaiah countered.

"Yah, I know," the bishop replied. "But when I asked what you needed, you said you needed to understand why your *daet* did what he did. And that struck a chord with me. I can sympathize with that. So, while he is shunned from the rest of the community, we are lifting the ban for you and your sisters. As long as you can be open with me and keep me informed on your progress in your mission to make sense of this, and not take advantage of the kindness that I mean it to be."

"So—" Isaiah licked his lips. "You're saying I can talk to him?"

The bishop pulled an envelope out of his jacket. "Your *daet* wrote to you and sent it to my address. I haven't opened it—it's meant for your eyes, not mine. But you can feel free to answer him and converse. And I will pray that Gott will give you the insight you need to fully make peace with this whole situation."

Isaiah took the envelope from the bishop's hand and looked at the writing on the front. He recognized his father's handwriting immediately, and it was addressed to him alone, not him and his sisters.

"Should I tell Elizabeth that she has permission to write back to my *daet*, too?" he asked.

"Yah. Please do," the bishop replied.

"Thank you, Bishop. This is very kind of you," Isaiah said.

"You come by if you need to talk," Bishop Lapp said, and he patted his shoulder. "Take care now."

The bishop headed back out to his buggy, and Isaiah watched as he turned it around and headed back up the drive before he opened the door and went back into the kitchen. Vernon and Bart were just shuffling a deck of Dutch Blitz cards and Dawn carried a pie to the table.

"What did he want?" Dawn asked.

"Uh—" Isaiah shot his younger cousin a quick smile. "Just to talk a bit."

"About what?" she pressed.

"Dawn, you can't ask that," Seth said. "Here—cut me some pie."

"Hold your horses," Dawn said. "There isn't enough cherry for everyone."

"Well, I want cherry," Bart said.

"Yeah, me too." That was Vernon, and the argument

over who would get one of the last three pieces of cherry pie commenced, giving Isaiah the opportunity to escape into the sitting room, and then out the front door to the front deck. He firmly pulled the door shut and sat on the steps. Light from the front window spilled over him, giving him enough illumination to read by.

This was it—a letter from his *daet* that he was given permission to read. This wasn't rebellion or sneaking. But somehow he still felt hesitant to open it. He wasn't sure what he'd find in this letter, though he was almost certain it was going to break his heart.

Isaiah tore the envelope open.

Dear Son,

I can't begin to tell you how sorry I am for all that I've done. I've repented, I've cried, I've begged the Almighty to wash this sin away, but it doesn't help when I can't talk to my kinner. *Everything I've ever done was for you and your mamm. I know you might not be permitted to read this because I'm shunned. I was informed of that by letter. But I'm trying anyway, because I cannot sit in this jail cell and do nothing. I know how deeply I've disappointed you, and I had to explain—or at least try.*

I didn't know about the scam at first. By the time I figured out that it wasn't legitimate, I'd already been encouraging you to talk to friends and family about it, and they told me that they'd point the finger at you. I couldn't let that happen.

But it was more than that, and I suspect you'll require a deeper explanation, because I would if

I were in your shoes and you are so very much like me.

The truth is, I wanted that charity to help families because it could have been a blessing for your mother if we'd had enough money for specialists back when she was sick. The more I've looked into it, the more confident I've become that your mamm *didn't need to die. She could have been saved! There were other treatments available—all very new, and some were experimental—and a few years later I found out that some of those treatments worked! But when I asked for more money to try those innovative treatments, I was told that I needed to stop. This was enough. Gott didn't make mistakes, and if He was taking her from me, then I needed to accept that. But isn't that rather convenient for the people who could have helped but didn't?*

So when I encouraged them to give, it was vengeance. It's a sin, and harboring that sin led to me feeling very little guilt about getting the people in our community to waste their hard-earned money. Why should it sit in their bank accounts growing fatter when they didn't help your mamm *when she needed them?*

That won't mean a thing to the elders or the bishop. I know that. And I'm not even sure your sisters would understand. But one day you will fall in love, my son—every Adam finds his Eve someday. Sometimes he is blessed enough to marry her, and sometimes he isn't. But when you do eventually

fall in love, I want you to ask yourself how you
would feel if the community you trusted let her die?
  Gott might not make mistakes, but people do.
I'm not sure I can ever come back to our
community, and I know that means I won't ever see
you again. I regret this—all of it. It wasn't worth
losing my kinner.
  If Gott could forgive David for his sin, and call
him a man after His own heart, I pray that Gott
can forgive me. Know that I love you, that I think
of you three every minute. Work out your own
salvation with fear and trembling, my son.
Eventually, we all must face Him.

Isaiah sucked in a wavering breath. Some fireflies
flitted across the lawn in front of him, and he looked up
at the star-studded sky. How many times had he looked
up, wondering about the *mamm* he hardly remembered
who had beaten them to Heaven?

His *mamm* hadn't needed to die? Why would they be
so selfish, especially when a *mamm* with three small
kinner was in danger of losing her life? Bountiful might
have a darker side than he'd ever realized, and the thought
chilled him.

The door behind him opened and he turned to see Elizabeth. She stood in the doorway, her feet bare. She looked
thinner than she used to be, and he felt a pang of protec-
tiveness. He and Elizabeth had been the closest in age,
and they'd been playmates growing up, taking turns to
boss around Lovina. Looking at her standing there, looking so worn, he was reminded of years ago when they'd
been young teens. She used to be thin like this then, too.

"You should see this," he said, and Elizabeth pulled the door shut and then came to sit on the step next to him.

"From Daet?"

"Yah. The bishop says we're allowed to write to him now."

"We are?"

"Yah. He figures it might help us make our peace with everything."

Elizabeth took the letter from his hand. "He's innocent, isn't he?" she said.

"Far from it, but he's human," Isaiah said. "Go on and read it."

And while his sister read the letter, Isaiah leaned his elbows on his knees and looked out at the flickering fireflies hovering over the grass.

Bethany settled in at her workstation the next morning and stifled a yawn. She'd stayed up late last night letting out some dresses. Mamm had suggested she start wearing the clothes and aprons she'd put away in her trunk, and it was just as well that she'd mentioned it because when Bethany and her mother had sewn those dresses, they'd left some extra space to let out in case of this exact situation . . . mind, in their plans, Bethany would already be married by the time she was pregnant.

But her current dresses were beginning to get a little snug, and she'd pinned them looser, but the pin holes from earlier wearing were visible, and sooner than she'd feared, too. She had to let out her dresses before her *mamm* noticed—or, worse, the other women in their community.

She'd tried to pray last night, begging Gott to give her

a way out, a solution of some sort that would rescue her. But she knew it wasn't the right prayer. What was she supposed to pray for, though? She prayed for a forgiving spirit to take Micah back, for her parents, for her little sister to make better choices than she had . . . she even prayed for Isaiah and his determination to stay on the narrow path. And all through those prayers, she felt a void inside her, as if she was praying in circles, avoiding the prayer that would give her poor heart some relief.

What am I missing, Gott? she'd demanded. *What will become of me?*

So, by the light of her kerosene lamp, after her parents and her sister had fallen asleep, she'd picked the seams free and resewn them, giving herself more room and hoping that no one would notice the tiny holes from the previous seam, or her slightly expanded waistline. She had taken several hours, and this morning she was exhausted and her fingertips were sore from all the needlework.

"You were up late last night," Daet said, counting the change in the till. His fingers flipped through the bills and made notes on a pad of paper.

"Oh . . ." So he'd noticed. She'd thought she'd been quiet enough. "I couldn't sleep, so I thought I'd be productive."

"Micah's not worth your grief, my dear," Daet said quietly.

"You really liked him, Daet," she countered. And that might be important if he came back and she needed to marry him anyway.

"You need a proper Amish man, not someone who questions every bit of truth," her father replied. "Being married to a man like that would be difficult. Yah, we all have to come to terms with our beliefs, but there are men who question absolutely everything, and that isn't a comfortable home. You need to count on something."

"I thought you wanted me to wait for him," she said.

"I've changed my mind about that," he replied. "A woman needs to be the heart of the home, not the spiritual muscle. She shouldn't be the one to hold her husband to the faith. It isn't right. He's got to be there because he believes it."

The husband should be with his wife for better reasons, too, she realized, but if he came back, she'd humble her own passionate spirit and accept the father of her child. Because anything less than that would only multiply her mistakes.

"What about the others who left?" Bethany asked. "Shouldn't they be welcomed back?"

"Yah, of course," he said. "But none of those have tried to marry my daughter, have they? Accepting someone in Christian charity and marrying them are two different things. Marriage is for life—and you have to trust someone with every stage of that life, every year of it, every trial and hill you have to climb together."

Daet had idealized views of what marriage was, too. He wanted his *kinner* to marry only the best, and if he and Mamm had ever had any struggles, they'd successfully hidden it from the children as they grew up.

Except there didn't seem to be any young people out there as perfect as Mamm and Daet had been. Micah had come close in appearances, and even her father had heartily approved of him. But look what he'd been hiding under the surface. Even Bethany had fallen desperately short on what a good Amish man would be looking for in a wife now that she was hiding a pregnancy. Bethany had become the kind of girl her parents had warned her brothers about:

Some girls can be hiding big mistakes, boys. They can pretend to be one way before the wedding, and you find out otherwise afterward. It's better to court for a decent amount of time. Time tends to uncover all the secrets.

And time would uncover hers, too. Every day, every week, her body would grow.

Bethany turned back to the book presses lined up along one side of the room, and she began to loosen the first press in slow turns of the handle until she slid out the freshly bound book. She ran her fingers over the smooth leather cover, then opened it, the cover page crackling softly, and she inhaled the scent of paper, glue, and leather.

The front door opened and both Bethany and her father looked up as Isaiah came inside. Isaiah closed the door behind him and glanced between them.

"Am I late?" he asked.

"No. You're on time," her *daet* replied. "Good morning. Flip that sign to open, would you?"

Isaiah did as he was asked and headed around the front counter toward the back room. Bethany gave him a small smile as he passed her, but he didn't return it. Maybe it was just that she was overly tired and preoccupied with her own problems, but Isaiah seemed different today— more reserved.

"Bethany, would you refill the muslin container and get me some more cover paper?" her father asked.

"Sure, Daet."

Bethany put the finished book down on the pile with the others and headed into the back room where Isaiah had gone to deposit his lunch and things. As she entered the room, Isaiah looked up.

"What do we do if someone gets hurt or sick and needs expensive medical care?" he asked.

Bethany blinked. "Um . . . what?"

"Just humor me here. If someone in our community gets sick and needs some expensive medical care, what do we do?"

"We have a fund for that. You know that."

"And if that fund goes dry?" he said.

"We all dig down deep and help as much as we can."

"And if that isn't enough?" he pressed. "If more is needed? If the husband has used up every last penny he has, if he's gone into debt and mortgaged the farm . . . If he's asked all his friends and they won't give any more money, then what?"

Bethany shook her head. "What's this about?"

Isaiah sighed. "My *mamm*."

"Is that what happened?"

"I got a letter from my *daet*, and the bishop says my sister and I are permitted to write him back. He told me about the financial aspects of my *mamm*'s death for the first time."

"Oh . . ." Bethany breathed.

"People wouldn't give any more," he said. "And she died. But Daet found out later that her type of cancer was treatable, if she'd had the right specialists. She didn't have to die!"

"But we aren't doctors, Isaiah," she reminded him. "How could anyone know that?"

"That might be true, but they gave up on her," Isaiah replied, his throat tight. "I don't have many memories of my mother. She died when Lovina was a toddler. I was about eight. But I do remember how she used to cuddle me, and the feeling of her hand on my forehead. I remember her voice—always tired, but maybe that was because she was so sick. And I remember her thin and gaunt. Daet used to tell us about when she was healthy and plump. She was quite round when she was well, you know."

Bethany stared at him in silence, her heart squeezing in sympathy.

"She didn't have to die, Bethany. I could have grown up with a mother."

"I'm sorry, Isaiah . . ."

"You didn't do it," he said gruffly. "And I understand when money runs out, but I do have to wonder if people really did give all they could. Because Daet seems to think they didn't. Their plans for their businesses and families were more important to them than my *mamm*'s life."

"That can't be true . . ." she whispered.

"I don't know." He put down his bag and headed for the door.

"Isaiah—"

He stopped and turned.

"Gott doesn't make mistakes," she said. "When our time comes we have to be ready."

Isaiah dropped his gaze and his jaw tensed. "They tell us not to question when someone dies, but maybe we should."

They. Who was he referring to? The bishop and elders? Their ancestors who came before them? The traditions and wisdom that formed an Amish community? When was the last time she'd heard someone bitterly refer to what "they" insisted upon? That was Micah—and Micah had left.

"Our ancestors lost people they loved, too," she said quietly. "They understood how all of this felt, and they still believed."

"Our ancestors didn't have the medical interventions we have today," he retorted. "Our great-grandparents died of things that need not kill us. And there is no selfishness in staying alive, or in wanting to keep your wife alive. A woman's life should matter more than anything else."

Isaiah headed out into the shop again, leaving her alone. She sucked in a wavering breath. He was angry— that was clear. A mother mattered . . . she was the heart of a home, and many people had judged Abe Yoder for not remarrying. He could have gotten another wife to help with his young *kinner*, to have more babies with him. But he wouldn't, and the longer he stayed single after his wife's passing, the more people talked. She'd heard people discussing it for years. It was selfish, they said. He didn't have the right to mourn forever. It was a form of idolatry to love a woman so much that he couldn't accept Gott's decision to take her home to Heaven.

Gott gives, and Gott takes away. Who were humans to question His will?

Bethany ran her hand over her stomach—it still felt flat, even though her waist seemed to be getting thicker all the same. There was a baby inside her that would grow up loving her just as deeply as Isaiah had loved his *mamm* . . . as deeply as she loved her own *mamm*.

What she might never have was a husband who loved her like Abe had loved his young wife, no matter how wicked that kind of adoration might be.

Bethany gathered the muslin and cover paper, then went back out into the shop. She restocked the supplies and gave her father a smile as she passed by him again.

Isaiah sat on his stool, and his expression was granite, but at least now she had a hint of what was stewing beneath the surface.

Micah left because of Abe, and she couldn't help but wonder if Isaiah was heading in the same direction. Their community had lost so many young people in the last several weeks . . . and while she'd resented Isaiah deeply when he'd first started working here, she didn't anymore. He was just another young person in this community who was reeling from Abe's crime—and of anyone, Abe's own *kinner* had more right to reel than anyone else.

"There's the strawberry and cream event tomorrow evening," Bethany said, approaching Isaiah's table.

"Yah." He looked up.

"We should go," she said.

"I don't know if I'm up to it," he replied.

"It would be good for both of us," she countered. "It would . . . I don't know . . . remind us that we're a part of something bigger than ourselves. I'm grieving what I lost, but so are you. And I think we should go."

Isaiah blinked at her, and a smile quirked up one side of his lips. "Are you asking to drive me home from singing?"

"No, I'm asking you to come be sociable with our friends," she replied, but she couldn't help but smile at his humor. "It would do me good to go out with people, too."

Isaiah met her gaze somberly for a moment.

"You look really tired, Bethany," he said softly.

Her eyes misted and she nodded. "I'm so tired."

"And you want to go to this strawberry thing . . . with me?" he asked.

It wasn't that she so desperately wanted to go to that event, because left to her own inclinations, she'd stay home and brew over her own misfortunes. But she wanted to help him, and maybe pretend for one more evening that all was perfectly normal.

Because one of these days soon, she'd have to break her parents' hearts and tell them the truth.

"Yah. I want to go with you," she said.

Isaiah met her gaze soberly. "Then I'll come pick you up."

Chapter Nine

The next evening Bethany stood at the kitchen counter slicing apples for a strudel. The evening sun hung low, bursting through the kitchen windows and bathing her hands in golden warmth as she worked. Coils of apple peel piled on a piece of newspaper, and Bethany thinly sliced the fragrant apples into a large, white bowl.

"I wish I could go tonight," Lily said with a sigh.

"You aren't old enough," Bethany replied. "Look—you're leaving peel on that apple. Come on, Lily. Do it right."

Lily muttered something, but she did go back to take the last bit of peel off the apple. Bethany wasn't usually short with her little sister, and she felt a little bad for having snapped.

"You'll be glad you can make an attractive strudel," Bethany said, softening her tone. "When girls put out their pies and you put out a perfectly braided strudel, you'll stand out! And what boy doesn't want a girl who can bake?"

"Not everything is about appearances!" Lily retorted.

"Enough of it is," Mamm said, interjecting into their

conversation. "The only ones who look at what's happening in your heart first are Gott and your *mamm*. For everyone else, you'd best begin with good appearances."

Bethany chuckled at that.

"And that goes for you, too, Bethany," Mamm added. "I don't like you going out with this Yoder boy so much."

"He's a friend . . . and our employee," Bethany said.

"He's a risk," Mamm replied. "What will people think?"

"I don't know. I didn't think they'd assume very much," Bethany admitted. "We're both in weird situations right now, and I think we understand each other because of it."

"Well, it's going to look like that understanding has blossomed," Mamm replied. "And the last thing you need is for someone to write to Micah and tell him that you've started up with one of his best friends!"

"He might come back for that," Lily said with a shrug.

"Zip it!" Mamm snapped, pointing a finger at Lily, then turning back to Bethany. "Bethany, I'm serious. He's been gone what—two weeks? This is not appropriate."

"He'd been very distant before leaving," Bethany said. "You know that! He already seemed like he didn't want to get married after all. How many times did he put off his baptism? He wasn't taking me to any of the youth events, and he just kept saying he was busy!"

"Marriage is stressful on a young man," Mamm replied.

"Well, getting married is supposed to be one of the happiest days of your lives, not something a man wants to avoid talking about!" she retorted. "And now we know why. It wasn't stress about the wedding or adjusting to the new responsibilities of having a family. It was because he was leaving me, and he knew it. And he didn't know how to tell me."

Mamm sighed. "But if he comes back—"

"I just want to go to a youth event this evening," Bethany said quietly. "I want to see my friends." She wanted to see Isaiah, truthfully. He was a strange comfort, and she found herself missing him at odd times.

"Then get your *daet* to drive you," Mamm said.

"Mamm, I want to go with my friend. I'm grown."

Mamm sighed. "It's up to you, obviously. You're right that you're old enough to make your own decisions on these things, but be aware of how this could look. Even if you don't want Micah back, you do want to get married, and looking like the kind of girl who can go from being engaged to one boy to dillydallying with another—it makes you look cheap. Excuse the ugly word."

Lily looked toward Bethany, her eyes large. *Cheap.* Bethany had never been called that before—especially not in this house. She swallowed. The problem was, these little considerations weren't going to matter at all when Bethany told her *mamm* about her pregnancy. And if the community learned about it, too, they wouldn't be judging who drove her to the strawberry social; they'd be talking about bigger issues, like whether she could be trusted as a role model to the younger *kinner* in the community and whether they should bother inviting her to the quilting circle.

"I'm not cheap, Mamm," she said, her voice trembling. "But I'm not going to tiptoe either. People are already talking about me because Micah left. Our faith is about our community, isn't it? We're supposed to be there for one another in hard times? Well, Isaiah is going through some tough times right now, too, and I suspect he has a good many reasons to leave, just like his sister did."

"He isn't your responsibility!" her mother said.

"Then whose is he?" she demanded. "We're supposed to look out for one another! If Isaiah leaves, who else will follow him? Do we want to lose all the young people in one go?"

Mamm sighed. "Fine."

"I know that doesn't mean you're fine with this," Bethany said.

"I also can't stop you!" Mamm retorted. "And if you think that the world actually works according to our ideals, you have a few surprises coming."

"Of course our community upholds our ideals," Bethany said.

"Upholds them, but falls short all too often," Mamm replied.

"Not you and Daet."

Mamm's cheeks pinked, and she looked toward Lily, who was watching them in silence.

"No, there are good Amish people out there who live by their beliefs," Mamm said primly. "But there are also people out there who don't. And not everyone who wants to know your secrets is your friend."

Bethany couldn't argue with that, but just as Mamm fell silent, the sound of a buggy and hooves could be heard outside.

"That's him, Mamm," Bethany said. "Don't worry. You know me—I'll be proper."

Mamm nodded. "I know you. But not everyone is inclined to think the best of you. Remember that."

Bethany put down her paring knife and went to the sink to wash her hands. Then she changed her apron and quickly tied on a freshly laundered one. As Lily turned to grab another apple, she swiped past a plate and it fell with a crash.

"Oh, Lily . . ." Mamm said, reaching for the broom. "You've got to be more careful!"

"Are we okay, Mamm?" Bethany asked.

Mamm looked up, broom in hand and a tired look on her face.

"Yah. We're okay," Mamm said. "Don't be home too late."

Bethany smiled. "I never am, Mamm."

If only Mamm's warnings didn't sound with so much wisdom. But Bethany wanted just a few more days of being able to live her life without anyone else knowing her secret, a few more days before the criticism began. She should relish this—she'd never have it again.

Isaiah reined in the horses and squinted against the low, slanted rays of sunlight that splashed over the lush pasture, stretching the shadows of the trees and fence posts long. The Glicks' home was a two-story farmhouse set on about five acres of land. They had some pasture, some stables, a chicken house, and a bit of wooded forest that they owned but wasn't much use to them besides the odd bit of hunting. The front door to the house was propped open with a brick, and from inside, he could hear the clatter of broken glass and a female voice gently chastising.

Elizabeth hadn't wanted to come along this evening. The combination of their chilly reception at the bonfire and the letter from their *daet* had left her quiet and subdued. So she'd opted to stay at the house with Aunt Rose.

Isaiah wasn't keen on this either, but he was looking

forward to seeing Bethany again. Strange how their friendship was starting to mean a whole lot more to him lately . . . and maybe what he needed was a good friend right now, not anything romantic. Romance might soothe some deep, lonesome place inside him, but it would be a betrayal of Micah, and if Isaiah was going to be different from his *daet*, he'd better start here and now.

Isaiah tied off the reins and hopped down from the buggy. The evening was still warm and sweat beaded on his forehead. He headed toward the side door, and it opened before he could knock. Bethany stood there, smoothing down her apron with one hand and a surprised look on her face.

"Hi," he said, and he glanced over her shoulder into the kitchen, where Barbara Glick and Lily were crouched down, sweeping up what looked like a broken dish.

"Hello, Isaiah," Barbara called. "Don't be too late, now. When it finishes we expect Bethany home promptly."

"Yah, of course," he said. "Don't worry about that."

Barbara didn't answer him, but she did cast Bethany an indecipherable look. Did Bethany's mother think this was more than two friends going to a youth event? Granted, it might look that way, but he'd figured that Bethany would have explained that much.

"Let's go," Bethany said briskly.

Isaiah let Bethany leave ahead of him, then he looked back at her mother, who was staring after her, her lips pressed together in a line.

"Good night," he said.

Barbara gave him a nod but didn't answer, and Isaiah closed the door behind him. He met Bethany's glance and they exchanged a small smile.

"Tension?" he said as they headed toward the buggy.

"Mamm is just worried about appearances," she replied.

"You told her that this isn't a date . . . right?" he said.

"Of course."

It might still look otherwise, he realized, and he gave Bethany a hand up into the buggy. She slid down the bench seat to the other side, then he hoisted himself up and untied the reins. When he glanced toward the house as they headed back up the drive, he saw Lily at the side door, watching them with her head cocked to one side, as if she was trying to figure something out.

"Lily's too curious for her own good," Bethany said.

"About what?" he asked.

"Everything, I'm afraid. There's no privacy in a house with a little sister."

"Yah, I know about that," he said, and they shared a rueful smile.

"Where's Elizabeth?" she asked.

"She didn't want to go," he said. "She needs a break, I guess."

Bethany was silent, and he looked over at her. She leaned back against the backrest and let out a soft sigh.

"Are you okay?" he asked quietly.

"Yah."

"Because the last few days—" He swallowed. "I don't know. You seem . . . upset about something."

"I just want to get out of the house—I love my family dearly, but I'm much nicer to them when I've had some space to myself."

Isaiah smiled at that. "Yah, I understand that, too."

He guided the horses out of the drive and they started down the road.

"I'm pushing you into going to this, aren't I?" Bethany asked.

"No . . . no. I mean . . . No, I'm happy to drive you."

"That sounds like a yes," she countered.

Isaiah chuckled. "I'm not feeling like eating strawberries at the moment, but it's fine. You're right—it's good to get out. And I was looking forward to seeing you, actually."

"I don't feel like eating strawberries either," she said. "I did half an hour ago, and I thought that seeing my friends might help, but I think I've changed my mind. . . ."

He squinted at her. "Do you want me to take you back, then?"

"No. I wouldn't mind a drive. It feels good to be out."

Yah, him too. He smiled over at her, and they carried on past the turn that would take them toward the farm hosting the strawberry event and he settled into the buggy's rhythm. It felt good to be out with her next to him. Of everyone in his community right now, she was the one who seemed to understand him the best.

They rode in silence for several minutes, Bethany's arm moving against his as they bumped over a dip in the road. He almost wished he could find another one and have her jostle against him once more. He felt freer out there than he'd felt in a long time, and having her with him was settling his nerves. She felt good next to him; she was a reason to stay strong.

They passed several farms of families they knew, but no one was out close enough to the road to see them. He reached over and took her hand. She smiled and dropped her gaze when his fingers closed over hers.

"So, what will you do now if you aren't going to be a preacher?" Bethany asked.

"That's the question, isn't it?" He ran his fingers over hers, feeling the softness of her skin.

"You must have thought of something," she said.

"I'm enjoying bookbinding," he admitted. "I wouldn't mind carrying on with your *daet*."

"You're good at it," she said. "You picked up faster than Micah did."

"Yah?" He smiled faintly. "But if Micah comes back, I suppose I could find another trade."

They were approaching a little bridge he used to play around with his friends when he was a boy. They used to drop rocks over the edge of it and see who could make a bigger splash. And when Isaiah went out there alone he'd stare down at the water rippling past and let his mind wander with the current.

Ahead, beyond the bridge, was the farm that used to belong to his father . . . the farm that used to be home. So much had changed.

"If Micah did come back . . ." Bethany said quietly, "you wouldn't work with him?"

"No." He didn't mean for the answer to be quite so curt, but it was the truth. "I couldn't do it. Besides, I'm just helping out right now. If he came back, I'm sure your *daet* would much prefer him."

Bethany was silent.

"I want to open my own business, though," he said. "I don't want to just work for some big, faceless company. I want my work to be who I am, to show what I stand for."

"Maybe you could open a shop—make those birdhouses the *Englishers* like so much," she suggested.

"Yah, maybe."

"Or you could open a landscaping business. *Englishers* pay good money for that."

"Hmm."

"I don't think a carpentry business would be good right now, because Enoch just opened that other one on the far side of town, but my *daet* was saying that there is steady work in construction—"

Isaiah inhaled a measured breath. "I don't need you to fix my future, Bethany."

"I'm not—" She pulled back her hand, and his hand felt empty without hers.

"You are!" he countered. He wished he could take her hand again, but it had been overstepping to begin with, and maybe his irritation was more with that than with her eagerness to fix his problems. "I don't need you to find something new for me to focus on for when Micah comes back. I can handle that myself."

And maybe he didn't want to think about that just yet . . . Maybe he didn't want to think past the here and now, because he knew what he'd promised Micah, and he knew that Bethany wasn't going to be a part of his future—not in the way he'd like anyway.

"I wrote to Micah," Isaiah said.

Bethany was silent for a beat. "What did you say?"

"That I was looking out for you," he said. "I wanted him to know that there was still some honesty he could count on in our community."

"I haven't heard from him," she said quietly. "I thought he might phone the neighbor or . . . something."

Isaiah looked back to the road, running it all through in his head, sifting through it.

"You said that if he doesn't come back for what you told him, you don't want him back," Isaiah said slowly. "What *did* you tell him?"

Bethany looked away, and for a moment he didn't think she'd answer him.

"I told him that I'm pregnant with his baby," she said, and her chin trembled as she said the words.

Her words were like a blow to the stomach and it took him a moment to register what she'd said.

"What?" He turned toward her, stunned. "Were you . . . telling him the truth?"

"You think I'd just tell a wild lie to get him back?" she asked bitterly.

"No, I just . . ." The thought was a shock—this didn't happen in places like Bountiful. "*Was* it a lie?"

Bethany's gaze misted and she shook her head. "No, it's true. I found out a few days ago."

His heart beat hard, trying to catch up to his brain. She was pregnant . . . That meant that if Micah came back, it was no longer a choice of what she wanted. The elders and the bishop would make sure that the couple got married and that the baby would be raised by married parents. And he'd just written to his friend, asking him to return.

It was the best thing—wasn't it? She did need Micah, more than he'd even imagined when he wrote that letter.

As they arrived at the bridge, Isaiah reined in the horses and guided them to the grassy side of the road. He turned toward Bethany and swallowed hard. "What are you going to do?"

Bethany sighed. "I have to tell my parents still."

"You haven't told anyone?"

"I told Micah in the letter . . . and you." She licked her

lips. "I shouldn't have said anything to you, though. I don't know why I did."

"It's okay," he said. "I won't tell anyone. You're safe with me, Beth."

Her chin trembled again. "Yah. I hope so."

"Seriously." He reached out and caught her hand again, and this time it wasn't just to be close to her. He wanted to pull her into his arms, tell her that he could help her fix this—but he couldn't! What was he supposed to do? Sometimes a man's instincts to make everything better were useless.

"I think my best hope is Micah coming back," she said.

"And marrying him," he said, his voice tight.

"Yah."

Of course. That was what made sense. Micah had gotten her pregnant, and he needed to be the one to marry her and raise his own child. And Micah would want that— if Isaiah knew his friend at all.

"He'll come back," Isaiah said. "If that's what you told him in your letter, there is no doubt."

"I'm not so convinced," she whispered. "For the last few weeks, he didn't want to even talk about the wedding, or anything. He was supposed to be making the eck— and he hadn't finished it yet."

"That doesn't mean he didn't want to get married," Isaiah countered.

"He knew he was leaving—I'm sure of it. He wanted me to go with him."

"At least he didn't marry you first," Isaiah said.

To marry her and then leave—or ask her to leave her Amish life—that wouldn't have been fair. In his friend's defense, at least he'd left her single. And he hadn't known that there was a baby coming . . .

"I have to tell my *mamm* and *daet*," she said. "I won't be able to hide it for much longer, I don't think."

He was still holding her hand, and he lifted her fingers and pressed his lips against them. It had been impulsive, done without even thinking, but she didn't pull away.

"Come here," he murmured, and he tugged her closer, then wrapped his arms around her, pulling her gently against his chest. He could feel his own heartbeat reverberate through her body, and he let out a pent-up breath. He'd promised Micah that he'd look out for Bethany, that he'd protect her and make sure she was okay, but Micah had left her pregnant, and if his friend didn't come back, she'd be in some big trouble.

Bethany leaned her forehead against his neck, and for a moment they both looked out at the lowering sun, the sky splashed orange and pink over the swell of the little white bridge.

The best solution for Bethany was to have her fiancé come back.

And even knowing that, Isaiah wasn't looking forward to Micah's return because these stolen moments alone with her would never happen again, and while Bethany would have her husband and raise her baby, Isaiah would go back to being very much alone.

Bethany leaned her head against Isaiah's warm shoulder, a cool breeze rippling across the fields and moving her dress against her leg. Not having to look at Isaiah was comforting somehow. It was also a strange relief to have told someone . . . a momentary lightening of the burden.

Except Isaiah hadn't said everything would be all right. She'd half-hoped he would—that he could show her how it would all work out and the dark worries be overshot. But of all people, Isaiah wouldn't lie.

"I shouldn't have said anything," she said quietly. A secret was only a secret when no one knew. In a community their size, one breathed secret could quickly make it around Bountiful.

"I'm glad you did," he said.

"No, I mean—" She lifted her head from his shoulder and pulled back. "If anyone found out—I know the pressure I'm putting on you, asking you to keep a secret like this, but my future depends on it."

"I know that," he said earnestly. "Look, if you can't trust my friendship with you, then trust my friendship with Micah. I told him I'd look out for you, and I'm going to do that."

Bethany rubbed her hands over her arms, suddenly feeling chilly, even though it was a warm night. The sun sank ever lower along the horizon, and the little white bridge glowed pink.

"Is this why you've been so tired lately?" he asked. "And not feeling well?"

She nodded. "Yah, this is why."

"And your *mamm* hasn't realized?"

"Not yet, but she will soon, I'm sure." Bethany looked down at her hands. "I want to tell her first. I don't want to be caught. I'd rather confess."

"And Micah . . . Do you trust him to stay, if he comes back?" Isaiah asked.

Bethany thought for a moment, her gaze moving over the silvery water as it flowed between the rocky banks, the light of the sunset flashing off the water.

"I don't have much choice," she said at last. "He's the father."

Because that detail did matter—who the father of this baby was. If the elders and bishop were told, they'd ask her very seriously to tell them who the young man was. No one else would raise a child like the father would. To any other man, this baby would be the child that constantly reminded him that his wife had been with someone else. The father of this child had a Gott-given responsibility to raise him or her, and to show this child what love was. They heard fatherhood preached about often enough—what it meant within a family, what it meant spiritually . . .

Isaiah was silent, and she looked over at him to find his jaw set. He leaned forward, his elbows resting on the dash rail. What was he thinking? Had his opinion of her just dropped? She rubbed her hand over her stomach— something she had started doing more often now that she knew about the baby.

"I didn't mean to end up like this," she said, her voice shaking. "He promised he'd marry me."

"And he will yet," Isaiah said gruffly.

"What are you going to do, march out to the city and drag him back?" she asked bitterly.

"Yah, maybe." He turned to look at her, his gaze dark and glittering.

Bethany shook her head, imagining Isaiah doing just that—stomping into some *Englisher* house and grabbing Micah by the collar. It was a ridiculous mental image because she didn't know what *Englisher* houses even looked like on the inside, and she had no idea how Micah had been living. . . .

"It isn't exactly the kind of wedding a girl dreams of, I can tell you that," she said.

"Micah is a good man," Isaiah said. "I know he left the Amish life, but he couldn't have left all his morals and his ideals behind, too. He knows what's right and wrong. And he has a heart—"

Isaiah's words broke off, and he reached out and wrapped a stray tendril of her hair around one finger, then released it with a gentle tug.

"Oh . . ." She took the bit of hair and tucked it back under her *kapp*.

"Are you okay?" he asked, his voice low.

She nodded, but then tears welled in her eyes, and Isaiah slid closer along the bench and cupped her cheek in his warm, work-toughened palm. He didn't say anything, but when she looked up at him, his lips came down over hers, warm, soft, and insistent.

Her eyes widened in surprise, and then she let them flutter shut. Isaiah slid an arm around her waist, and when he pulled back he rested his forehead against hers and let out a ragged sigh.

"Why did you do that?" she whispered.

"Because I realized that when Micah comes back I'm not going to be able to do that again. I'm not going to be able to take you for drives, or talk to you, or—you'll be off-limits."

"I'm *already* off-limits!" she shot back. "I'm pregnant with your best friend's baby!"

"You think I don't know that?" His gaze flashed and

he straightened, pulling back. "You chose the wrong guy back then, you know that?"

Bethany stared at him, stunned. "A girl waits to be chosen. That's how it works with us Amish."

"And the first guy who came calling, you agreed to marry!" Isaiah shook his head. "Look, I'm not saying Micah wasn't a worthy man, but he wasn't the right one."

Bethany felt anger steadily rising up inside her. "And in a community this size, I was supposed to turn away a good man who wanted to marry me? I was supposed to take those chances?"

"Did any of it feel wrong to you?" he demanded. "Choosing him, I mean . . . Wasn't there any hesitation, any sense that he wasn't the man for you? Because I could have told you that much!"

"In hindsight, yah. But my parents loved him! They thought he was ideal—" Her voice choked, and she clenched her teeth together in anger. She'd trusted her parents' instincts because they knew what love and devotion looked like. They had experience. And there was a thrill in being engaged . . .

Isaiah rubbed his hands over his face. "I get why you accepted him. I just wish you'd waited a little longer—made him work for it."

"Do you?" she demanded. "Because I could have just as easily ended up single for the rest of my life, just because I turned down an eligible man! And waiting for who, exactly?"

"For me!" Isaiah's hot gaze raked over her, and she felt her cheeks heat in response.

"You never showed interest!"

Isaiah raised an eyebrow. "Yah, I did. You just didn't notice."

"How? How did you show it?" she demanded.

"I talked to you, I smiled at you, I went out of my way to spend time with you," he said.

"You did that to all the girls," she said incredulously.

"No, I didn't. And if you'd stopped to look, you would have noticed that. Yeah, I might not have been the first one you noticed—"

"Not the first man?" she said. "Do you know how the girls saw you? They all had crushes on you! All but Mary Fisher, and she had a wild crush on Micah. But the others? It was you! And I wasn't going to put out my pie with all the other girls and hope you chose me. Because I wouldn't have won that!"

A family of ducks—some adults and a scattering of yellow ducklings—came down the stream, the soft quacks surfing the breeze toward them.

"You would have," Isaiah breathed.

Bethany stared at him. He would have chosen her? Out of all the girls in the community, all the girls who baked better and were prettier, he'd have chosen *her*?

"It's a little late now," she said, and she felt tears rising inside her.

"Yah. Maybe."

"What do you mean, maybe?" she demanded. "It is too late! I'm having a baby and you're trying to prove that you're more Amish than your preacher father ever was. You're going to court a girl who's pregnant with your best friend's child? I'll make this easy for you, Isaiah. You can't choose me. Not anymore. If you want to get the respect of the community, you've got to find someone beyond reproach, and that is no longer me."

The words tasted bitter in her mouth, but they were true. She was no longer one of the "good girls" in the community—that was over. She was officially a scandal now, even if no one knew it yet.

Isaiah didn't answer her, and the sun sank steadily lower behind the hills in the distance. They sat in silence in the near darkness, and Bethany felt a welling of grief building up inside her.

"Do you feel anything for me?" he whispered hoarsely.

"Does it matter?" she asked.

"Yah. I think it does."

But she wouldn't answer him because he was wrong there—it didn't matter. She'd listened to the honeyed words of her own fiancé and look where that left her! Her best-case scenario was having Micah come back, in which case admitting to any of her convoluted feelings would only hurt her future with the father of her child. And if Micah didn't return, she still couldn't be the woman for Isaiah. She knew what he needed as well as he did, and whether she married Micah or not, Isaiah would find a proper Amish girl with a good reputation, and he'd marry her.

Would he love that other girl, though? Really and deeply?

She looked over to find Isaiah's miserable gaze locked on her.

"You need to admit it," she said. "Admit that I'm not the kind of girl you need anymore."

"Are you going to admit you feel something for me?" he asked, his voice low and rough.

She smiled bitterly. "Fine. I feel something. You?"

"Yeah, I feel something." He reached out and touched the top of her hand.

"You know what I'm saying," she said. "You can't marry me and you know it."

"I can't marry you, but not for the reason you think," he retorted.

"Then humor me," she said, her voice strengthening. "Why not?"

Already, the other girls who had mooned after him were winning. She could feel it. And she was no longer stupid enough to listen to those sweet words. Words meant nothing.

"I made a promise to Micah," he said. "And I intend to keep it. I have to be the kind of man I want to live beside in this community. I'm nothing if I can't stand by my word."

Isaiah was standing by his principles. Why did that hurt?

"I think I should go home," she said, leaning back in the seat.

"You sure?" he asked, and when she looked over at him again she saw his dark gaze moving over her face, his strong hand resting on the seat next to hers. His shoulders were broad, and it was oh, so tempting to just forget about all the reasons why this wouldn't work and enjoy the feeling of someone wanting her again.

"I wouldn't kiss you again," he added. "We could just talk. We can get out and stand on the bridge—no temptation that way."

It was a paltry offering—as if a bridge was public enough to take away any temptation—but if he gave his word, she was inclined to believe him.

"You won't kiss me?" she whispered.

"I promise."

The sky was darkening to a medium blue behind them, and the sun came lower, blushing the horizon in red. Somewhere not far away, there was a strawberry social happening, but here in the cool evening, there was only a little creek babbling across the rocks, and the horses that stamped their feet and swished their tails against the insects that were attracted to their warmth.

"We might not get more chances like this one," he said. "And I don't mean for kisses and that sort of thing . . . I mean for talking, and for being alone. We don't have much more time like this where we'll be together."

And he was right. Her pregnancy was about to change everything.

"I suppose we could talk," she said quietly, and he smiled.

"Come on. Let's get out," he said, and he led the way, hopping down from the buggy and holding out his hand to her to help her down. He was very proper, and he released her hand once she had her balance, and they strolled toward the creek together.

"I used to play by this bridge when I was little," he said.

"Me too."

Her arm brushed against his warm, strong biceps.

"I used to drop little paper boats over the edge and watch them float away," he said.

"I used to pretend I was a horse and gallop down it while I waited for my *daet* to buy produce from a farm up there—" She nodded up the road. And when she got older she used to imagine that she was being courted, and the boy would propose to her in the center of that bridge. But that was a memory she wouldn't share with anyone. . . .

"It used to look bigger," Isaiah said, and he looked down at her, his gaze tender. "And grown-up responsibilities felt like an eternity away."

Bethany leaned her head against Isaiah's shoulder and turned her gaze to the rippling water. Once upon a time she and Isaiah were both just *kinner*, trusting in this Amish community and hardly knowing there was anything beyond it. She certainly hadn't imagined her fiancé disappearing on her, and she'd only heard the word "Mennonite" whispered among the adults, hardly even understanding what it referred to.

So much had changed now that they were grown, and Bethany wished with every fiber of her being that she could go back and try living this life again. Maybe she'd make some different choices and come out happier.

Chapter Ten

The sky was dark, moonlight casting long shadows, when Isaiah came back onto his uncle's property after dropping off Bethany. The air had cooled off, and the cattle lay down in the field beyond, dozily chewing their cud. From the house there was a light shining from the kitchen, and Isaiah felt a wave of guilt. He was late, but more than that, he hadn't gone where he said he would either. Seth might have told his *daet*, or one of the girls, that Isaiah hadn't been at the strawberry social. And while Isaiah was plenty old enough to make his own decisions, he was still under his uncle's roof, and he hadn't seen Mel angry yet.

That thought was mildly daunting.

The memory of Bethany's kiss was still strong in his mind. Her lips were soft, and at first her kiss had been tentative, but there had been a moment when he felt her relax and lean into him . . . Even thinking about it, his pulse sped up. But it was wrong—he was supposed to be a better man than that. Delivery on a promise shouldn't be complicated—he'd said he'd protect his friend's fiancée, and he'd never been the kind of man to find a loophole to let him out of a promise. Kissing her was wrong, and that wasn't who he wanted to be.

But he hadn't done it again after that first kiss. They'd stood together on the bridge in the twilight, talking, their arms pressed together as they shared a bit of warmth, but he hadn't given in to the temptation to taste those lips again. And when he brought her home again, he didn't walk her to the door—but he stayed watching until she disappeared inside before he headed back to his uncle's land.

Isaiah unhitched the horses, rubbed them down, gave them some extra oats, and when all was finished in the stables, he headed back toward the house with that accusing kitchen light.

"You're back," Uncle Mel said. He sat at the table with the Bible open in front of him, his hat hanging on the back of the chair and the bald top of his head shining in the kerosene light.

"Yah . . . I'm back." Isaiah pulled off his own hat and ran a hand through his hair.

"Have you seen Seth?" Mel asked.

Isaiah looked over in surprise. "He's not back?"

"Not yet. The girls got a ride back with another family, but he's still out."

"He's driving Mary Fisher home," Isaiah said.

"Yah. And I'm sure Elmer would like his daughter home more promptly than this," Mel said dryly. He nodded to a chair. "Have a seat, would you?"

Isaiah did as his uncle asked and pulled out a chair. Collette and Dawn could have told their *daet* that he wasn't there, but he didn't sense that sort of mood in his uncle. Mel looked at Isaiah thoughtfully.

"Elizabeth told me that your *daet* has been sending you letters," Mel said.

"He sent me one."

"And some to your sister."

"Yah, but the bishop has allowed it," Isaiah pointed out. "It's not going against any rules."

"What does he say?" Mel asked.

Isaiah frowned. "Why?"

Mel blinked. "Because he's my brother."

"That never meant much to you before this," Isaiah countered. "You can't stand my *daet*."

Mel sighed. "A brotherly relationship can be a complicated one. Maybe that is why the Good Book refers to members of the church as brothers. It's never simple."

"Can we leave the Good Book out of it?" Isaiah asked bitterly.

Mel shrugged. "We live our lives by it, Isaiah. It seems hypocritical to leave it out."

Frustration rose up inside him. The last thing he needed tonight was an argument. His uncle would win it, because if he didn't, Isaiah would have nowhere to go. This was pointless.

"You asked what my father said in his letter . . ." Maybe this was easier than debating religion with the man. "He told me some things that explained his behavior. It doesn't excuse it, but it explained it."

"What was that?" Mel asked, leaning forward, and there was a haunted, hopeful look in the older man's eye.

"He said that my *mamm* didn't need to die," Isaiah said.

"What?" Mel shook his head. "She died of cancer, Isaiah."

"Yah, but she could have been treated if she'd gone to

some specialists, he said. It didn't need to be fatal, but the community wouldn't give him the money for it."

"The community already gave all they could," Mel said. "Did you?"

Silence descended, and Mel licked his lips. For a few beats he didn't answer, and then he shook his head.

"Let me tell you what happened—from the way I saw it. Your *mamm* was very sick, and your Aunt Rose would go and be with her in the hospital for days at a time. Your *daet* was beside himself with worry and grief. He loved your *mamm* more than was healthy."

"He loved her with his whole heart. How is that wrong?" Isaiah demanded.

"He loved her to distraction," Mel said. "It's an English phrase I heard, and I think it describes it well. He loved her more than he believed in Gott's goodness. He couldn't trust her to her Maker's hands."

"And the money?" Isaiah said.

"There were some experimental treatments, but they hadn't been proved," Mel replied. "And the medical fund for our community that we all contribute to was empty, and I'd given him everything extra I could from our own money. But I had to feed my family, didn't I? I had to have something set aside in case we had any emergency of our own. So I told your *daet* I couldn't. And I wasn't the only one—everyone else seemed to come to the same conclusion. It was very sad, but when someone's time comes—"

"Gott doesn't make mistakes," Isaiah said, his voice low.

"Your father wasn't being reasonable," Mel said.

"Would you be, if it were Rose?" Isaiah demanded.

"I like to think I would."

Isaiah shook his head. Maybe his uncle just didn't love his wife as much as Abe had loved Isaiah's mother.

"You're angry, too," Mel said after a moment. "I can see that."

"Am I being 'unreasonable' like my *daet*?" Isaiah snapped.

Mel's expression softened. "You're grown, but you're still the same boy I remember. Stubborn, smart, talented."

Isaiah had never heard his uncle refer to him that way. Normally, his uncle mentioned his name with a huff of disgust. *He's got a fancy spirit, just like my brother.*

"Isaiah, in order to be Amish, there are three things that must guide our lives," Mel began slowly. "The first is to love Gott with all our hearts and minds and souls. The second is to follow the Ordnung's leading to protect our community. The third is to love one another. That combination is a strong one, and it helps to keep us grounded in reality as well. It keeps us being reasonable. One person can't be of more value than another, for example. And the good of the community is more important than the good of just one or two."

"It was my mother's life!" Isaiah burst out.

"And we didn't think that those experimental treatments would work," Mel said quietly. "We know that Abe hoped they would, and it was only a decade later when some of those treatments proved to be successful. But how could we know that then? We had limited knowledge, and we made the best choice we could."

"What did my *mamm* want?" Isaiah asked hollowly.

"She was ready to go," his uncle said quietly. "Rose said that she was in a great deal of pain. It was terrible. She didn't want to prolong her pain anymore, but your *daet* was making a very big mistake. He wasn't trusting in Gott. He was demanding that his prayers be answered, and if not, he would bend the will of the Almighty."

Isaiah was silent.

"Love is a beautiful part of marriage, Isaiah," Mel said quietly. "But there must be a balance with reason, too. Love is not enough. That's why we have the Ordnung. That's why there are rules within a marriage—fidelity, respect. When the balance in a marriage is off things go wrong. For example, when someone makes being reasonable too high of a priority, they end up being too cold and demanding, and it becomes a loveless marriage, and that's misery. It's certainly not what Gott intends a man and wife to be. And when someone makes love too high of a priority and the person they marry doesn't meet the other reasonable requirements for a happy life together—having similar interests, similar views of Gott and family, similar hopes for the future—they end up in a broken marriage, and that is a surprisingly similar misery."

"Are you saying my parents' marriage was broken?" Isaiah asked dully.

"I'm saying that your *daet* let go of reasonable behavior, and it made it very difficult for your mother at the end," Mel said quietly. "Instead of being her rock while she faced death, she had to be his. It wasn't right."

Isaiah had only been told stories about his *mamm*—and seeing her through his father's eyes, she'd been beautiful and perfect. Isaiah had never questioned if his *mamm* had been happy . . . He'd been raised to believe that to love a woman with all your heart was success in marriage. And shouldn't it be? But maybe there was more to it that he'd never seen before.

"Is this why your *daet* defrauded everyone—anger over your mother's death?" Mel asked.

"It's not why he started. He was duped, too, at first. But then they threatened to pin it all on me if he didn't continue with them. And that was when he had to decide if he was going to wholeheartedly continue to convince his neighbors to invest in a fraud, but it was because they had stopped helping Mamm that he went on with it so . . . passionately. That's what he said, at least."

"And you . . ." Mel met his gaze. "Do you think he was wrong?"

"Definitely," Isaiah replied. "But I also think he was hurting, and I think he was scared, and I think he'd lost faith, too. You can be wrong and still be worthy of love."

Mel nodded. "I agree—we can be in more than one state at once. And so can you. Remember that. You can love your father and learn from his mistakes simultaneously."

Outside, the sound of a buggy's wheels and horses' hooves came into the drive, and Mel straightened.

"I wish it were simpler," Isaiah said.

"It never is," Mel said quietly, and he rose from his seat, carrying his mug over to the sink. Seth would be back now, and the talk was over. Isaiah was just as happy to be able to go upstairs to bed.

His uncle was right and Isaiah knew it. Isaiah looked like his father, and he sounded like him, too. And he was prone to love like his father loved as well—too deeply, too passionately, with too much demand. And look where that had led Abe . . .

Being reasonable was important. It didn't matter how Isaiah felt about Bethany—her happiness lay in allowing her to take a reasonable step and reunite with the father of her child, and his lay in finding the woman he needed to give him a respected life here in the community. That was reasonable. It might not fill his heart, but it might fill Bethany's.

And perhaps Gott would answer his prayers and allow him to find some comfort in Bountiful at long last.

Bethany couldn't quite forget Isaiah's kiss—not after he dropped her off at home, not even when she lay in bed that night. She'd played it over in her mind—the way his hand had cupped her face, the way his thumb had moved over her cheek so slowly, so lightly . . . the look in his eyes before his lips came down over hers. She'd never been kissed quite like that before. . . .

Isaiah's kiss had been filled with a longing that made her heart want to explode even remembering it, and the next morning, as she and Isaiah worked on that order of literary journals, she couldn't help but remember what his lips had felt like as they moved over hers. She'd never seen Isaiah as a romantic option in the past—not a realistic one, at least—and to now know what his kisses felt like . . . He'd been in control of that kiss, and she'd felt something that had scared her just a little—abandon.

She couldn't let herself follow those feelings. She'd done that once already . . . why was she even allowing herself to entertain whatever it was that was stewing between her and Isaiah? She knew better!

"I'm just going to the storage room," Bethany said. "Does anything need refilling?"

"Not here, Bethany," Daet replied, not even looking up from foil pressing.

"Yah—I could use more leather," Isaiah said, and when she looked over in his direction he caught her eye. He didn't smile, but there was something tender in his gaze that brought the heat to her cheeks. She turned away and headed for the back room.

Gott, help me to stop this, she prayed in her heart. *What is it about me that keeps doing this? I know I'm wrong! But I need strength . . .*

Because there was something about that man that seemed to empty her brain these days. She shouldn't have stayed out with him so late. She should have insisted he drive her home right away—he'd offered, hadn't he? He hadn't even tried to kiss her again, and they'd only talked as the moon rose, but her *mamm* was right about appearances. If they'd been seen . . .

All the possibilities were just now tumbling through her head, and she felt the hypocrisy of her prayers for Gott to remove the consequences of her own stupid mistakes while she insisted upon making more of them. The time for praying was beforehand, not afterward!

Bethany carried a pile of leather over to Isaiah's workstation, and as she turned to leave, she felt his fingers brush against the side of her hand. Nothing more than a tickle, but her heart hammered hard in her throat.

"Did anyone ask you about last night?" Isaiah whispered.

"No." She glanced over her shoulder, but her father was turned away from them, focused on the gold foil. "Did anyone ask you?"

Isaiah shook his head. "I'm sorry I kept you out like

that. Your *mamm* said she wanted you home promptly, and we don't even know when people went home."

"It's okay." Bethany sighed. "We didn't do anything wrong."

"That doesn't always matter," he said.

And while Bethany's instincts had always been to guard her reputation, she realized it might be silly at this point. Her reputation was going to be beyond tarnished—it was going to be irreparably dashed to pieces.

"It was nice all the same," he added with a smile. "I like being with you."

"Me too," she admitted, and she dropped her gaze.

"Maybe we could take a walk sometime, or another drive—"

"No." She shook her head and saw his expression fall. "Isaiah, I don't think we should be playing with this. . . ."

"Because I kissed you . . ."

"Because—" She swallowed. "Because I liked it."

Isaiah smiled ruefully at that. "Me too," he whispered.

"So you see the problem," she breathed.

"I told you I wouldn't do it again and I stood by it, didn't I? I know we have to stop that. You don't have to convince me."

One kiss had been enough . . . besides, she could imagine a walk with him—all the opportunities to duck behind a tree and let him kiss her all over again. The very thought sped up her pulse. These feelings were dangerous!

"I don't want to take chances," Bethany said, glancing over her shoulder again to check that her *daet* was still occupied. "It isn't just about what people will think. Things are complicated right now for me. If we can be friends, and only friends . . . but I'm not sure we can do that."

"I could try," he said, but the look in his eyes was a little too tender for her to feel entirely safe.

The front door opened with a jingle of the overhead bell, and Bethany stepped quickly away from Isaiah's workspace, pasting a smile on her face before she even saw who it was. Mary Fisher came inside the shop, and she smiled when she saw Bethany.

"You should have come to the strawberry and whipped cream night, Bethany!" Mary said. "It was such fun! And the strawberries are really sweet already. I thought they'd be a bit bland, but . . ."

Bethany hurried up to the counter and lowered her voice. "No need to holler about it, Mary."

Mary met her at the counter and grinned.

"Seth held my hand," she whispered.

"That's wonderful." Bethany tried to smile. "I . . . couldn't make it."

"Obviously, but the next one—you've got to come. We're thinking of going to the creek next time and bringing a big, potluck picnic."

It sounded like innocent fun for a Christian group of young people, but there wasn't going to be a next time for Bethany. The next time the youth group got together, Bethany probably wouldn't be able to hide this pregnancy anymore. And she couldn't explain that. Once she was noticeably pregnant, she wouldn't be welcome.

"What's this about the event last night?" Daet asked, coming over to where they were standing.

"I was just saying that I wished she was there," Mary said. "It was fun . . ." Her voice trailed away when she saw Nathaniel's face, and her gaze flickered toward Bethany again. "Oh . . ."

"You didn't go?" Daet asked, frowning.

"I'd better get going," Mary said with a weak smile. "Bye . . ."

Mary fled for the door and Bethany rubbed her hands over her face. "Daet, I meant to go. We were on our way, but neither of us actually felt in a very strawberry mood—"

"What is a strawberry mood, exactly?" Daet asked curtly.

"Um." She looked over to where Isaiah sat, but he'd risen to his feet, his expression as grim as her own. They'd been caught. "Daet, I didn't mean to lie. We were on our way and we changed our minds. That's all!"

"And where did you go?"

"For a drive."

"For three hours?" Her father looked over toward Isaiah. "That's quite the workout for your horses."

"Nathaniel, it isn't what it looks like," Isaiah said, coming around the table in their direction. "We just talked for a while, and I'm sorry. I probably should have just taken her home when we both agreed we weren't feeling like going to the young people thing."

"Or you could have gone," her father said dryly.

"Daet, I'm sorry. Isaiah offered to bring me home. I said no."

Her father pressed his lips together in the way that meant he was angry, but he was counting his words, too. "I'm going to say this to both of you," her father said, his voice low. "And I'm saying it to both of you, because it applies to you both. Reputation matters. My daughter's fiancé only just left Bountiful, and he may very well come back. We're praying he does—other young people have made a mistake and returned. Micah may very well do the same, but if he comes back home to hear rumors about his fiancée and his best friend having picked up a romance while he had barely stepped away, how will he feel? He'll feel betrayed! And while I know I've struggled with my anger about him leaving, if he comes back and you *want him*, my dear girl, you'd better act like it now! Because people *will* talk. They always do. And nothing spreads faster than a juicy story. You need to have a choice, not have it taken away from you."

Bethany felt her cheeks heat. She didn't need this lecture, and she wasn't some teenaged girl who needed reminders about how people worked either.

"Daet—" she started, but her father cast her a flat look, and she shut her mouth.

"As for you, Isaiah," he went on. "You wanted a second chance, and you asked me to trust you. This is how you repay that? I gave you a job, and I gave you a start after everyone was furious with you!"

"I'm sorry, I really didn't intend—" Isaiah began.

"And my daughter is not part of you regrowing your reputation around here," Nathaniel added, cutting him off. "She's hurt right now, and she's vulnerable. Everyone can understand the pressure she is under, and she has to look to her own needs, not to yours!"

"I'm not trying to lean on her," Isaiah said. "If I can help in any way—"

"You can help by taking a step away from her!" Nathaniel retorted. "A true friend protects a girl's reputation, and if she appears to be rebounding after a lengthy engagement, whether that is true or not—" Nathaniel softened his tone. "And I recognize that it might not be true. I'm not accusing you of doing anything inappropriate. I'm only pointing out that many people will be glad to talk as if it is happening. And that could be horrible for our daughter."

Her father met Isaiah's gaze, and Bethany could see something unspoken passing between the men. Isaiah dropped his gaze and her *daet* gave a decisive nod.

"I'm sorry if I was harsh," her father said. "I won't bring this up again, seeing as you are both grown. But I felt it needed to be said straight."

There was a couple of beats of silence as Bethany swallowed uncomfortably. To be lectured by her *daet* was one kind of indignity, but to be lectured by him with Isaiah included in it . . . Anger welled up inside her. She hadn't done anything wrong, and Micah was no longer her fiancé. He'd left her! She was the one who'd stayed Amish, who'd refused to leave with him. And now she was being treated like some sort of risky girl because of that?

She'd just been telling Isaiah that she couldn't go out with him anymore. She had this under control, and she didn't need her *daet* bounding in to fix it for her, as if she were a girl before her Rumspringa!

"Now, there is another shipment of leather that arrived at the bus depot this morning," her father went on.

"I'll go get it," Isaiah said quickly.

"Thank you, Isaiah," her father said. "I appreciate that."

Isaiah turned and briskly headed for the door, his back rigid and his heels sounding loudly against the floor.

"He's angry," Bethany said as he stepped outside and the door swung shut behind him.

"He knows I had a point," her father replied. "Any man with an ounce of sense can take a direct word from a girl's father without wilting."

And while that may be true, Bethany knew it was time

she talked to her parents. Tonight, she'd have to come clean and tell them the truth about her pregnancy. She couldn't avoid this any longer. If her *daet* was going to worry, it was best he leave Isaiah alone and worry about the truth.

Isaiah headed across the street, his heart hammering in his chest. He'd never been lectured by a girl's father before. Up until his own *daet*'s disgrace, he'd been a respected young man in this community, and there were plenty of families who would have been thrilled to have him court their daughters.

And he *hadn't* been courting Bethany—they were friends! Heaven forbid a man and a woman talk! But he knew how it looked—he shouldn't have been so stupid. But all the same, he didn't require a dressing down like the one he'd just received.

Everyone wanted Micah back, and Isaiah, apparently, even though Isaiah was loyally Amish and doing his best to outlive his *daet*'s mistakes, he was worse for Bethany's reputation than the man who dumped her to go English. That was a bracing revelation, but perhaps one he needed to recognize. This was the position he now held in the community, and it was a stomach-churning descent from the position he'd been used to.

He paused and waited for some cars to pass before he jogged across the street and headed up toward the bus depot.

Gott, what has become of me?

It wasn't fair. Isaiah was suffering because of his father's sins, not his own. And he was doing his very best to walk the narrow path, to do the right thing, to pull a life together for himself and his sisters, and he didn't have many friends left. Was he supposed to do all this without any kind of friendship?

Did he have to let go of Bethany completely?

Isaiah nearly bumped into an Amish man who was carrying a bag of flour over one shoulder, and he muttered his apologies as he carried on toward the bus station. He'd work hard for Nathaniel, and he'd back off and let Bethany do what she had to do. Wasn't that the message he'd been receiving since last night? Maybe Gott was trying to tell him something.

He pulled open the heavy glass door to Bountiful's bus station and stepped into the air conditioning. Air-conditioned *Englisher* spaces were his guilty pleasure this time of year, and maybe he'd have to find his own small bits of comfort where he could. He headed for the counter where Bethany had picked up the last box.

"Hi, there," the woman said with a smile. She wore a blue polo shirt with the bus company's logo on the chest.

"Hi." He tried to smile naturally, although he wasn't sure he was managing it. "I'm here to pick up a box for Nathaniel Glick at the book bindery."

"Yep, he just called." She smiled and tapped a box already on the counter. "That one is for you. I'll add it to Nathaniel's bill."

"Thanks." Isaiah hoisted the box up onto his shoulder and as he turned, he spotted a trail of new tourists descending from a bus. He didn't know why he stopped to watch them—he had no real reason, besides enjoying a few extra moments of air conditioning, but then his heart thudded to a stop.

A man stepped down from the bus in Amish clothing, and he was just replacing a straw hat on his head as he came down the last step. Isaiah knew him immediately, and when he looked up, their eyes met.

Micah Weibe was back.

Chapter Eleven

Micah wound his way around the other passengers who were milling about, picking up their luggage, and he crossed the depot toward Isaiah. It was like no time had passed—the last couple of weeks had never happened. Micah had the same friendly look on his face, the same straw hat with the dent in the side. And after a moment of numbness the first thing Isaiah felt was a blast of anger.

Micah came back *now*? After leaving Bethany, abandoning their wedding, and letting her look like the fool? He came back now? But on the heels of the anger came another sensation—grudging relief. That flow of young people leaving their community was frightening for more than just the older folks. It left everyone feeling off-balance, grief-stricken, and afraid for the future for all of them. If Micah could come back, maybe the damage Abe had done was reversible. Maybe there was hope for Lovina to come back, too. Or any of the others who'd already left. He scanned the other travelers, hoping to see his sister's face among them, but there weren't any more Amish on that bus.

"Isaiah!" Micah said, and he forced a smile that didn't

look natural. He had rings under his eyes and he looked like he hadn't been sleeping.

"Hi—" Isaiah swallowed. "You're back."

"Yah." Micah reached out to Isaiah's hand and they shook, then had an awkward hug with a few thumps on the back. "I'm back. And I'm glad you're the first one I'm seeing."

"I don't imagine I'm the one you're here to see," Isaiah said.

"No, but maybe we could talk a bit before I go find her," Micah replied.

He looked like the same old friend—the same clothes— except when Micah pulled his hat off again and rubbed his hands through his hair, Isaiah noticed that he had an *Englisher* haircut now. That would take a while to grow out.

"So where did you go?" Isaiah asked, and they moved off to the side, away from the chatter of other people.

"I'm in Pittsburgh," he replied. "There are some Mennonite churches that help out Amish kids who leave, and . . . so yeah. They've been really helping me out. I got a job at a hardware store, and the pay isn't bad. Plus, I'm staying with this family, and their kids are grown, so they like having someone young around . . ." His voice trailed off. "How are things here?"

"Not great," Isaiah admitted. "No one trusts me, but I'm doing what I can."

"I know your *daet* is shunned, and I know you won't break the rules right now, but honestly, Isaiah, if it were me, I'd be talking to my father," Micah said with a shake of his head. "The bishop and elders can't tell you how to relate to your own *daet*."

"Have you seen Lovina?" Isaiah asked. "Because the bishop thought maybe she'd gone to find Daet, and—"

"No, I haven't seen her," Micah said. "I'm sorry. She's . . . she's left, too?"

"Yah." Isaiah let out a shaky breath. "I have no idea where she went. I was half-hoping she'd gone with you."

"No." Micah swallowed. "So, is she going to be shunned, too, then? She was baptized—the rules are stronger for her than for me."

"No, she's not," Isaiah said irritably. "And as for the bishop controlling my relationship with my father, you're wrong there, too. He's authorized my sisters and me to talk to him, even with the shunning. And he wants you all to come back."

"He authorized it?" Micah looked surprised at that. "That's . . . really good."

"They aren't the unfair, hard-nosed people you seem to think," Isaiah said. "Some things just take time. But they do care."

"Right." Micah slapped his hat against his leg. "Look, I haven't changed my mind about the bishop's authority and all that. I'm not going to knuckle under for that man."

"It's not about one man, it's about our entire community," Isaiah retorted. "Are you telling me you have that out there with the *Englishers*? People who love you, who have known you since you were a baby?"

"They might not know me as well, but there's a community, yah," Micah replied. "The store I'm working at belongs to a Mennonite man. He helps out the Amish young people who leave. And there was this lady who gave me a free haircut"—Micah's face colored—"it still feels strange. And the older couple I'm staying with, the lady is helping me learn how to do some cooking on those electric stoves—so weird. There's no flame!—"

"Is there another girl?" Isaiah asked curtly.

"It's been three weeks," Micah said, swallowing. "You think I hit the city and picked up a girl? Even the *Englishers* don't work that fast."

Isaiah wasn't sure if that was good news or not. Good news for Bethany, definitely, but he did feel a stab of guilt about how quickly things had developed between him and Bethany.

"What about Lovina?" Isaiah asked. "Do you know where we could start looking?"

"I don't know. There's a few different places—she could have gone anywhere," Micah said. "Look, I feel terrible that she left. It wasn't because of me, was it?"

"It was because of my *daet*," Isaiah said bitterly. "Not you."

"She's old enough to take care of herself," Micah said.

"She's only twenty."

"She could be married with *kinner* at twenty," Micah countered.

"Yah, well, she's not!" Isaiah snapped, and then he sucked in a breath, looking for some calm. "We thought she'd be marrying Johannes soon, but that's off, obviously. And having an Amish home is a whole lot safer than wandering some *Englisher* city! You know that."

"So, Johannes must be a wreck," Micah said.

"A whole lot like Bethany, yah," Isaiah retorted.

Micah fell silent, and they stared at each other for a moment, the noise as the *Englishers* headed out to the street flooding around them.

"Did you get my letter?" Isaiah asked.

"No . . . I got hers, though," Micah replied, and his cheeks colored. "And she sounded angry."

Isaiah couldn't help but smile bitterly at that. "Yah, she's angry."

"I never meant to do this to her," Micah said, lowering his voice. "I didn't! When I proposed I meant every word of it, and I thought I'd be with her for the rest of my life. I thought—"

"Yah, I get it," Isaiah muttered, cutting him off. "You meant to be the kind of guy she could trust."

"I did. I really meant to."

"So what changed?" Isaiah demanded. "My *daet* lets you down and you walk out on your promises?"

"It . . . Didn't your *daet* shake your faith at all?" Micah demanded, anger flashing in his eyes. "We've been told all our lives that Amish living means safety, that we're different from the heathen out there. And all the while your *daet* was working some scam with a bunch of *Englishers*! Isaiah, Bountiful is no different! Our community just works harder with fewer comforts, and that's it!"

"That's not true," Isaiah replied. "Being Amish means a whole lot more than that and you know it. It's about family and community and pulling together when times are hard. We support one another. We stand by our word!"

"Did your *daet*?"

"No!" Isaiah snapped. "He didn't. He let us all down, and me even more than you, so you can stop using my father as your excuse for all this. But there are other people in the community who embody everything we stand for—people you can trust!"

"Like who?"

"Like *me*!"

Isaiah was tired of holding it all in. He was trying to be the man everyone needed, even if they didn't want him right now. He was trying to be as good of an Amish man as he knew how, and it was tearing him apart.

"I know," Micah said, softening. "You're a good friend. You always were . . . Bethany mentioned you in her letter, you know."

Isaiah's heart gave a little lurch. "Oh? What did she say?"

"That you stayed." Micah sighed. "That you were facing all this, and I guess that you were a bigger man than I was for doing that."

That wasn't so bad . . . He'd been half afraid that she would have told him about whatever it was that seemed to be blossoming between them, but that couldn't help anything.

"This has been really hard on her," Isaiah said. "People were talking after you left, and she had to face everyone. You really broke her heart."

"How about her parents?" Micah asked. "Do you know how they're dealing with it?"

"I'm working with Nathaniel at the shop," Isaiah said.

"You're doing *my* job?" Micah squinted.

"Someone has to!" Isaiah said. "And I needed work. Our farm is gone. I've got to make some money, and Nathaniel needed the extra muscle. We're working on some pretty big orders at the moment."

"Right." Micah chewed the inside of his cheek.

"When you leave like that you're going to be replaced, Micah," Isaiah said. "You should know that."

And as the words came out, he heard the implied threat. Micah could be replaced in Bethany's heart, too.

"So how is Nathaniel, then?" Micah asked uncertainly.

"He's angry, too, but . . . you'll have to face him, I guess."

"I guess."

Isaiah wasn't feeling a lot of pity for Micah right now. He had to expect some sort of fallout from walking out on his fiancée! But now that Micah was back, Isaiah was going to have to find a new job. In a rush, staring his friend in the face, he realized that whatever time he'd had working side by side with Bethany was now over, and his heart sank inside him.

Isaiah bent down and hoisted the box of leather to his shoulder. "I have to bring this back to the shop. Nathaniel needs it."

"Right."

"Are you going to see your parents first, or Bethany?" Isaiah asked.

"Bethany."

That was the right answer, at least.

"Why don't you get your luggage and we'll head on over?" Isaiah said.

Micah headed wordlessly toward the last bag sitting alone beside the luggage sign, and Isaiah watched him as he gathered it up and made his way back. For a man who'd just discovered that he was a father and had come back to see the mother of his baby, his steps were rather slow.

Did Micah want to be here? It was hard to tell, but Micah *was* here.

"I know what Bethany said in her letter to you," Isaiah said, his voice low.

Micah stared at him, his face blanching. "You do?"

"You owe her, Micah," Isaiah said, the words coming

out in a growl, then he pushed out the glass door and into the sunny heat.

Isaiah and Micah walked down the sidewalk together, and for the first time in days, there were only *Englishers* on the street and no Amish. One buggy rattled past, but the driver didn't look in their direction.

When they approached Glick's Book Bindery, Isaiah adjusted the box in his grip and opened the door. Bethany looked up from her seat and gave Isaiah a wary smile—likely still thinking about her *daet*'s lecture, but then her gaze slid past him to Micah, who came up behind him, and her face paled.

Isaiah went inside first, depositing the box on the counter, and Nathaniel turned; then he froze, too.

"Hello," Micah said quietly.

"Micah . . ." Tears welled in Bethany's eyes, and she clamped a hand over her mouth. Isaiah's heart gave a squeeze at the sight of her tears.

"Did you just arrive?" Nathaniel asked. "Come in—flip that sign to 'Closed,' Isaiah."

Isaiah reached over and flipped the sign, then locked the door behind him. The family would need some privacy for this reunion. He shouldn't be here for it either, he knew, but he wasn't sure what else to do.

"Hi," Micah said with a weak smile. "Bethany . . . I got your letter."

Bethany didn't say anything for a moment, and when she uncovered her mouth, her voice shook. "You, idiot . . . you *left* me!"

Isaiah felt a lump constrict his throat. Micah and Bethany had history, and it was time for him to let them sort it out between them. She'd never been his to begin with.

* * *

Bethany hadn't meant for the words to leave her mouth, and when she glanced toward her father, expecting him to be glaring at her for her audacity, he didn't look fazed. Instead he beckoned her forward.

"Micah, I'm sure you're here to see Bethany," her father said. "And you two will need some time to talk."

"It's good to see you," Micah said, giving her father a hesitant smile.

"Yah, it's good to see you, too, Micah," her father said, but his tone remained somewhat tight, and he didn't reach out to shake his hand. "Have you seen your parents yet?"

"No."

"They'll be relieved to have you home, son," Daet said quietly. "But first things first, I'm going to lend you my buggy, and you and Bethany can go for a ride and talk in private."

Bethany glanced toward Isaiah and found his gaze locked on hers, but his expression was wooden. He hated this—she could feel it radiating from him. She felt it, too, but her melancholy came with a dose of guilt as well. She'd had no right to be getting closer to Isaiah—but she had. Sure, she was single, but her situation was far too complicated to make whatever was developing with Isaiah okay.

And with Micah back—her breath caught in her throat and she felt a wave of misgiving. She'd wanted this, hadn't she? She'd asked him to return. But now . . .

"Bethany?" Daet said.

She'd missed something, and she looked back toward her father.

"Yah?"

"Go with Micah. Isaiah and I can keep working on this order. In fact, Isaiah can drive me home after we close up. Right, Isaiah?"

"Yah," Isaiah said, but his voice sounded strangled.

"Go on, now," Daet said.

She could see the hope in her father's eyes. He'd been angry with Micah before, and now it seemed that all was forgiven . . . but it wasn't for her. She'd hoped that Micah would answer her letter—even come back—but now that she was looking him in the face, she felt a deep and rising anger.

Micah ambled around the counter just like he'd never left and paused when he got to where she stood.

"Does your *daet* know?" he asked softly.

Bethany shook her head. "Maybe we'll tell them together."

Micah didn't answer that, but he nodded toward the back door. "Come talk with me?"

She nodded, and before she followed him toward the door, she stole one more glance in Isaiah's direction. Isaiah's gaze was still locked on her, but as her eyes met his, he looked away. Was he angry?

Bethany followed Micah out the back door and she shut it firmly behind her. Micah paused and came closer, leaning in as if to kiss her, and she turned her face so that his lips brushed her cheek instead.

"I missed you," Micah said.

"Not enough to come back on your own," she replied.

Micah licked his lips. "I had no idea you were pregnant, Beth. Are you sure? Is there any possibility of a mistake?"

"I took the test," she said. "And my waist is getting thicker. I've been letting out my dresses."

Micah nodded a couple of times. "I can't remember when we—" His cheeks reddened. "Is it early still, then?"

"Yah, it's early," she said, but she instinctively slid a hand over her stomach.

"So there is the possibility that it might—I mean, this early, things go wrong sometimes, don't they?" he asked.

She winced at the words. "Are you hoping?"

"I'm just trying to be realistic," he said.

"Well, I love this baby already, so you can stop wishing it gone, Micah!"

"I'm not, I'm—" Micah shook his head. "I'm sorry, Bethany. I'm sorry for saying the wrong things, and for having gotten you into this situation to begin with. It's my fault—I know it!"

"And the thought of having a child?" she asked, her voice trembling.

"I—" Micah swallowed. "I don't think either of us are ready for this."

"If we'd gotten married, we would have been *praying* for this," she countered. They were plenty old enough to marry and have *kinner*, and up until a few weeks ago, he'd been more than eager to take a husband's privilege with her.

"Yah, but we aren't married," Micah said.

The words were like a slap in the face. He didn't want to come back and marry her—she felt the truth of it in a rush. His promises, the love he said would never change . . . it had changed.

"Let me get the buggy hitched up," Micah said. "We obviously need to talk."

Bethany waited, and as she stood there in the mid-morning sunlight, she felt like the world was spinning around her. If Micah came back, she'd somehow imagined everything being exactly the same. But it wasn't—Micah had changed, and so had she. In such a short period of time, it was like talking to a relative stranger.

When Micah brought the buggy around he reached down to give her a hand up, and she accepted his help, then settled in with a more than proper eighteen inches between them. She didn't have any desire to scoot closer, to feel his arm against hers.

"Bethany, I am sorry for this," he said, giving the reins a flick. "When I left I know it was a shock. When I asked you to marry me, I thought I'd get over my doubts. I really did."

"There's a baby coming," she said bluntly. "I don't think it is about your doubts and certainties anymore. A baby is coming, and you and I are going to be parents."

"Yah." He glanced over at her. "And I want to do the right thing, but I need you to meet me in the middle."

Bethany frowned. "There is no middle ground between right and wrong."

"There's more than you think," he replied.

"Is that what the Mennonites say?" she asked.

"Bethany, listen. I'm willing to marry you. I promised I would, and now there's a baby coming, but I can't live here," he said.

Perhaps she should be grateful for that much—he was still willing to get married. But she didn't feel the same elation she'd felt the first time he'd proposed, and she realized that if she weren't pregnant and he came back again, she wouldn't want to marry him after all.

Something had changed between them—something she couldn't quantify, but it was different all the same.

"You want to go to a different community and start over?" she asked, and she felt a pang of loneliness at the very thought. She'd already be marrying a man she no longer loved—did she have to give up her family, too? "It's just that I want to be close by my *mamm*. And Lily could babysit—I know she'd love it. I don't want to be away from my family when I'm having my first baby. There is a lot more pressure on a woman than men seem to realize. My sisters—"

"I don't want to go to a different Amish community," he broke in. "I want to go back to the city."

Bethany stared at him. "What?" she asked feebly.

"I'm serious. It isn't what you think out there. The church that has been helping me has some really good Christian people in it, and there's more opportunity for me out there—"

"You had opportunity here," she cut in.

"Bethany, I don't believe in it anymore!" he said. "Can't you see that?"

"But I do," she said.

"Yah . . ." He sighed. "I'm trying to be fair here. I'll marry you and do right by you, but not here. We can be Mennonite; we can live simply and raise our *kinner* to be good Christians."

But not Amish. Her heart hammered hard in her chest, and it was only then that she started to look around to see where Micah had been driving them. They were headed toward her home, and she felt a wave of panic.

"My parents don't know about the baby yet," she said. "I haven't had a chance to tell them." She brushed a stray hair out of her eyes. "That's not true, actually. I haven't been brave enough to tell them."

"We'll tell them together," Micah said.

"I'm not sure I want that now," she said.

"Why not?" Micah demanded. "I'm the father. We're going to raise this child together—"

"Are we?" she demanded. "Because you've gone Mennonite and I haven't!"

"What's worse, going Mennonite with me or staying Amish and being a single mother?" he shot back.

"Going Mennonite!" she retorted. "Micah, what are you even thinking? You expect me to leave my faith, my family, and my salvation—"

"You won't go to hell, Bethany," he said irritably.

"I'm not debating theology with you!" she retorted. "You asked me to marry you and be your *Amish* wife. And now that I have very few choices, you're going to change that on me?"

"I'm trying to do the right thing here!" Micah shot back. "I thought you might appreciate that!"

"This is *not* the right thing," she said, her voice shaking.

Why had he come back if he was only going to make impossible demands? Or was this his way of getting out of the whole marriage and making it her choice instead of his own?

Micah expertly guided the horses around a pothole and they headed up her drive.

"I thought we needed to talk," she said.

"I thought we needed to start telling our parents the situation," he countered.

"I told you, I haven't told them yet," she said. "I wanted to talk to them alone."

"Yah?" Micah said, turning. "We don't have a lot of time!"

"Why not?" she demanded.

"Because I have a job to get back to and I don't want to lose it!"

There it was—Micah was here on a mission—a very short-term one—and he was going to head back just as soon as he could. His life wasn't here anymore and Bethany was going to have a very serious choice to make.

Micah reined in the horses just before the drive and turned toward her. "What do you want, Bethany? Do you want me to go back to Pittsburgh? Do you want me to drop you off and let you have a conversation with your *mamm* alone . . . or do you want me to go inside with you and we'll tell her together?"

"Let me tell her alone," Bethany said. "You go on home to your parents and tell them, too. I think it's better that way."

Micah gave a curt nod. "Okay. Fine."

"I don't think you have a right to be angry about this," she said.

"I know. It's fine. I'll come back here when I'm done with my parents and I'll face yours like a man. I'm not going to dodge that."

She had to admire his bravery right now, and she nodded. "Thank you, Micah. I'll see you later, then."

Then she climbed down from the buggy and started down the drive toward her house. She'd been avoiding this for too long. It was time to tell her *mamm* the truth.

* * *

In the kitchen, with late-morning sunlight spilling over a freshly mopped floor, Bethany sat down at the table and pressed her damp palms against the cool wood. The kitchen smelled of bleach—the counters were all clear and the sinks empty. Lily leaned against the table, her apron dirty from kitchen work.

"Is it very serious, then?" Mamm asked. "What's the matter?"

"It's private, Mamm," Bethany said, and she cast her younger sister an apologetic smile.

"I won't tell anyone," Lily pleaded.

"Lily, go do some weeding in the garden," Mamm said.

"I could go out and play instead," Lily said plaintively. "I don't see why I should be punished because Bethany's got a secret."

"The weeding has to be done anyway," Mamm said. "Go on, now. Outside."

Lily heaved a sigh, but she knew better than to argue twice, and she headed outside, pulling the door shut behind her as she headed toward the garden with a bucket. Mamm watched her go, then turned back.

"She won't hear a thing," Mamm said. "Now, what's going on?"

"First of all, Micah's back," Bethany said, and her mother broke out into a smile.

"Is that all?" Mamm asked.

"He's back because I wrote to him," she said, swallowing. "And I told him I'm pregnant."

Mamm's smile faded, and she put a hand up to her chest. "Is that why you've been pale and putting on some weight?"

"Yah." And it was rather irritating to know that her *mamm* had noticed her weight so quickly.

"How long have you known this?" Mamm breathed.

"A week." Bethany felt her eyes mist. "I'm so, so sorry, Mamm! I know it was wrong of me, and I wouldn't have done it if Micah hadn't promised to marry me! But it was stupid and I know that, so I don't need you to lecture me and tell me everything I already know—"

"Oh, my girl . . ." Mamm stood up, circled around the table, and wrapped her arms around her, pulling Bethany's head against her, smoothing her hand over Bethany's face the way she used to do when she was a little girl.

"I don't know what to do," Bethany said, and she pulled back, wiping at the tears on her face.

"Micah's here, isn't he?" Mamm asked. "He came back for you. I'll tell you what you do—you marry him!"

"He came back to marry me, yah," Bethany said. "But he wants me to go Mennonite with him."

Mamm's face blanched, and she sank into the chair next to her. "And you said?"

"No, of course," Bethany replied. "He asked me to go Mennonite with him before, and I turned him down. He's back, but he won't live an Amish life."

Mamm rubbed her hands over her face. "This is bad. . . ."

"I know," Bethany said.

"Why did you wait a whole week before telling me?" Mamm asked.

"I—" Bethany's chin trembled. "I was ashamed of myself."

Mamm sucked in a breath. "I don't think we have time for shame, my dear. If we can convince Micah to stay Amish, your problems are over. A quick wedding will be easy enough to throw together, and everyone will turn a blind eye at an early baby. At least the two of you will be married. He was happy enough to work at the shop with your *daet* before—"

"I don't think he will," Bethany said. "And I'm not sure I want to force him. If he doesn't love me—"

"He made a baby with you," Mamm said. "I don't care if he has soft and gooey feelings for you or not, he's the father of your child, and he made promises that he is obliged to keep."

"The only way that works is if the boy wants to stay Amish and is afraid of being shunned!" Bethany said. "Micah's not afraid of that!"

"It also works if the boy has any kind of conscience at all!" Mamm shot back, then she lowered her voice. "You're scared, but you did the right thing by coming to me. Your father and I will discuss it and we'll come up with a plan. It's a good sign that Micah came back at all. So, while he might be saying that he doesn't want an Amish life now, we have some time to convince him." Mamm pressed her lips together into a determined line. "As do the bishop, the elders, and his own father."

The community pressure would be applied, and if all went well, Micah would do as the community ordered, marry her, and remain Amish.

Bethany's stomach knotted inside her. "Not quite a girl's dream, having a boy ordered to make an honest wife of her."

Mamm reached over and put her hand over Bethany's. "We're no longer dealing with wishes and dreams, Bethany."

Chapter Twelve

That evening, after closing up the shop with Nathaniel, Isaiah flicked the reins and the buggy pulled forward as he and Nathaniel started out. Nathaniel had been cheery, but as the afternoon wore on, he became more solemn and quiet, and now he stared hard at the road ahead of them as the horses found their rhythm. The dragonflies were out, darting along the tall grass that stretched out of the ditch at the side of the road, and the sun shone warm and low. Both Isaiah and Nathaniel waved to an Amish man out checking his cattle in the field.

It was one of those days that would be satisfying and pleasant for everyone else, but Isaiah felt like he would snap, he was so filled with tension. Working hour after hour, not knowing what was happening with Bethany, had been excruciating. But Bethany wasn't his business—she never had been! So he'd best stop this preoccupation with a woman who was going to marry another man.

"What did Micah say to you?" Nathaniel asked for the third time that day.

"He's come to see Bethany," Isaiah said. "That's about all, really. And I asked about my sister, of course."

That was something he hadn't mentioned earlier.

"Of course," Nathaniel said, his tone softening. "Any news about her?"

Isaiah shook his head. "No."

"Has she written?" Nathaniel asked. "Or called?"

"Not yet. I'm hoping she will."

"Yah. She will. I'm sure. She'll miss you. It's understandable that she'd be confused after everything that happened with your father. Give it time."

"That's what the bishop says, too," Isaiah said.

"Micah came back, didn't he?" Nathaniel said. "Your sister can come back, too, for the very same reasons."

Not quite the same reasons, but then, Nathaniel didn't know the whole story, did he? However, Lovina had left behind a fiancé of her own, so maybe she'd come back for Johannes. It was possible, wasn't it?

Micah and Bethany had news of their own, but it wasn't Isaiah's place to share it. And maybe by the time Isaiah dropped Nathaniel off at his house, there would already be wedding plans commencing, and all Nathaniel's worrying would be for nothing.

The thought made Isaiah's stomach hurt, but he'd brought this on himself. If he had been keeping his promise about looking out for Bethany without overstepping those lines, he would be nothing but happy for a reconciliation between the couple. And maybe this was a lesson learned.

Except his feelings for Bethany had always been a little complicated, and even if Micah had stayed and the wedding was going forward without a hitch, Isaiah was going to feel a few pangs about it. But now, after this time with her, it would be a whole lot more painful to see her married off to the man who'd never love her quite enough.

"You've been a real help lately, Isaiah," Nathaniel said.

"I'm trying," Isaiah replied.

"This has been a difficult time for all of us, so having you help out at the shop while Micah was away—it helped to keep things rolling. I appreciate it. You've had your own troubles, too."

And with Micah back, he'd likely have a few more of those troubles again.

"If Micah's here to stay," Isaiah said and cleared his throat. "I imagine I'll need to find a new job."

"One step at a time," Nathaniel replied. "You've shown some real aptitude for the trade. I'd hate to lose you completely."

"And I like the work, but . . ." Isaiah swallowed, measuring his words. He couldn't say what he was really feeling—that while Micah might be fine working with him, Isaiah might not want to work day after day with the man who got to go home to Bethany every night. Maybe it was common jealousy, but it wouldn't be easy for him.

"If Micah's back like we hope, I might still need another set of hands around the place. I'd really hate to lose someone who's got your work ethic." Nathaniel looked over him, and for a moment his gaze seemed a little too perceptive. "But if it doesn't work out, I'll give you a good reference."

It was better than no reference, and it might help him to secure another job somewhere in town. He might have more luck with *Englishers* than he did with the Amish. He'd be wise to start thinking ahead, but his mind kept slipping back to Bethany, wondering what was happening, if she was getting what she needed after all.

Because Isaiah had sensed something in Micah—something reticent, holding back. Micah didn't trust Isaiah—not completely. Was that because he knew that Isaiah had always harbored some feelings for his fiancée, or was it something deeper? While Micah had returned, something was definitely different.

When they pulled into the Glicks' drive that long, over-hanging branch from the huge oak tree tickled the top of the buggy, and Nathaniel turned and gave him a smile.

"Isaiah, I appreciate your flexibility today with all this. You've been an unexpected support for my daughter while Micah was away, and for me, too, in the shop," the older man said. "I hope you'll come in and join us for supper."

"I thought maybe you'd need some privacy," Isaiah said.

Nathaniel considered for a moment. "If Micah returns, even if he and my daughter marry, things will be different, Isaiah. And I think it's good to start things out with an understanding of that. Micah can't flounce out of here and then come back and expect nothing to have altered."

"So this is . . . punishment for him?" Isaiah asked with a wry smile.

"No. This is reality," Nathaniel replied. "A meal is the least I can offer after all you've done today. My wife would be appalled if I didn't bring you in to eat. Please. I won't take no for an answer."

With an invitation like that, Isaiah couldn't very well turn him down, but when he saw that the Glick buggy was back under the shelter, his stomach tightened.

"It looks like Micah is here," Isaiah pointed out.

"Yah. And that's a good thing," Nathaniel said. "Look, Isaiah, if you're going to find your footing here in Bountiful, you'll have to face Micah. He'll need to be welcomed back. That's reality, too."

Did Nathaniel suspect Isaiah's deeper feelings for Bethany, or was this simply the Amish, pragmatic approach to relationships? Or perhaps this invitation to dinner was part of a greater plan to start that reconciliation that would be necessary to bring Micah back. He met the older man's gaze, and Nathaniel's expression was sympathetic.

"Yah. You've got a point," Isaiah agreed.

"So let it start now. It'll be easier if you don't put it off."

Like whipping off the covers on a cold winter morning, or plunging out into a downpour when there were chores to be done, Isaiah would have to face reality, too. They unhitched the buggy and put the horses into the paddock, and then they headed toward the house.

The house didn't smell of cooking when they came inside, and there was no laughter or cheerful banter coming from the kitchen, as Isaiah expected. He glanced over at Nathaniel, who had pulled off his boots, and Isaiah suddenly knew what was about to happen. Nathaniel was going to learn what Isaiah had known for a few days now, and their family's hopes were about to get a whole lot more practical. Isaiah didn't bother taking off his boots because he didn't expect to stay.

When Isaiah looked out of the mudroom and into the kitchen, he spotted Barbara with red, puffy eyes. Bethany stood next to her mother, but her expression was grim, not teary. She lifted her gaze to meet Isaiah's and held it.

"What's wrong?" Nathaniel asked, looking around the room.

Micah sat at the table, an untouched sandwich in front of him, and Lily leaned against the chair next to him, looking mildly confused.

"We need to talk," Barbara said. "But Lily needs to go get a start on mucking out some stalls in the stables."

"By myself?" Lily said, shaking her head. "Mamm, that's not fair!"

It was an effort to get her out of earshot—and not even a politely disguised one.

"You can start and we'll help you finish," Mamm said. "Off you go."

"Why?" Lily demanded. "I know a lot about life, you know! I'm not too young to know this, too!"

"Get your boots on," Nathaniel said gruffly. "If your *mamm* says you need to head out, you need to head out. I'll take over in a few minutes if you've worked hard. If not, you'll be working with me until it's all done."

Lily looked around the room, seeking someone on her side, but found none, so she heaved a sigh and brushed past Isaiah. She pushed her feet into a pair of black rubber boots and tromped out the door, letting it bang shut behind her.

"I should go, too," Isaiah said. "This is family business."

"I've asked Isaiah to stay to supper," Nathaniel cut in.

Barbara crossed the room and murmured softly with her husband for a moment, and Nathaniel sighed.

"I'm sorry," Nathaniel said. "You were right about us needing some privacy. Maybe we can have this dinner another day."

Isaiah nodded. "Of course. Have a good night. I'll go hitch up."

He didn't belong here for this conversation, and as he moved toward the door, Bethany's clear gaze followed him. Bethany was pregnant . . . but this wasn't unheard of in the community. Micah had come back—although perhaps a family needed some time to adjust to news like this. He forced a smile, but she didn't return it.

Once outside again he did as he said he would and started hitching up his buggy again. Lily came out to watch him as he worked, and he gave her a weak smile.

"You'd best get some work done," he said.

"They just want me away from the house so I don't hear what they're talking about. But I know already."

Lily's hair fell free around her face and she pushed it back, looking victorious.

"You do?" he asked hesitantly.

"Yah. I'm not a baby, you know," she said. "*Kinner* know a whole lot more than the grown-ups ever think. Micah doesn't want to marry my sister after all."

Not quite, and Isaiah felt a wave of relief that she'd missed out on the crucial element here. It was best that Lily didn't have a handle on all this.

"We'll have to see about that," Isaiah said. "Adult business can be very complicated."

"Doesn't seem that complicated to me," Lily replied. "If he doesn't want to marry her, she should find someone else."

"Maybe it's the hearts that make it all more complicated," he said.

Lily stared at him for a moment, then nodded. "Yah. I hadn't thought of that. I guess they would, wouldn't they?"

"Every time," he muttered.

But complicated or not, he had no doubt that they'd sort it out and the wedding would be back on. Of course Micah would marry her. It was he who'd have to take a nine-year-old girl's advice and just move on to someone else. So much easier said than done.

Inside the house, Bethany sat at the table across from her father and next to Micah. She folded her hands on the table in front of her, and when she glanced in Micah's direction he didn't look in hers.

"So . . . you won't marry her," her *daet* said, his voice hollow. "After asking me for her hand in marriage, and after planning a wedding with her and getting her pregnant, you've decided not to marry my daughter."

"It isn't that, exactly," Micah said. "I will marry her, if you'll all agree to it, but my life is going to be in Pittsburgh. I want to marry her, and I want to be the one to raise my child."

Bethany pushed back her chair and rose to her feet. Her mother glanced up and Bethany turned away from them. This was humiliating. Obviously, if Micah loved her as he claimed, he'd come back to the life he was raised to and marry her. But he had a way out—the Mennonites. Whatever they were telling him gave him an easy exit, and Micah knew as well as she did that her parents would never give their blessing for her to go English.

"You know that your eternal salvation lies in being united to your community," her *daet* said. "Have you talked with the bishop about this?"

"I've talked with the bishop, with my uncles, with my

father, my mother, my friends . . . I know the arguments, but there is another way of looking at this. The Mennonites believe that we are all part of the church—the *Englisher* Christians, too."

"'Narrow is the path that leads to life, and broad the path that leads to destruction,'" Daet paraphrased.

"Yah, but what if that narrow path is not the Amish life but Jesus himself? We aren't saved by our works."

"I'm not questioning our Savior's sacrifice," Daet said, unamused. "And I don't appreciate word games."

"It isn't a word game. There are many Christians who truly and sincerely believe that the narrow path is Jesus himself. He's our salvation. He's our way to life. Not a list of difficult rules."

"Our behavior matters, Micah. Are you saying we can believe in Jesus and go about hurting others and living like the heathen? A pious life focused on Gott—"

"A pious life is not stopped because of electricity or gas-powered vehicles!"

"The Ordnung says—"

"The Ordnung is not the Bible, though, is it? And we are told to follow Gott, not man-made rules!"

"The Ordung is *tradition*—hard won, hard earned. Our ancestors discovered that by limiting our lives here on earth, our spiritual experience is deeper. We don't need to reinvent the wheel, Micah. You aren't the first one to wonder if all of this is necessary. Generations before you have struggled with the same questions. But over and over again, they came to the same conclusion—our community is sacred. Keeping apart from the world is absolutely necessary to keep ourselves from becoming *like* the world."

"So our produce and our crafts—that's our witness to

the world?" Micah asked. "Do we open our doors to others? Do we encourage them to join us, and grow this church of ours? Or do we hide ourselves under a bushel? Is that what Gott really wants of us? Does He love us more than the *Englishers*?"

"Of course not, but—"

Bethany blocked their argument out of her head. She'd heard all this before. What Amish young person hadn't grappled with some of these bigger questions? But this wasn't really about theology at all. It was about whether or not Micah would abide by his promise to marry her properly.

She headed toward the side door and stepped into her shoes before she slipped outside, closing the door softly behind her and blocking out the murmur of arguing voices. She couldn't do this—sit there and listen while her parents argued with Micah over his choice to leave them all. She wouldn't beg.

Isaiah was securing one last strap and Lily stood next to him, her arms crossed over her chest. If Bethany weren't already so upset, she might find the sight of them amusing.

"What's going on?" Lily asked when she saw her.

"They're talking."

"About what?" the girl pressed. "Trying to make him marry you?"

"Yah," she admitted. "That's what it amounts to."

"You should tell them that you don't want him!" Lily said, and tears rose up in her eyes. "What kind of husband is he going to make anyway? You said it yourself—he left! He doesn't even want to be Amish. You should be the one to call off the wedding, not him! Just tell them you changed your mind!"

"Hush," Bethany said with a sigh. "This isn't your business."

Lily's face blotched red and she dashed her hair away from her face with vehemence.

"I think you're beautiful, Bethany," Lily said, her voice shaking. "I think you're just wonderful. And any man who doesn't think so is either blind or stupid. One of them. Don't you think so, Isaiah?"

A smile tickled the edges of his lips and Isaiah's gaze softened, moving over Bethany slowly, appraisingly. "Yah, I'd agree with that."

Bethany felt her cheeks warm and she looked away. "Lily, go on into the stables and start working. Daet will be out soon, and you know he'll make you stay out until it's all done if he doesn't see that you put in some real effort."

Lily heaved a sigh. "This is only to keep me away from inside. Why do I have to work?"

"Because Daet said so," Bethany said, her voice firming. "Now, go on!"

Lily headed back into the stable, casting one last look over her shoulder before she disappeared inside. Isaiah nodded toward the fence and they ambled slowly in that direction. His arm was close enough to hers that his shirt brushed against her sleeve, but she didn't dare move any closer to him, no matter how reassuring that broad shoulder might be.

"So, what's really happening?" Isaiah asked, his voice low.

"They're trying to convince him to marry me," she said quietly. "And he's arguing very passionately against it."

"What?" Isaiah asked, stopping in his tracks and turning to face her. "I thought he was back to do just that—marry you!"

"He's not," she said. "He said he'd do his *duty* by me and marry me if I go English with him. He's not back to do it right."

Isaiah let out a slow breath. "Why?"

"He thinks the Mennonites make a good point," she said with a weak shrug. "And he won't be argued out of it."

"He knows about the baby, though. . . ." Isaiah clenched his jaw.

"Yah. He knows. He's asked me quite earnestly to marry him here, then leave with him."

"And you won't?" Isaiah confirmed.

"How could I? I'm Amish! When he proposed it was an Amish future he promised me!"

"Let me talk to him," Isaiah said.

"I don't think it'll make much difference," Bethany said. "If you heard him in there—he's a Mennonite already. He's saying that . . . that . . . we're wrong."

"Yah, but he did come back, and I can still try," Isaiah said. "You deserve everything your little sister is convinced you deserve, Bethany. You deserve a man who will love you and stand by you and . . . and . . . raise your child together!"

"Yah." Tears misted her eyes. "But in order for him to marry me, I'd have to leave and hope that I could convince him to come back to the Amish life after a few years. If at all."

It was a huge risk to take, one that depended on Micah's heart and their connection as a couple—neither of which she was certain of anymore. It also relied on a woman's ability to lead her husband—which turned everything she'd been taught on its head. Her parents would never approve of it.

Still . . . her options were shrinking.

Isaiah reached out and touched her hand, his hand warm and firm, and she longed to lean into his arms and feel his strength close around her.

But even Isaiah wasn't the answer here! He needed a girl to give him a place in this community, and she knew better than to rely on these sorts of feelings. She'd felt drawn to Micah in much the same way—believing his words, slipping into his arms and imagining what their marriage would be like. It had been foolish on her part. Attraction might make a baby, but vows made a life together. And whatever convoluted soup of emotions had tugged her into her last mistake with Micah, she would not follow it again with a different man.

Because Micah was currently in her kitchen, explaining to her *mamm* and *daet* why he couldn't possibly make a proper Amish wife of her. This was humiliation enough.

"Beth . . ." he murmured, and he caught her fingers in his strong grasp, tugging her closer. This was what she wanted from Micah—some longing, some desire! But he wasn't the man she'd thought he was either.

"Isaiah, stop," she said, her voice shaking.

"I'll talk to him," he repeated. "Who knows? Maybe I'll get through to him yet."

And if Isaiah was successful, she'd have a husband, but not the kind she'd dreamed of all these years—no strong, reliable Amish man who would keep the family united and pious. She'd have the husband she rightly deserved—the one who'd gotten her pregnant. She could no longer hope for much more than that.

The side door of the house opened again, and Bethany pulled back her hand and stepped away from Isaiah, her heart speeding up. Micah appeared on the porch, looking as decently Amish as he ever did, his hat on his head and his suspenders just a little bit crooked. Micah looked toward them, and she felt a lump close off her throat.

She'd wanted so much more than this—but here she was.

"I wonder if you might be willing to drive me back to my parents' place, Isaiah?" Micah said.

"Yah. Sure." Isaiah looked at Bethany, and she sucked in a wavering breath. "I'll talk to him," he said, his voice low enough for her ears only.

Bethany shrugged. For whatever good it would do.

Isaiah headed for the buggy and Micah followed. Micah paused and met Bethany's gaze as if he expected her to come say something, but she didn't move toward him.

No matter how dire her situation became, she would not beg that man to love her.

Isaiah got up into the buggy and waited until Micah joined him. He looked back, watching as Bethany headed toward the house again, and her father opened the side door for her. Nathaniel met Isaiah's gaze worriedly, then turned his attention to his daughter as he drew her inside, and the buggy crunched over the gravel, heading for the road.

Was Nathaniel worried that Micah would tell him about the baby? Perhaps. These secrets had a way of getting out.

"Is it true, then?" Isaiah asked as he reined in the horses at the road before flicking the reins again and guiding them toward the west. "Are you wanting her to go English with you?"

The lowering sun caught Isaiah in the eyes and he tipped his hat down to give him some relief.

"It isn't the den of evil that you think, you know," Micah said quietly. "There are good people there—solid Christians."

"So it's true."

"I can't live my life Amish, Isaiah. I know you can, and in a way I'm envious of you. Trust me, it would be easier for me if I could! But I can't just turn off everything I've learned. There's no going backward on this."

"If I, of all people, can stay Amish—" Isaiah began.

"Please, Isaiah. I've just spent the better part of the day arguing with my own parents and now Bethany's. I don't want to argue with you, too."

Isaiah sighed. "Just tell me this—do you want to marry her still?"

"Yah!" Micah replied. "Of course! I'm not some animal who courted her and changed his mind. I'm not that kind of man. You know me better than that. I don't think she wants to marry me, though."

Isaiah felt a thrill at those words, and then a twinge of guilt. "Why?"

"She won't come with me. If she loved me like she said, wouldn't she at least try things this way?"

"If you marry her and it doesn't work, she can never marry again," Isaiah countered. "And you're asking her to leave everything she knows. If you loved her like you claim, you'd stay for her—for your child."

Micah didn't answer at first, and Isaiah guided the horses closer to the side of the road as a car came up behind them. It eased into the other lane to pass and carried on ahead.

"I'm going to be a father." Micah's voice softened.

"Yah." Isaiah looked over at his friend. "And you have to ask yourself, if she stays here and you leave, will another man raise your child?"

Micah's expression darkened. "I don't want that. I'm going to be that child's father and I'm not going to just disappear and pretend that child isn't mine."

"Wait . . . you mean, if she doesn't marry you and go English, you'll come back to see that child and make it clear that you're the father?" Isaiah asked, the words choking in his throat.

"I'm going to be a father," Micah said, his voice strengthening. "I'm not turning my back on my own flesh and blood!"

"If you do, you'll ruin Bethany's chances at marriage," Isaiah pointed out. "So if she doesn't marry you, she can have no one?"

"She has a chance to get married!" Micah retorted. "She just doesn't want it!"

So this was where it stood—Micah didn't want to walk away from his child, even if he walked away from the mother.

"A *daet* matters!" Micah went on. "Can you imagine being a boy growing up thinking his own father never loved him? My son won't grow up that way! You of all people know what a father means to his *kinner*!"

"Then *stay*," Isaiah said simply. "Be a proper *daet*."

"Whatever I do, I'm not giving up on my child," Micah said. "If I go Mennonite, I'm coming back to visit my child. My son or daughter *will* know me."

"You'll ruin Bethany's life," Isaiah said.

"Then she can come with me. But I'm not going to be beaten into submission here. I don't know what it's like to be a *daet* yet, but I know I already feel something for that child, and I won't be told that I can't be a father because we made a mistake. If she wants to live within these rules, she's welcome, but if she comes with me to Pittsburgh, no one will treat her like she's worthless because of an indiscretion before marriage. And forgive me for thinking that's a positive thing!"

They passed another Amish farm—the Peterschwims—and Isaiah could see a man walking with buckets in each hand and a little boy following after him. The child couldn't have been more than three or four, wearing boots that were too big. The *daet* slowed down and looked behind him, waiting for the boy to catch up.

Isaiah looked over at Micah and found him watching the same scene, his eyes filled with conflicting emotions.

"Your child will follow *someone* like that," Isaiah said, his voice gruff. "I don't mean to be cruel—I'm just pointing out the truth. It will either be you or someone else."

"Yah . . ." Micah swallowed hard.

They didn't say anything else on the ride back to the Weibe farm, and as the horses plodded steadily forward, Isaiah couldn't help but think of that little boy following after his *daet*. So small, so trusting.

One day Isaiah hoped to have *kinner* of his own. The problem was, his sons would need to be able to look up to him, to trust him to be the man he said he was. Isaiah already knew what it felt like to be let down by his father; he wouldn't do that to his own *kinner*.

He'd be the man they could trust to do the right thing, even when it was hard, even when it meant sacrifice. He'd be the one they could count on to be exactly what he claimed to be. Isaiah would have to make up for Abe in a hundred different ways. He'd have to be everything an Amish man should be to bring some family pride back to the Yoder name.

When Isaiah dropped Micah off at his family's farm, Micah paused and put his hand on the side of the buggy.

"You're a good friend, Isaiah," he said, his voice tight.

"I do try," Isaiah replied.

And he would continue to try—with every relationship within this community. He'd take the narrow path, he'd climb the steep way. He'd prove that he was trustworthy for the sake of the next generation of Amish *kinner*. And it started now, with Micah.

"Good night," Micah said.

Isaiah waved, then flicked the reins, heading back toward the road again.

He was hungry, tired, sad, and rather lonesome. But now he had a purpose, at least. An Amish life was not an easy life, but it was worth the work.

Chapter Thirteen

Sitting at the kitchen table, Bethany rubbed her hands over her face and blinked back some fresh tears. Daet met her gaze, but all she saw was sadness in his lined face. How badly had she disappointed him?

Her value was not in her virginity—she knew that. And yet it would factor in for a potential husband. As her *mamm* always said, only Gott and one's own mother cared more about what was inside her heart; for everyone else, there was proper behavior. Her *daet* would never love her less, but one ill-thought-out choice had certainly changed what was possible for her, now. Instead of that hope chest reminding a husband of her value to her parents, how much they adored her and how much her husband should as well, it was now a reminder to her alone, and for the first time since she'd discovered her pregnancy, all this felt very, very real.

Daet stood by the door, his expression grim. The table was empty, all except that plate with the sandwich that Micah hadn't touched. At a time like this no one was hungry . . . except Lily, perhaps.

"Micah doesn't love me," Bethany said quietly.

"He loved you enough to make a child," Daet said. "And right now he wants everything—his freedom, a wife, a child, connections with his Amish upbringing, an English life. . . . He wants too much. Part of growing up is realizing that you can't have everything. And Micah better face that fact quickly."

Bethany didn't answer, and Mamm sighed. "Lily's out there, Nathaniel."

"Yah . . . let me go finish up the stable with her. I'll keep her out there with me for a little while so you two can talk." He gave Barbara a meaningful look and she nodded.

"We'll sort this out, Bethany," Daet said. "Okay?"

"Yah, Daet."

Somehow, a lecture might be easier to endure than her father's earnest reassurances because the latter meant that he was scared. No matter how old a woman got, she wanted her parents to feel more in control of things than she did. This time, they didn't.

Daet headed back outside, the door thumping shut behind him, and Bethany wiped a tear from her cheek.

"I told you Micah couldn't be trusted now that he'd left," Bethany said. "He's not the same. He's changed."

"Yah, you did tell me." Mamm sighed. "Sit down, my dear. I can see the writing on the wall as plainly as you can. And so can your Daet—don't be fooled there. We'll have to come up with a plan that doesn't rely upon Micah coming back again."

Outside the window, Bethany saw her *daet* approaching the stable. The door opened and Lily appeared. Their voices carried through the air but were too muffled to make out the words. Lily looked at their father with an adoring smile. Bethany could remember helping her *daet* in the stables at the same age—and feeling that same adoration for her father. She'd wanted to marry a man just like her *daet* one day.

"What will Daet think?" Bethany asked.

"He'll be thinking the same thing I am—that we need a plan. And that this needs to stay a secret."

"He's disappointed, though," Bethany said.

"You need not concern yourself with that," Mamm said with a gentle smile. "Everyone will have opinions your whole life long. And those opinions are none of your business. He'll run through a lot of different feelings surrounding this—we all will. But your *daet* will love you no matter what. And that's all you need to worry about."

Bethany nodded, and she slid her hand over her belly, feeling a slight swelling now. Was her body changing so quickly? "So what do I do?"

"From what I can tell, you have a few options," Mamm said. "First of all, be completely honest with me, because I don't want you disappearing and worrying us sick. Do you want to go Mennonite with him?"

"No, Mamm."

"Are you sure? You can tell me."

"I'm positive."

"Good . . ." Mamm exhaled a pent-up breath. "Then there are a few options here at home. The first one is that you have this baby and give it up to another family in another community."

The very thought felt like a knife in her chest and Bethany shook her head. "Never."

"I'm only putting it on the table as something to look at," Mamm said. "I know that isn't your first choice, and it would break my heart, too. The next choice is to simply have the baby, tell people the truth, and accept that you will never get married. You can get baptized again after a short shunning, and—"

Bethany's eyes brimmed with tears. "A short shunning. Mamm! Do you hear yourself?"

"We're being realistic here," Mamm said. "That would be the straightforward way. You would raise your child, at least."

"And my child would grow up with a *mamm* with a badly tarnished reputation!" Bethany said. "What life is that? If it's a boy, he'll resent me. If it's a girl, she'll have a hard time finding a husband of her own because of me. I'll never be trusted by the other women—you know what gossip does. I'll go from being a girl who trusted her fiancé to a girl who can't be trusted around other women's husbands. Married women are nervous around the un-marriageable women. You know that."

Unmarriageable women were seen as desperate—and perhaps they could be. But the properly married women were cautious with them, and Bethany hadn't thought she'd join their ranks, though it looked like she would.

Mamm licked her lips. "True . . ."

"Is there any other option?" Bethany asked.

"You could relocate to another community with a . . . story," Mamm said, and as she said it, her cheeks pinked. "And come back with your baby and a different story."

"Lie to everyone," Bethany breathed.

"Yah."

And while the thought chilled her, her conscience veering away from it, the words came out of her mouth without missing a beat: "What would I say?"

"It's been done before," Mamm said slowly. "I have an older aunt who lives in Indiana. You and I would go out to visit her together and get her to help us. If she agreed—and I think she would—you'd stay with her until you've recovered after having your baby. You'd use a different name so gossip couldn't follow you back. The story would be that your husband died and you are fighting with your family—something like that. So you'd have to make us look quite terrible for a while, and then, when the baby is a little bigger and you've recovered, you come home with a new story."

"Which would be?" Bethany asked weakly.

"That one of your cousins got pregnant out of wedlock and gave birth. You fell in love with the baby and decided to bring it home to us. Your *daet* and I would raise the child, and he or she would be raised thinking that you are an adopted older sister. A very loving, caring older sister."

Bethany's stomach clenched and she felt bile rising in her throat. Her *mamm* would be the one to give the rules, to give the security, to be called "Mamm" in that piping little voice. . . .

"I wouldn't be this baby's mother. . . ."

"No." Tears misted Mamm's eyes. "But you would be able to find a good man and get married and have more *kinner*. You could have a very close relationship with your child—you know I'd never hold you away from your baby!"

"But not the *mamm* . . ." Bethany's chin quivered.

"It's an option," Mamm said softly. "That's all I'm saying. And we are going to have to come up with an option quickly, because you are going to start to show soon."

"What if I went to another community . . . and stayed?" she asked hesitantly.

"And who will provide for you?" Mamm asked. "You can't take care of a baby and work a job. Someone has to care for that child, and you'd never make enough to pay someone. Are you willing to give up all that time with your little one in order to be called Mamm?"

Was she? Maybe! She didn't know. What path would hold the least pain for her in the future? What path would be the best for her baby as the years rolled on?

"I don't know!" Bethany sucked in a breath. "In order to stay Amish and have any kind of life, I'd have to live a lie. And if I go with Micah, I have to live English. Neither of those will please Gott."

"It is your choice, ultimately," Mamm said quietly. "But can I suggest something?"

Bethany remained silent, but she met her mother's gaze.

"My suggestion is that you live with a secret," Mamm said quietly. "You have your baby and you bring that baby home. Maybe one day we can tell your child the truth. I know it isn't right, and I know we raised you to be honest no matter what, but in this situation, my precious girl, I'd advise you to lie."

Through the side kitchen window, Bethany saw her father and younger sister coming back toward the house. Lily looked dirty but happy, and she laughed at something Daet said to her.

Bethany had lost something today—a certain amount of innocence in her father's eyes and a certain amount of integrity in her own. She'd crossed a line, and a simple, honest life was no longer a possibility for her. Not if she wanted to keep her child and have any kind of future. But the quote from Proverbs 31 was talking about a wife of noble character, and Bethany could still have a chance at being a wife—a good wife, a kind wife, a woman who would be compassionate and understanding because she had endured more than anyone would ever know. . . .

Did a man need to know everything for her to be a blessing to him, all the days of her life?

The side door opened, and Daet and Lily came inside.

"Take that apron off," Mamm said. "And go upstairs to wash up, Lily."

"You're a hard worker, Lily," Daet said with a fond smile.

Lily grinned over her shoulder and bounded up the stairs. The bathroom door shut and the water turned on; then Daet's smile fell.

"What have we decided, then?" Daet asked.

"I don't know yet," Bethany admitted. "But I can't give my baby away, Daet. I can't!"

Daet put an arm around her shoulder and kissed her forehead, his beard tickling her eyelashes. "Of course, Bethany. We're going to do our best to help you. Your *mamm* and I will discuss this, but I think we're all in agreement that Lily can't know, aren't we?"

"Yah," Bethany said with a nod. There was no way Lily could keep a secret of this magnitude.

"Is there a solution you like better than others, Bethany?"

Bethany pulled away from her father and wrapped her arms around herself. "That I go away to have the baby and when I come back we say my cousin had an illegitimate child that you and Mamm will raise." Bethany felt the tightness in her chest.

"You'd see your baby all day, every day," Mamm said. "And we'll find you a husband—that's better than a life alone."

Bethany nodded. The lie—that was the preference. The lie that saved her reputation and hid the natural consequences of her mistake.

Gott, will You bless this? Will You be with me through it?

She didn't feel anything in response to her prayer—just an empty silence. The Amish life was the narrow path . . . and somehow this easier way, this convenient untruth, felt like the kind of mistake she'd regret much later. But regrets could be a luxury, something to wrestle with after she was sure she had a life to live and her child was safely close to her in her parents' home.

Gott would forgive her afterward . . . wouldn't He?

The next morning Isaiah arrived early at Glick's Book Bindery and stabled his horses and cleaned out the stalls in preparation for the Amish businessman who would come by in a couple of hours with a wagon to cart away the soiled hay.

Isaiah hadn't slept well the night before. He had too much running through his head. He was Micah's friend and, as his friend, he needed to be there for him, to help him see what he needed to see—namely, the girl he was obliged to marry. And that baby was going to be born regardless of what Micah chose to do—Micah *would* be a daet. Had he meant it when he said he wouldn't allow Bethany to raise the child quietly, let her have a life of her own? Had Bethany made a mistake in telling Micah the truth?

And yet Micah deserved to know that he was going to be a father. And even if he wasn't living an Amish life, didn't his child deserve to know him, too? Micah had been right about one thing: a child who grew up thinking his father didn't love him would have a piece of his heart broken all his life.

Isaiah gave his horses some oats and listened to the slow grind of large teeth; then he stepped outside just as Nathaniel arrived. Bethany wasn't in the buggy with him, and Isaiah couldn't help but feel some disappointment, even though he hadn't expected her to be there. Not after yesterday's revelations.

"Good morning," Nathaniel said as he reined in his horses. "I see you mucked out the stalls. That was kind of you."

"Yah. Just doing my job," Isaiah said.

Nathaniel gave him a nod of thanks and hopped down from the buggy and started unhitching the horses. Isaiah headed around to the other horse and lent a hand. When the horses were comfortable in the stable, Nathaniel paused at the door and looked over at Isaiah.

"My daughter told me that she trusted you with . . . a secret," Nathaniel said quietly.

"Yah, she did," Isaiah confirmed.

"And she feels confident that you'll keep that secret," Nathaniel added.

"She can trust me," Isaiah said.

Nathaniel nodded again and put a hand on Isaiah's shoulder. "Good. That is a relief."

The older man started forward toward the shop as Isaiah added, "I talked to Micah."

Nathaniel stopped, turned back. "Yah?"

"I don't know what you'll do for Bethany, but Micah seems intent on being in the baby's life," Isaiah said.

Nathaniel stilled, his lips compressing together. "He said that?"

"He says that if she goes with him, he'll marry her, but if she stays here, he doesn't want to give up his rights to the child. From what I understand of *Englisher* law—"

"I don't care about *Englisher* law!" Nathaniel retorted, then shut his eyes for a moment, gathering his self-restraint. "Why is he doing this to her?"

"I don't know," Isaiah said, shaking his head.

"What does he want?" Nathaniel asked. "You're his friend!"

"I don't know. I think he's overwhelmed by all this, to start," Isaiah said. "I think he's afraid he won't fit back in here as Amish—his ideas have changed too much. And he's hoping that Bethany will go with him."

"I don't think he wants that at all," Nathaniel replied with a bitter downturn of his lips. "He argued quite passionately for his way of seeing things last night, and the impression I got was that he wanted a way out of this engagement. He wants us to turn him away and take it off his conscience."

"He's off-balance right now," Isaiah said. "Maybe if you give him time to think this through properly . . ."

"And Bethany isn't off-balance?" Nathaniel demanded. "She was engaged to him! The wedding was going to happen. He had promised to marry her, and she gave in a little early. And now he gets to feel all sorts of conflicting emotions and leave her hanging this way? No! That is not how an honorable man conducts himself!"

Isaiah was silent. Nathaniel was right, of course, but

he had nothing to say. This wasn't his business, strictly speaking. Bethany wasn't his fiancée and this wasn't his baby.

"What did you say to him?" Nathaniel asked after a moment.

"I . . ." He cast back, trying to remember the conversation. "I think I pointed out that the baby is coming whether it is convenient or not, and that someone will raise that child. I was meaning to encourage him to come home and let that father figure be him. But he took it differently than I'd intended."

"If Micah stayed and married her properly . . . even now . . ." Nathaniel smoothed a hand over his grizzled beard. ". . . that would solve it all. And he might be insulting everyone, right and left, but there might still be hope that he'll stay."

"Maybe," Isaiah conceded. "Sometimes, after a good sleep, or a few days to think, a man will see reason."

"Did you get the impression that he might change his mind?" Nathaniel asked.

"I don't know," Isaiah confessed. "He's . . . he's so different from what he was. He isn't thinking like an Amish man."

"Can you talk to him again?" Nathaniel asked. "Encourage him to do the right thing?"

"I've already done that," Isaiah said. "But I promised him I'd look out for Bethany, and I'm standing by my word. I'm trying to be the friend he needs right now."

"What does that mean for Bethany?" Nathaniel asked, his brows furrowing.

"I think Micah should do the right thing and marry her

here," Isaiah said. "But I don't know how long it will take for him to see that."

"And Bethany is the one to pay for it," Nathaniel said.

"He's wrong," Isaiah said. "He's wrong and confused and turned in circles. He's thinking like an *Englisher* already—planning for parental rights and being separated from the mother instead of marrying her. But maybe he'll change his mind yet. He's Amish, deep down. You know that."

"He might have been raised to be Amish," Nathaniel said curtly. "But deep down, that boy is selfish."

Isaiah couldn't help but agree. He knew that Micah was doing wrong, but he also knew that if they let him down now, Micah might never return to them . . . not to be part of the community. And if he came back to visit his child, if he brought *Englisher* courts into it and demanded partial custody or visiting rights, he'd make it impossible for Bethany to do anything else but go with him into the *Englisher* world.

Because when a woman was faced between losing her child and losing her community, her child would win. Even if she no longer loved the man who forced her hand, and the thought of Bethany being pushed and prodded, forced to act against her will, angered him.

And yet Micah wasn't the only one facing the draw of *Englisher* ways—Lovina was out there, too. Was she changing just as quickly as Micah was? If Isaiah ever saw her again, would he even recognize his little sister?

They started walking toward the shop, and Nathaniel's keys jangled in his hand. Overhead the sun was low in the sky, the cool morning air feeling good against Isaiah's face. It was like any other summer morning—fresh and sweet. But it was no longer simple—not the way it used to be even a few months ago. The orderly Amish life that gave Isaiah purpose had started to wrinkle and tug.

"What will happen if Micah doesn't marry her?" Isaiah asked.

"It depends on whether he lets her disappear or not," Nathaniel said quietly. "Because if he insists on being a *daet* and not a husband, then he'll ruin the rest of her life. You were right—someone *will* raise that child, and it may very well be me. But my little girl—the daughter I loved and raised"—his voice broke—"is going to live with a heart in tatters. And I'll never forgive Micah if he does that to her."

The only answer was to bring Micah home—Isaiah knew that. As Micah's friend, as the one who'd promised to be all that the Amish community should be, Isaiah had to do what was right for Bethany and Micah, not what his heart might long for . . .

Because if Isaiah followed his heart, he'd find a way to make Bethany his, but he'd lose the very integrity that made him Amish.

Chapter Fourteen

Bethany put a plastic bag of fresh dinner rolls into the basket, then added a Mason jar of blackberry jam from last year's bumper crop of berries. They still had a whole row of jam jars downstairs in the cellar. Lily stood by the basket, watching as Mamm and Bethany filled it with baked goods, but as Bethany loaded up the food, her mind wasn't on the gift.

Tessa Weibe sat silently at the kitchen table, a cup of tea in front of her and a piece of untouched pie next to the tea. She looked tense, every nerve stretched to its limit, but she didn't say anything. Nothing could be said with little ears present.

"And tell Susanna that you're offering to stay and help her clean," Mamm said. "She's been sick with this cold for over a week now, and what she really needs is a nap. You tell her I said that."

"Okay." Lily tested the basket. "It's kind of heavy."

Bethany lifted it, and her sister was right. It was rather heavy for a nine-year-old to carry to the neighbors. She reached inside and took out the fresh cauliflower from the garden and one of the jam jars and tried it again. It was better.

"Now you hurry over and be helpful, all right?" Mamm said. "You're a good girl, Lily."

A good girl . . . When Bethany had been Lily's age, that had been her goal, too. Even as she got older, she'd wanted to be the kind of girl a boy would gladly marry—virtuous, kind, neat, a good cook . . . And now, it seemed, she was being thrust upon Micah like some unwanted cast-off.

Lily looked uncertainly toward Tessa, then back at Bethany. Bethany knew that her sister was adding up the information—at least the amount she had—and trying to figure out what was going on. Lily wasn't a dumb girl, and she knew she was being gotten out of the way so the adults could talk. Bethany gave her sister a sad smile, which Lily returned, and tears misted the girl's eyes.

"It's fine, Lily," Bethany said softly, picking up the basket and carrying it to the door herself. "Come on, now. It'll be fine."

"You sure?" Lily asked, looking up at her.

"I don't lie, do I?" Bethany asked. "It'll be fine. Off you go."

And up until this point, Bethany had never been one to lie. She'd believed in being honest because it was the right thing to do—who were you if you couldn't be trusted when you said something? Except she and her parents were planning a massive deception, and she'd never be able to say that again. Because after this Bethany *would* be a liar.

Lily took the basket from Bethany and headed out into the summer morning. Bethany watched her go a few paces in the direction of the neighbor's house and then shut the door firmly behind her. When she turned back, she found Tessa and Mamm staring at her fixedly.

"So . . . Micah told you, then?" Bethany said weakly.

"Yah, he told us." Tessa nodded. "And if there's a baby, I'm sure we'll convince him to stay."

"Convince him." The words were bitter in Bethany's mouth. "So he's still determined to leave, is he?"

"Well . . ." Tessa licked her lips. "I'm not sure he knows what he wants."

Bethany disagreed there. Micah seemed quite certain what he wanted.

"Has he . . ." Mamm cleared her throat. "Has he said anything about his feelings for Bethany?"

Tessa's cheeks pinked. "He says he's willing to marry her if she leaves with him."

"Willing," Bethany said.

"Oh, Bethany, I know it sounds callous and rough," Tessa said. "I think he's just overwhelmed. What man is ever good with words? They have such trouble articulating their feelings, don't they?"

"He was rather articulate about his love for me when he wanted to sleep with me," she said hollowly.

Tessa dropped her gaze. "He wasn't raised to do that."

"And if I leave and go English?" Bethany said, shaking her head. "I'll lose everyone! My *mamm* and *daet*, my sisters and brothers, my friends . . . It isn't fair to even ask it of me!"

"I'm glad you don't want to go," Mamm said.

"So am I," Tessa added. "I may have to face that my son is leaving us and I'll hardly see him again. But I don't have to lose my grandchild, do I?"

Bethany was silent.

"You aren't thinking of giving the baby away, are you?" Tessa asked earnestly. "Because if you are, I could raise the baby. We could find a story that would explain it, and you could visit—"

"No, she's going to bring the baby home to us," Mamm broke in. "We'll say it's the illegitimate child of a cousin from Indiana."

"Oh . . . Yes, that's a good plan, too," Tessa agreed. "Daniel and I will help any way we can. I'll babysit! I'll make baby clothes, I'll—"

"Tessa, people will be watching," Mamm said. "If Bethany comes home with a baby in approximately nine months and her ex-fiancé's parents are deeply attached to that child, they'll do the math."

Tessa's face blanched. "I know . . ."

"We'll have to take things slowly, but you and Daniel will have to be a little distanced," Mamm went on. "Bethany's reputation has to be preserved."

"Micah might decide to stay yet," Tessa said, her voice firming. "I know he's behaved badly here, but I know my son. He's a good boy, and he loves us. I know this looks bad, but I know him."

"He isn't staying!" Bethany broke in. "He made it clear from the minute he returned—he's going back to Pittsburgh."

"And if he leaves for a few months and then returns?" Tessa asked. "Sometimes a Rumspringa isn't enough to get the curiosity out of a man's system. If he comes back—"

"After having done what, exactly?" Bethany burst out. "After he dates *Englisher* girls and tries to make a life with them, and then comes back all brokenhearted because the

Englisher girls don't want him? That's when I'm supposed to take him back again?"

"What other option do you have?" Tessa demanded. "There's a baby!"

Bethany bit back a retort. She was supposed to be grateful if Micah eventually decided to take her back after all? What about *her* heart? This was the life of a woman— waiting, always waiting, to be chosen. Waiting to be accepted. Waiting to be proven worthy of being a wife.

"Let's not argue," Mamm said, her tone quiet. "We have to be realistic, and Tessa, I appreciate you wanting to believe your son will return, but I think our plans need to assume he won't."

"Nine months is a long time. If he comes back, are you going to pretend that child isn't theirs?" Tessa asked.

"If he comes back, Bethany will marry him," Mamm said. "And our problems will be over. But if he doesn't come back—"

"People would forgive this in time, as long as the parents are properly married," Tessa said. "I'm just putting this out there as a possibility, because I heard of a couple in a similar situation. It was the girl who left, but she came back with a toddler and married the father. Yah, for a while it was tough, but the end result was that they were accepted into the community again."

"I heard of them . . ." Mamm said. "Out in Benton, right?"

"Yah, I think so. But you see what I mean? As long as they're married, even if there were some bumps to get there—"

"Bumps?" Bethany said.

"Dear, marriage is not always the easy path it seems

from the outside," Tessa said. "I'm sure your *mamm* knows what I'm talking about."

Mamm shot Tessa a warning look. "Marriage to the right man is easy enough."

Tessa eyed Mamm with a mildly confused look of her own, then looked back toward Bethany. "Daniel and I almost didn't get married. We were engaged and we had this huge fight about his *mamm*'s opinions about me, and the wedding was nearly called off. We made up, and here we are today."

"It's not quite the same," Bethany said.

"Well, your parents had a tough time, too. I'm sure you know about that."

"No, I don't know about that," Bethany replied. And she looked over at her mother quizzically. "What is she talking about?"

Mamm's face had turned white, but not from shock. This was anger—Bethany had never seen her mother quite this enraged before, and Tessa looked stunned, as well.

"Nothing," Mamm said tightly. "Your father is a wonderful man, and I was a good girl. There is nothing to tell."

Tessa shook her head. "You won't tell her, even now?"

Mamm shot Tessa another glare. "When a husband and wife have a falling out, it is no one else's business."

"You and Daet had a falling out?" Bethany asked.

"It was nothing," Mamm snapped.

"Even when it might give her some perspective with Micah, you won't tell her? Are you that prideful, Barbara?" Tessa demanded.

Mamm clenched her teeth together, then heaved a sigh. "Fine. It was our first year of marriage. We were living with my *mamm* and *daet*, as Amish newlyweds do, and your father and my father had a big fight. I wouldn't speak against my father because I was a good girl! I loved my *daet* very much and I thought your father was wrong. Your father moved out of my parents' home and I stayed."

"For how long?" Bethany asked.

"For three months."

"For three months!" Bethany shook her head. "Mamm, that was a serious fight!"

"And it wasn't your business to know about!" Mamm shot back. "We worked it out. That's all that matters."

"What made the difference?" Bethany asked.

"I was pregnant." Mamm's chin trembled.

A baby had reunited them. Perhaps that was why she was so convinced that this baby could bring her and Micah back together. But it didn't explain why her mother had made her marriage seem so utterly perfect that it was impossible to replicate.

"And you went to Nathaniel, if I recall," Tessa said quietly. "You both moved into that little house on the edge of the Kaufmann property."

Mamm licked her dry lips. "There can be bumps. And they never need to be spoken of again. That's the point."

Her *mamm* had been holding on to a secret like that . . . And while Bethany could agree that it wasn't her business, her *mamm* had certainly made her feel like she'd been falling short of the perfection of her mother's life for a very long time now.

"You made things seem easier than it was," Bethany said, anger edging her tone. "You made it all seem so much easier for you."

"I told you what you needed to know," Mamm snapped. "I do deserve some privacy."

"I felt like . . . like a failure!" Bethany said, her voice shaking. "I felt like I was doing it wrong every time Micah and I disagreed! I felt like I was somehow not so virtuous as you, not so feminine. And I wanted to please Micah like you'd pleased Daet. So I . . . I . . ."

She'd given in. She'd given up her virginity to him.

"Because girls need to know that if they behave well, they can have a happy life!" Mamm said.

"And I didn't, did I?" Bethany shot back. "I'm pregnant—so I'm a bad girl! I'm not one of the good ones!"

"Bethany, I'm not saying—"

"But you are," Bethany interrupted. "And all my growing-up years, I believed this story of marital perfection that you and Daet put forward. And I thought I could find a man like Daet—kind, mature, stable, pious. I thought I could find a *perfect* man."

"You can!" Mamm said.

"Not anymore, Mamm!"

"Well . . . you have a little sister. And *she* still can. So we are going to give her an example to strive toward. She never needs to know about our stupid mistakes when we were young."

The fact that Mamm, who had been a virtuous and proper girl, had gotten married and had such a massive fight with her new husband that he stayed away for three months . . . that wasn't going to matter either, because it didn't give the proper lesson. And Bethany's secret was going to remain hidden, too. She'd simply be the girl who was strangely attached to her cousin's child, who'd eventually marry someone proper and kind, who wouldn't look too closely at any stretch marks or scars she might have acquired through her pregnancy and delivery.

Everyone was going to pretend for the good of the young people.

"I'm going out," Bethany said, standing up. "I'm going to help Daet at the shop."

"You don't have a buggy," Mamm said.

"Tessa, would you drive me?" Bethany asked.

"It's out of her way!" Mamm shook her head. "And you are at a very delicate stage! You need to rest. Your *daet* left you at home for a reason."

"You can drive me, Tessa, or I'll walk," Bethany said, her lips wobbling as she tried to hold back the tears that threatened to break through.

"Barbara," Tessa said quietly. "It's probably better if I drive her. She'll be with her *daet*. He won't let her overdo it."

Did Bethany have no more choices in her life? She was pregnant, and now Mamm and Tessa were the ones to decide her every step, all the way to marrying a man who didn't want her. And in her heart she no longer wanted Micah either, but this one mistake would connect them regardless, for the rest of their days.

"Fine." Mamm stood up, bumping the table and making the dishes clatter. She put her hands on the table-top to settle it and slowly turned her gaze to Bethany. "But you be careful."

Because this baby that was complicating everything was already loved . . . by all of them. It wasn't the baby's fault that the adults had made such a mess. But this child would be forced to live with the fallout regardless.

* * *

The morning at the book bindery seemed to drag for Isaiah, and he noticed that Nathaniel seemed restless, too. The work was coming along and the pile of boxes of bound books kept growing—ready to be shipped in a matter of days. Strange how Isaiah was already feeling like the outcome of this shipment reflected on him as well as Nathaniel's business.

Isaiah was at the sewing frame this morning, pushing the thick needle through the holes in the folios to hold the pages tightly together. His hands knew the work by this time, and in a way the methodical movement was soothing. But Isaiah's mind kept drifting back to Bethany.

If it weren't for Isaiah's father's crime, Micah would still be Amish. He'd still be engaged . . . in fact, he might already be married, considering the baby on the way. If Abe had forgiven the community instead of harboring a grudge, if he'd done the right thing even when it was hard . . . if Abe had practiced what he preached even a little bit, these lives would be moving merrily forward.

A community was a safe place—the strength being in people who stuck together and took care of one another. But communities suffered together as well. What hurt one person hurt everyone, and perhaps Abe's crime had proven that more clearly than anything else could have. Isaiah wasn't the only one floundering because of his father's sins.

The clock showed nearly noon, and Isaiah's stomach rumbled. He clipped off the last thread and removed the pages from the frame. It was a neat, tight job of sewing, and he couldn't help but feel some elemental pride at doing a job well. He was hungry, though.

"Nathaniel, I thought I'd get some lunch," Isaiah said.

Nathaniel looked up at the clock on the wall. "Yah. It's that time. Go ahead. I'll finish up here first. When you get back you can start working on those covers. How many literary journals are left?"

"Twelve journals. So, six more bindings of two journals per book. We're almost done."

"Yah, we'll be able to deliver this order with a few days to spare, so we'll be in good shape. Good. I'm pleased. Go get yourself some lunch."

Isaiah headed out of the shop and down the street toward the bakery. He stood in line with a few *Englishers* and some Amish women who looked over their shoulders at him and gave him a stiff hello. Whatever conversation they were having in Pennsylvania Dutch died off, though, and they stood in silence the rest of the time.

Isaiah ordered a roast beef and cheese sandwich, a bag of chips, and two fresh brownies, and when he'd collected his food and paid he headed back toward Glick's Book Bindery. He headed around the back of the store to eat in the little strip of grass between the stores when he spotted Bethany getting down from a buggy. He stood there watching her as she said something to Tessa Weibe, who was driving, and when Tessa's gaze moved over Bethany's head and met his, he saw something there he didn't expect: antagonism.

Bethany turned and Tessa flicked the reins, and by the time Bethany had seen him, the buggy had already masked Tessa from view.

What had that been about?

He headed over to meet Bethany and she gave him a wan smile.

"I came to help Daet," she said.

"I'm glad." And he was—deeply, strangely glad. He'd missed her. "You hungry?"

"Yah, actually."

"I have more food than I can eat," he said with a small smile. "Come on. Let's go sit by the stables."

"I could go get my own lunch, you know," she said, but a smile tickled her lips.

"It's okay. You know the bakery—the sandwiches are massive."

There was a little bench that lined one side of the stables and they headed in that direction. When they sat down Isaiah gave Bethany half his sandwich and put the rest of the food between them.

"I didn't think you'd come," he said.

"I had to get away," she said. "Mamm and Tessa will have my life planned between them, and they both seem to think they have a right to it because I'm carrying their grandchild."

"Is it that bad?" he asked.

Bethany took a bite and gave him a dry look as she chewed.

"I guess it is," he said. "At least you have people who care."

"Tessa is convinced Micah will come back," Bethany said. "I'm not so convinced."

"What will you do?" he asked.

"I'll go away for a while," she said.

His heart sank. "For how long?"

"A little less than a year—long enough to recover," she said.

Isaiah swallowed his bite of sandwich with difficulty. "Will you let me know where you went?"

"The less anyone knows the better," she said quietly. "Too many people know about this already. If I'd been smarter, I wouldn't even have told you."

"Don't say that . . ." He reached out and put his hand over hers. "You can trust me."

"You're Micah's friend, so I guess . . . you're safe, in a way."

He pulled back his hand. "Micah's friend? Is that how you see me at this point? Nothing to you?"

"I'm just staying, you care about how this turns out," she said, and tears misted her eyes.

"Yah, I do." He cared more than he had any right to, and the thought of Bethany just disappearing somewhere was a difficult one to embrace. Her family loved her, and she'd have a plan . . . but the man in him wanted to be part of it. Even though he had no right to ask.

"Have you talked to Micah?" Bethany asked.

"When I drove him home," he said.

"And?"

"He—" Isaiah sighed. "The fact that he'll be a father made an impact. He doesn't want to just leave his child to be raised by another man."

"That doesn't mean he'll come back," she said hesitantly.

"No . . . I agree there," he said. "He is very certain he wants to be in his child's life, though."

"He'd ruin me . . ." she whispered.

"I'll try to talk to him again," he said.

"What use is that? He isn't listening to anyone!"

This whole situation had gotten incredibly complicated. All he knew was that if Micah did go back to Pittsburgh, he'd find a letter waiting for him from Isaiah promising him that he'd stand by his word.

"I promised him that I'd look out for you while he's away," Isaiah said. "Maybe that will be enough for him to give you some space, if he knows I'll tell him how you are and . . . how the baby is."

"Do you think?" she asked, leaning forward. "Would that be enough?"

"I don't know. But it's something," he said, and he nudged her hand holding the sandwich. "Eat, Bethany. You need energy."

She smiled faintly and took another bite. They ate in silence for the next few minutes, and Isaiah felt a strange relief at just being next to her on this bench. She caught him looking at her and a smile turned up her lips.

"What?" she said.

"Nothing. I just think you're probably my last friend right now." He opened the chips and then passed her one of the brownies.

Bethany accepted the brownie and looked at him somberly for a moment. "Isaiah, we've been raised to be honest always. But I wonder if that wasn't just a ploy to make us be good *kinner* while we were young and everything was simple."

"Is that all it was?" he asked. "I don't think so. If we can't trust one another with little things, what about the big ones? We have to stand for something."

She swallowed. "I know."

"My *daet* got sucked into more trouble because he

wanted to save me," he said. "And because he was bitter. But small things turned into very big things more quickly than he anticipated."

She nodded. "I did want to be a good woman, Isaiah. I'm not sure I'll manage it, though."

"You already are a good woman," he said, shaking his head. "What are you talking about?"

"Just keep my secrets, Isaiah," she said, her eyes filled with pleading. "I'll live with the consequences, but please keep my secrets. I'm tired of everyone deciding for me. I'm sick of it! I'll choose what I do; I'll choose what I tell my child, too. That will be mine, and I'm not being pushed into anything."

"You know I will. . . ." He frowned. "I'm not pushing you into anything!"

"You're the only one who isn't right now," she said, and nudged his arm with hers. "You're a good man."

And she might be the only one who thought that right now, too. Isaiah took the wrappers from her hands and dumped their trash into a garbage can. He looked up as a car honked from the street, beyond, and they carried on toward the building through the patchy sunlight.

"Beth . . ." he started, and he looked over at her to find those deep, brown eyes meeting his. Her lips parted, and for a millisecond that felt like an eternity, they looked at each other. She was beautiful—more so than he'd ever thought before in his younger days of that wild crush he'd had on her. She was stronger than he'd realized, too, and more vulnerable. She was deeper and kinder and more compassionate . . . and while he might have pined from afar for years, looking down into her dark brown eyes today, his gaze flickering down to her pink lips, this was a much more dangerous position to be in.

From afar, he had no hope. But standing inches from her in the warm summer sunlight, his heart pattering in his chest, he could do something he'd been longing to do again ever since that night in the buggy.

Isaiah stepped closer and tentatively touched her waist. When she didn't pull back he dipped his head down, his lips hovering over hers until he closed the whisper between them and she leaned into his kiss. Her breath tickled his face when she let out a sigh, and he wrapped his arms around her, pulling her closer against him.

She tasted like the chocolate brownie she'd just eaten, and she was warm and soft and fragrant, so that his head echoed with the pounding of his own heartbeat. When he pulled back she blinked blearily up at him, and then her fingers fluttered up to her lips.

"Why did you do that?" she whispered shakily.

He could ask her the same thing, but it wasn't gentlemanly to do so. "Because I wanted to," he admitted, his voice low and gruff. And he wanted to do it again, pull her back into his arms and keep her there, forget about the demands of the world around them.

"Isaiah, I can't—" she started.

"I know," he said, and he ran a finger down her soft cheek and let his hand drop. "I'm not asking you for anything. I promise. I just . . ."

He'd wanted to kiss her. It was wrong, it was ill-timed, it was bad for both of them. And yet he'd wanted to kiss her so badly that it had overridden everything else in his head.

The back door opened, and Nathaniel poked out his head.

"Oh, Bethany. You're here? I thought I heard voices."

"Yah." She stepped away from Isaiah, making him feel like a flood had suddenly swept between them, and she licked her lips. "I came to help, Daet."

Nathaniel nodded. "Your *mamm* thought this was a good idea?"

"Not really," she said. "But I had to get out, and she agreed that if I was with you, I couldn't come to too much harm."

Nathaniel smiled at that. "Your *mamm* is a wise woman. Come on, then. We'll see if we can finish this order today. Are you done with your lunch, Isaiah?"

"Just finished," he said, and he cleared his throat. Had Nathaniel seen them?

Bethany went inside ahead of Isaiah and Nathaniel pulled an envelope from his pocket. "This came for you while you were out. The bishop dropped it off."

Isaiah looked down at the envelope and recognized his *daet*'s printing immediately.

"Thank you," he said, but his voice sounded distant in his own ears.

A letter from his *daet* . . . He looked up and found Nathaniel's gaze still locked on him, a meaningful look in his eye.

Yah. Nathaniel knew more than he was saying, and Isaiah felt his face heat.

"We'd best get to work," Isaiah said hurriedly and followed his boss inside.

Chapter Fifteen

Isaiah went back to his workstation, and for the next couple of hours he worked on leather bindings, ensconced in the strange perfume of glue, leather, and paper. Bethany worked with equal fervor, and a few times he'd look up at her to find her gaze flicker in his direction and her cheeks would flood with pink.

What was it about Bethany that made him take these risks with her? He wasn't the one for her—she needed to find a future with Micah, not him. And he needed to find a future, period. But he was also wondering what Nathaniel thought of him right now. Bethany was vulnerable and pregnant, and if Nathaniel thought the worst of him . . . He just hoped he didn't.

Isaiah finished with his last binding, putting it in a book press to keep it flat while it dried over the next several hours. Then he headed over to Bethany's table to collect the last of the sewn folios for his next batch.

Bethany clipped the last thread, and when he stopped at her side she leaned toward him, almost imperceptibly, and he felt like all the blood in his body yearned toward her in response. Whatever this was that drew them together, it was dangerous, and he knew it. Even her father's back didn't seem to dampen it.

"You said you'd try to help me," she whispered.

"I will."

"This—whatever this is—isn't helping!" She looked up at him and pressed her lips together.

"You kissed me, too," he whispered.

She looked away. "Well, I won't do it again."

"Okay."

He wasn't sure he believed that, though, because even as she said it, he brushed her fingers with his behind the table and her hand stretched toward his. He twined his fingers through hers, but she wouldn't look up at him again. They simply stood there, their hands clasped together and his heart pounding in his chest.

Nathaniel turned and glanced toward them, and Isaiah released her hand and picked up the stack of sewn folios. She was right, of course. Whatever this was brewing between them wasn't helpful to her, and it wasn't who Isaiah wanted to be either.

The hours chugged by, and when they finished the last bound collection of journals, putting them into the book presses and winding down the wheel, Isaiah let out a sigh. This had been a huge order, and the sight of boxes of bound books waiting for shipment left Isaiah with a sense of pride. Those journals would sit on a library shelf somewhere, their sleek, burnished bindings speaking of quality. They would last for generations.

"Those last books will come out of the book presses in the morning," Nathaniel said with a satisfied nod. "Thank you both for your hard work. I think we can leave early today—we've earned it. And Bethany, I'll just feel better when you're home."

"I can get started on the next project," Isaiah said, "if you want to take Bethany back—"

"You should rest, too," Nathaniel said. "You'll do better work rested, I promise. But first, I owe you your wages."

Nathaniel nodded toward the back room. "I'll write you a check."

"Thank you."

"Come on, Bethany, let's get our things. . . ." Nathaniel gave his daughter a pointed look, and she startled slightly and then followed him. It looked like Nathaniel wasn't going to leave them alone.

Isaiah didn't want to be the guy who was a threat to Bethany's happiness in the future, but it seemed her father might suspect he was just that. Bethany glanced back at him before she disappeared into the back room, but her expression didn't betray her feelings. Isaiah sighed.

He had no choice but to wait.

Isaiah touched the letter in his front pocket. He'd been waiting to read it when he was alone, and as Bethany and her father headed toward the back room to collect their things and for Nathaniel to write that check, Isaiah sliced open the envelope.

What would this letter be—more explanations? More excuses? He unfolded the cheap prison paper, and as he scanned the handwriting, his heart hammered to a stop.

Dear Son,

    I've been wondering if I should tell you about this, and I've started and stopped writing this letter about five times already. I'm not sure they'll give me more paper if I crumple up this one. I've been praying, asking Gott what I should do, seeking His guidance and His will, asking what would be right, and I have no answer from above. Either I'm no longer able to hear Him when I'm surrounded by concrete and inmates, or I have crossed a line and He has given me up. I think the right path to take is so far in the past that it may no longer even matter.

But I'm worried about you, Isaiah. Gott must be our all in all, but the physical body still needs certain comforts to survive. I know that the farm is gone, and that things must be hard for you and your sisters. You must be strong in the faith, regardless. Don't let this time of trial beat you down. I have let you down, but Gott is still true. I know our community, and they have either sided with you and wrapped you in support or they have all taken a step back. From what your sister tells me, I believe it is the latter. And your sisters will need your support now more than ever.

What was it about his father's way of speaking—the spiritual language, the preacher's cadence, that turned Isaiah's stomach so much these days? Words were supposed to be more than flowery decoration. What was it his uncle had always said about his *daet* . . . that he was "fancy" in his heart? And Isaiah could see exactly what his uncle meant now, because the religious tone meant very little to Isaiah right now. He wanted to hear from his *daet*, not from the preacher. The preacher was a fraud. His *daet* . . . well, they had a history together, at the very least.

He turned back to the letter:

> *I've let you down—all of you—and I worry
> about you constantly. I pray for you, but I don't
> know if Gott even listens to me anymore. I'm not
> worthy, but then I never was, and we are all
> sinners, short of the glory of Gott, are we not? I
> can only hope that Gott will remember my* kinner.
> *It's wrong that you all be punished for my
> mistakes. They should have left you some of the
> land, at least, to live on, but there is nothing I can
> do about that now. However, I do have something
> that might help you . . . something for you alone.*
>
> *Do you remember the tree you used to climb—
> the one where you would look down from the
> branches and say, "Daet, I'm never coming down
> again!" Do you remember?*
>
> *I left a memento there—something that might
> comfort you in this difficult time. It won't mean
> much to anyone else, but I thought you might like
> to have it.*
>
> *I deserve the punishment I'm suffering. You
> do not.*
>
> *I hope this helps.*
>
> *Daet*

A memento . . . What was his *daet* even talking about?
That tree was on the far corner of their old farm property—
along a side road that was very little traveled. It now belonged to someone else—an *Englisher* family. Was there
a Bible hidden out there or something? If there was, Isaiah

might want to retrieve it out of respect for the Bible that would molder and rot if he didn't go get it. Or maybe it was something else . . . something meant to spark an emotional reaction in him.

He used to find his father's spiritual diction comforting, but now it felt like a wall between them—a way to talk without saying anything at all. It was blather. It was fancy.

Bethany came out of the back room with a bag over her shoulder, and Isaiah looked at her uncertainly. What did the letter mean? It was like he didn't even know his father anymore. Or maybe he never had. Maybe he'd had an image of his *daet* and he'd simply chosen to believe he was everything he needed him to be. Because underneath the spiritual talk, what was there? Just a man in prison, serving time he deserved to serve.

Nathaniel came out of the back room, a check in his hand. He passed it to Isaiah with a smile.

"That's for eighty-seven hours of work," Nathaniel said. "I've been keeping track of your overtime, as well, and you'll find that you've been paid fairly."

"Thank you." Isaiah looked down at the check; it was a fair amount. It would be a good start to saving up for a place to rent for himself and his sisters. And it would allow him to give his uncle some money toward the extra expense of helping them in the meantime. If he could keep getting a regular paycheck, they'd be okay. Eventually. *This* was what he needed—a job, a paycheck—not some memento.

"Let's go," Nathaniel said, and Isaiah left the shop, his heart heavy.

The bishop thought that if Isaiah talked to his father, he might find his answers, but Isaiah wasn't so sure anymore. All he seemed to find were more questions, more disappointments, and more realizations that everything he'd depended on all these years might have been in his own imagination.

Bethany leaned back into the seat as the horses pulled the rattling buggy along the cracked road on their way out of town. She could see Isaiah's buggy ahead of them, and her heart felt heavy. Isaiah was a surprisingly good friend . . . she hadn't really expected that depth from him. If things had been different, if she wasn't pregnant with Micah's child, she might have chosen Isaiah.

The memory of his arms around her, his lips moving over hers, still gave her goose bumps. She hadn't imagined that his kisses would be quite like that. . . . The serious boy who wanted to be a preacher—there was such passion underneath that shell of his that she'd never imagined. If she'd looked closer a little sooner . . .

But that wasn't the mistake that had changed her course. A boyfriend—even a fiancé—was a correctable mistake. A pregnancy wasn't.

"I spoke with Isaiah today," Daet said quietly. "He mentioned that Micah might not be willing to let you raise your child without him."

He glanced over at her, and she saw the worry in his clear gaze.

"He told me the same thing," she said.

"What do you want to do, Bethany?" he asked. "I've been trying to stay ahead of this, find a back way out for you that allows you to raise your child and keep your secret . . . to have a life still. . . ."

"I do have an idea, Daet," she said. A desperate idea, a last-ditch hope of regaining some sort of life for herself after all this . . .

"Oh?" He didn't sound hopeful.

"Isaiah is the link between Micah and me right now. He's friends with him—determinedly so. Micah asked Isaiah to look out for me if anything should ever happen to him, and that pact between them seems to mean something to both of them. Isaiah doesn't want to let Micah down."

"And?" Daet said.

"And if Micah trusts Isaiah, maybe he'd agree to give me some space to raise our child if Isaiah would keep him updated on things. I mean, I could send Micah letters from time to time, but Isaiah could confirm what I'm saying. It might help Micah to trust that I won't just disappear with his child, and give him another point of contact that wouldn't be me—that would allow me to simply move on with my life. Because if I marry again, and if I'm keeping this secret, I might not be able to write him very often, and maybe he's thinking about that possibility."

Daet was silent and he pursed his lips.

"Like a godfather of sorts," Bethany added.

"And why is Isaiah special?" Daet asked.

"I don't know. But after all he's gone through, he's still determined to be Amish to the core—to be honest. And that seems to be shining through right now. I'm not saying it will work, but I don't know what else to do. It might be my only hope of maintaining any kind of reputation."

Because the other option was to let her secret out and

endure the consequences. The very thought made her hands sweat.

"He would also be someone we could both visit if Micah wanted to see his child," Bethany added. "If we both went to see his parents, that might be suspicious. But if we had a mutual friend . . ."

Would it be enough? If Micah truly didn't want to marry her anymore, if he didn't want to bring her to Pittsburgh with him as his wife, it just might be.

"It's worth a try," Daet said at last, and as they approached the gravel road that led toward the Weibes' farm, Daet guided the horses around the corner. "And if it's to work, we need to know now. Because we are running out of time, Bethany."

Bethany ran her hand over her stomach. It was growing—slowly, but she could feel the change. And she knew from her sisters' experiences with childbirth that one day a belly appeared seemingly out of nowhere, and when that day came Bethany needed to be safely out of town with a story to cover her. But was she ready for this conversation with Micah?

"Daet, have I told you how sorry I am?" she asked.

"You don't need to apologize to me, Beth," he said gruffly.

"I do, though. You had higher hopes for me," she said.

"Yah, but I haven't lost you either, have I?" her father asked, giving her a sad smile. "You're still here with us. You aren't going English, or joining the Mennonites. And I'm grateful for that. We'll sort this out. A baby is a blessing. Always. Do you understand me?"

She nodded. But sometimes along with the blessing came heartrending sacrifice, and that was her deepest fear.

* * *

At the Weibe farm the chickens clucked contentedly from the coop, pecking at the ground of the small enclosure. Bethany looked around—there were no men in sight, and she could smell cooking coming from the house. The windows were open, and there was the murmur of voices from indoors. The horses were left with feed bags because it seemed her father didn't think this would take very long, and Bethany followed him to the door. When the door opened Tessa was drying her hands on a towel.

"Oh!" She smiled hesitantly, then stepped back. "Come in. How are you?"

Micah and his father were in sock feet at the table and Tessa appeared to still be cooking. Micah straightened when he saw them and stood up. He looked from Bethany to her father and back to Bethany.

"We need to talk," Daet said simply. "As a family. With all of you."

Tessa exchanged a look with her husband, and Daniel rose to his feet, pulling out two more chairs.

"Please, sit down," Daniel said. "Can we get you anything? Something to eat, maybe?"

"No, thank you." Daet saw that Bethany sat down first and then took his seat. "This shouldn't take too long, actually."

Daniel leaned forward and Tessa put down her towel and pulled out the chair opposite Bethany. Bethany's stomach tightened and she stole a look at Micah. He was staring at the table in front of him.

"Micah doesn't want to marry our daughter," Daet said, and for a moment silence hung around the table.

"We've tried to talk to him about this," Daniel said. "You know that we want the same thing you do."

"But he doesn't *want* to marry her," Daet repeated. "And we can accept that, but the thing we can't accept is his threat to continue to visit this child after he's left the community."

"With the *Englishers*, a father matters," Micah said.

"More than with the Amish?" Daet said, his disgust barely masked. "Micah, you have the choice to marry her and be a *daet* to this child. But you don't want to do that. Not properly. Not here, where we can see that she's being treated well. You want to make her Mennonite."

Micah chewed the side of his cheek.

"Or perhaps you're counting on her refusing you," Daet went on. "Regardless, I'm going to stop being diplomatic and I'm going to tell you how I see things. This baby came about because both of you put the buggy before the horse when it comes to marriage. Both of you! Now, in our way of life, that means that couple gets married, but we can't make that happen if you go English, can we?"

"I'm not trying to escape my responsibilities," Micah said. "I'll send money. I'll come visit—"

"Enough." Daet shook his head. "You promised my daughter and our family that you'd marry her. Then you took a husband's right with her. But if you go English, no consequences follow you. You can marry an English girl, start a family, grow a business . . . Your life will go on. But what about her? You're threatening to come back and keep her forever in the shadow of the mistake you both made together."

Bethany felt her face flush with humiliation. Tessa and Daniel wouldn't look at her and she wished she could slip out of the room unnoticed—but that wouldn't happen today.

"Is that fair?" Daet pressed. "You get a life, but she doesn't? You break a promise to her and she has to pay for your broken promise for the rest of her life?"

"If she'd stopped me—" he started.

"Shut your mouth, son!" Daniel boomed, and he pinned Micah down with an icy glare. Bethany's breath caught as she stared at the normally placid man. His face was blotched with red and he stood up partway, as if ready to throttle his own son. "You will *not* blame this on Bethany! You are a man, you made a promise, and you made a choice!"

Bethany swallowed and Daniel slowly sat back down. Tessa reached over and put a hand on her husband's arm, but Daniel's jaw still twitched with repressed anger. It was good to be defended, but Bethany felt bile rising in her throat as she looked over at Micah.

He was slouched in his chair, his *Englisher* haircut looking too short, too bare. His lips were pressed together, almost in a pout. This was the man she'd believed would be her husband? The man who said he'd face her parents with her when she told them about the baby, but who blamed her for their mistake when sitting at his parents' table? Micah still wouldn't look at her, and she swallowed back the tears that threatened to rise.

"So you want me to forget about this baby?" Micah asked after a moment of silence.

"No," Daet replied. "I don't. I understand that you will be a father whether you are here or not, but you will not be a *daet*."

"I can try—" Micah started.

"I have a solution," Daet cut in. "One that we think is fair."

"Go ahead," Daniel said.

"Not so long ago, when you were still in love with Bethany, you asked your friend Isaiah to look in on her if anything should happen to you. From what I understand, he's been keeping that promise."

"He's got a crush on her," Micah said bitterly.

"He's been keeping his promise," Bethany said. "He's helped Daet in the shop and he even brought you to me. He's been the friend you didn't think you had in this community."

Micah's expression softened, so it seemed like she was right there.

"You don't want to lose contact with your child," Daet went on, "but if you come back and visit her directly, everyone will know that the child is yours and she will never be able to marry. Ever. You know that."

Micah dropped his gaze.

"You'll marry, I'm sure of it," Daet went on. "But she won't."

"That isn't fair to her," Tessa said softly, speaking for the first time. "And for the love you once shared, it isn't right to do that to her, son."

"I'm not wanting to hold her back," Micah said, his voice tight. "But I won't walk away from my child either."

"Then here is my solution," Daet went on. "What if Isaiah kept at his post, looking out for Bethany? What if when Bethany can't write to you to tell you about the child, Isaiah does? And when you want to come to see the child, you go to see Isaiah, and Bethany and the child will visit, as mutual friends? There will be less gossip that way, and you will have someone you trust to keep you apprised of how your child is doing."

"Isaiah . . ." Micah frowned.

"He's been on your side so far," Daet said.

"Will Bethany give the baby away?" Micah asked hollowly.

"No!" Bethany broke in. "Never! I love this baby already and I won't give him up! I promise you that. But if I go away to have the baby and come back with a story to explain a child in my arms, you can't ruin my chance at finding a marriage afterward. Please."

"And you'll let me see the baby sometimes?" Micah turned toward her for the first time.

"Yah."

"Will you tell the child I'm the father?" he pressed.

"No!" Bethany felt the tears rise and her lips trembled. "A child talks, Micah. You know that! But you will be . . . an uncle, maybe. Or a family friend? And you can forge a relationship. Until the child is old enough to keep a secret. We'll find a way. But if you insist upon forcing yourself onto us, the *Englisher* law might be on your side, but I'll be ruined. Completely."

"And Isaiah will act the part of . . . go-between . . . for us?" Micah asked.

"I'm sure he will," Bethany said. "He's been a good friend so far, and I'll talk to him about it. I'm sure he'll agree."

Micah let out a sigh. "Isaiah is the one man I trust not to hide you away while I'm gone."

"You think *we* would?" Tessa asked, looking wounded.

"You might," Micah said quietly. "You'd feel terrible, but you'd do it."

Daet put his hands on the tabletop. "Then do we have an agreement, Micah? We will stop pushing for this marriage and you will allow Bethany to have a life here."

"If Isaiah will keep me posted on what's happening," Micah said. "Then yah."

Isaiah was the key, after all . . . if he was still willing to help.

"Good," Daet said. "Then you can go back to your life in Pittsburgh with our blessing, Micah. And I do wish you well. I wish you blessings and happiness wherever you might find them."

"I don't!" Tessa said, her voice choked with tears. "You're going against Gott, Micah!"

"Mother . . ." Daniel put his hand on hers. "We've found some middle ground. It will have to be enough."

Daet looked over at Bethany and gave her a reassuring nod. "Then our business here is done."

Where would she be if it weren't for her *daet*? He loved her . . . even when she took a wrong turn. In his eyes she'd always be more precious than rubies—she knew it. And this evening they had a solution that would give her a chance at marriage and a future. It would allow her to keep her family, too.

And it all hinged on Isaiah.

Chapter Sixteen

Isaiah didn't show his father's letter to his sister when he got home from work that afternoon. Elizabeth seemed happy enough chatting with their cousins, and Aunt Rose had complimented her on her bread baking skills. It seemed cruel to pull her away from a perfectly pleasant evening just to show her more of their father's emotional manipulations. Let Elizabeth have a bit of happiness. Besides, he hadn't quite digested it all himself yet.

Abe wanted his *kinner* to miss him—and they did—but that didn't mean Abe had been right in what he'd done. And it didn't mean that Isaiah was ready to write to him either. He'd started mentally composing a reply to his father, but he couldn't commit it to paper yet. There were too many emotions jumbled up in it, too many cross-arguments that wouldn't resolve anything. And he and his daet had always talked with spiritual language twined through their discourse. Isaiah just didn't have it in him.

Isaiah couldn't allude to Bible verses and talk about Gott's will and timing. It would be false. Not because he didn't believe very deeply in Gott, but because he wasn't going to use his faith to cover over his real feelings.

And his real feelings right now were clouded and angry.

After supper was finished and Isaiah had helped his cousins with the evening chores, his emotions almost were swallowed up in the work. The letter his father had written to him had churned through his mind, and he worked with a dogged determination that left his younger cousins eyeing him uncertainly.

Isaiah hung back as Uncle Mel, Bart, and Vernon went back inside, but Seth didn't follow his brothers. He crossed his arms and fixed Isaiah with a stare.

"What's wrong?" Seth asked.

"Nothing."

Seth smiled faintly. "Come on. What is it? You've got my brothers on eggshells just looking at you."

"My *daet* wrote to me," Isaiah said. "And I hate to say it, but I think your father was right about mine."

Seth's eyebrows rose. "Well, I mean, he did defraud everyone."

"No, I mean . . . more than that. More than the crime, more than the sin . . . He's a fake," Isaiah said. "He acts the part of a religious man, but that's it—it's an act."

"If it makes you feel any better, I thought my *daet* was wrong about your father, too," Seth said. "I thought he was just jealous."

And maybe Mel had been jealous. That couldn't be completely discounted, but they were brothers, so his feelings would have been more complicated than that. Just like Isaiah's were. His father was a fraud, a fake, and Isaiah was disappointed, furious, confused . . . and still he loved him. Abe was still his father, even as a complete failure as an Amish man. Those conflicting emotions were hard to make peace with.

His *daet* had left something for him by that tree, and maybe it would be nothing at all, or maybe it would be something that would only make him angrier, but he couldn't just leave it there either.

"I'm going to head out for a couple of hours," Isaiah said. "And I'm not asking permission. Just tell your parents you saw me leaving and I'll be back."

Seth nodded. "Where are you going?"

"Just out for a while."

"You want company?" Seth asked.

He did, but it wasn't his cousin's company that he was longing for. He'd go see if Bethany wanted to come. Even if she couldn't come out with him—which was what he suspected would be the case—maybe they'd offer him some pie and he could sit in a quiet kitchen for a few minutes with the one girl who seemed to understand him most. He wouldn't have much more opportunity to do that before she'd be whisked off to wherever she'd have the baby. Then, after a few grateful minutes with Bethany, he'd head out to see if he could find whatever his father had left at that tree.

"I'll be okay," Isaiah said. "Thanks, though."

Whatever these feelings were that he was developing for Bethany, he'd be smart to smother them. She wasn't his . . . and maybe her time away from the community would be good for him. He could rinse his heart clean of these confusing emotions and get back his balance. He knew who he wanted to be . . . he just had to get there. And he couldn't take shortcuts or he'd end up just as fake as his own father.

* * *

When Isaiah pulled into the Glicks' drive Bethany and her sister were taking laundry off the clothesline in the lowering summer light. The clothesline squeaked as Bethany pulled it, the sound carrying on a warm breeze, and she pulled off a shirt and handed it down to her sister, then pulled the line again to reach a dress.

Bethany paused in her work when she heard the horses and shaded her eyes against the sun. He waved and she waved back, then she gave the clothesline another squeaking pull.

It was a peaceful scene, one that warmed him on the inside. Micah was giving this up—a chance at an Amish wife taking care of an Amish home. . . . What could be so alluring out there with the English that he'd give up this kind of paradise?

But maybe it wasn't peaceful scenes like this that Micah was escaping—maybe he just couldn't face the parts of their world that didn't match up with the idyllic appearances. For the first time Isaiah felt like he could understand that sentiment. Because no matter how appealing all this was, if you couldn't trust it to sustain you, what was the point?

The difference was, Isaiah did still trust their community. He just no longer trusted his own father.

When Isaiah pulled up the horses he tied off the reins and hopped down. Bethany pulled the last shirt from the line and shook it out, then folded it before dropping it on the top of the laundry basket.

"Hi, Isaiah," Lily said with a grin.

"Hi, Lily." He smiled back. "How are you doing?"

"I'm good." Lily blushed and twisted her hands in front

of her. "Did you know I'm going to have a new little niece or nephew?"

"Yah?" His gaze flickered toward Bethany and she subtly shook her head. So Lily didn't know . . .

"My big sister is pregnant," Lily said. "She and my brother-in-law have four *kinner* already, and Mamm says we can go visit her to help her with the baby."

"Enough chatter, Lily," Bethany said. "Take this."

Bethany held out the laundry basket to Lily, who hoisted it in her strong little arms and headed for the door. Lily looked back, the screen door propped open against her shoulder.

"And my *mamm* says I can help make baby clothes this time, and when my sister has the baby I'll help take care of the little ones," Lily added with a grin, darting a look at Bethany, then adding, "I already help with the little ones, but I've never helped sew the baby clothes before. I can stitch well enough now, though!"

Then Lily disappeared inside, the screen door slamming shut behind her.

Bethany smiled faintly. "She loves babies, that girl."

Isaiah met her gaze, but he didn't comment. Lily would have another baby to cuddle and play with if all went according to plan. But how painful would that scenario be for Bethany, pretending that the squirming infant was nothing more to her than a cousin's child? Would she be able to pull off the act? Or would Lily catch on? *Kinner* that age weren't as naïve as their families might hope.

"I—uh—came by to see if you wanted to go for a drive," he said.

"A drive?" She squinted up at him.

"My *daet* said he left something for me at the farm—

on the far edge, so I won't be disturbing the new owners or anything. But I thought you might want to come along."

"Hold on," she said, and she headed inside, leaving him on the gravel drive. He looked around, watching some brown hens peck at the ground while a rooster strutted nearby, surveying him with a glittery black eye.

The door opened again and Bethany came back out. "Yah. I can go."

"Really?" He shot her a look of surprise.

"Yah." She met his gaze evenly enough. "Shall we?"

"Uh—of course." He glanced toward the house and saw Barbara in the door. She gave him a solemn nod and then disappeared again. It looked like he had her parents' permission, although he wasn't sure why. Whatever—he'd take it.

Bethany pulled herself up into the buggy without his assistance and he got back up into the driver's seat and cast her a smile.

"So, how come they let you?" he asked as he untied the reins and got the horses doing a U-turn to head back up the drive. "I figured they'd be keeping you pretty close to home."

"You didn't want me to come?" she asked.

"No, I just expected to have to make do with pie."

She smiled at that, then shrugged. "It's because my little sister is always around, and she's all ears, that girl. She's figured out something is up and she's determined to sleuth it out. And . . . I needed to talk to you about something."

They got to the top of the drive, and he made a clicking sound with his mouth as he guided the horses down the road in the direction of the land that once belonged to his family. He glanced back as they turned, and he saw Nathaniel standing in front of the house watching them.

"What did you need to talk to me about?" he said.

Bethany's hands were clenched in her lap, and when they went over a bump, she grabbed the seat to steady herself, knuckles white.

"My *daet* took me to talk to the Weibes this afternoon, and we . . . well, we came to an agreement," Bethany said.

"Like . . . a marriage agreement?" he asked hesitantly. His mouth felt dry and he glanced in her direction, wishing she'd just spit it out.

"No, not that," she said, and he felt himself relax with relief. He felt mildly guilty about it, because those two getting married would be the right thing for everyone. So, being relieved that no wedding was on the horizon for Bethany was cruel at heart. He had no right to wish she'd stay single just so they could continue with this friendship that skirted all proper lines.

"Okay, so . . . what kind of agreement?" he asked.

"It hinges on you, actually," she said, casting him an apologetic look. "Micah says he won't come back to Bountiful and visit me and make it obvious that he's this child's father if you're willing to keep doing what you've been doing."

Falling for her? Because that's what he'd been up to these last weeks.

"What exactly does Micah need me to do?" Isaiah asked.

"You said you'd look out for me, before. And if you kept doing that—" Bethany licked her lips. "He doesn't trust my parents or his to have his best interests at heart in this. I suppose they're too close to it. That's what it comes down to. He knows everyone wants us to get married, and he doesn't want that. He won't live an Amish life. But if you would be willing to stay in contact with him and send him some updates on the baby, he'd trust things more. And if he wanted to see the baby, he could come back and visit you. Because he isn't baptized yet, he wouldn't be shunned, and I'd stop by to see you, as an old friend, and . . . no one would be the wiser."

Her voice had gotten breathy, and he looked over at her. Her cheeks were pink and her gaze was locked on her hands, which were clasped in a white-knuckled grip in her lap.

"So . . . Micah needs me involved?" Isaiah asked.

"He trusts you." Bethany turned her gaze toward him pleadingly. "And I know it was presumptuous of us to make this deal with him without even talking to you first, but you'd been so helpful lately, and you said you'd be willing to talk to him for me, and . . ."

"So . . . with me standing clear and giving him confirmation that all is well, he'll let you get married and have a life and not meddle with your future," he concluded.

"Yah." She swallowed.

Right. It all came down to his original promise—to be a good friend to Micah first, and to make sure that Bethany would be okay.

"The thing is," she went on, "Micah makes us all nervous. He's not thinking like an Amish man. He knows that the *Englisher* law would be on his side to see the child and to be a *daet* to this baby. And the only thing that made him feel better was the thought that you'd report back to him."

"Because he trusts *me*."

"Yah . . . You're the one who doesn't have a personal stake in this, I suppose. And maybe it's because you were such good friends before, but he trusts you more than he trusts his own parents in this right now."

"It's funny," he said quietly. "All I've wanted lately is for someone to trust me again. But this wasn't quite what I had in mind."

Isaiah swallowed. He had to start somewhere, didn't he? Trust, once broken, had to be earned back. This was a start—a good one! He had a job and he could be a part of another family's solution to a difficult problem. If he felt only friendship for Bethany, this would be an answer to a prayer, a way back into the community he loved so much. . . .

Except he felt considerably more for her than friendship.

"Isaiah, would you do it?" she asked earnestly.

"Would I be that friend that Micah can count on?" he said.

"Would you be the friend that *I* can count on . . . ?" She met his gaze. "Please? It's the only way I can see out of this. I know it's asking a lot, but . . ."

She was right. It was the only way he could see of her getting out of this with her reputation intact and her baby in her arms.

"Yah, I'll do it," he said, and he reached over and put a hand over hers.

Bethany was asking him to be a friend—to be her hope. How could he refuse her?

Bethany let out a slow breath and felt the weight of her worries lift ever so slightly. Isaiah's hand was warm and rough, and she turned hers over so that their palms connected. Out in the field beside them, a tractor growled and *Englisher* men's voices called back and forth as they tried to pull a tree stump out of the ground in front of a house. Bethany let her eyes flow over the scene, but when one of the men looked up and saw her, she quickly averted her gaze.

"I suppose this isn't very appropriate of me, then, is it?" he asked, squeezing her hand gently. She looked down at his broad, sun-browned hand engulfing hers. In a way it was incredibly strange to be sitting here holding Isaiah Yoder's hand, and yet it also felt like the most natural thing in the world. She pushed back a wave of melancholy. Whatever this was, it couldn't move beyond this. . . .

"No," she admitted. "But no one will know."

"And if I'm going to be the friend I promised Micah I'd be, we can't be more than friends. . . ."

"But you *are* my friend," Bethany said quietly. "Except maybe we have some weird boundaries."

He laughed softly at that, and he loosened his grip, running his thumb down her hand.

"All right, then. As friends, I'll tell you why I picked you up," he said. "I got this letter from my *daet*, and he still sounds like Daet, you know? He's still religious, and quotes the Bible, and . . . In some ways, it feels like he's just gone preaching at another community. And all of this was just a bad dream."

She watched as his thumb moved rhythmically over the top of her fingers.

"Anyway," he went ont, "he said he left something for me, and it was all a little cryptic. Something sentimental, I think. And at first I just felt angry, you know? I mean, my father ruined us—all of us kids! Our farm is gone, our reputation is gone, our relationships are all tense and uncomfortable because of what he did!"

Isaiah looked over at her, his gaze filled with complex emotion.

"But you want to see what it is," she said.

"Yah. Like some kid, you dangle a surprise under my nose and I can't help myself," he said. "Or maybe I'm hoping to find something that will make me feel better. If that's even possible! I lost my father, and maybe I want to find a way to understand him, or excuse him. . . ."

"Or forgive him," she murmured.

"I'm not there yet," he said.

"Where did he leave it?" she asked. "You said it was on the edge?"

"The north side," he said. "Just by a side road, there's a big oak tree I used to climb as a kid. Daet used to take us out there when he was planting, and we'd sit up there in the branches and watch the men work. Until we got old enough to actually help, that is."

"So a spot that was meaningful?" she asked.

"I didn't think it was, actually," he replied. "It was no more meaningful than the house, or the barn, or the fence my sisters and I broke over and over again by jumping on the middle rung . . . I mean, it was a part of our life, but . . ." He sighed.

"It's accessible by the road," she said quietly.

He looked over at her quizzically. "Yah . . ."

"I mean, if it isn't important because of a special memory, maybe the importance is that it's easily accessible from the road."

"And far from the house," he said, then he shook his head bitterly. "That's probably all this is, isn't it? And when did he stick it out there? Because it wasn't like he knew he was going to be arrested, was it? And once he was in custody, he never had a chance to come back and put anything out there. That means it's been there for a while."

His hand stopped moving over hers and he pulled it back, leaving her fingers cool.

"It doesn't mean he didn't put something out there for you," she said.

"It does, actually," he replied woodenly. "If there was something he wanted to give me before he got arrested, he'd leave it safe in the house, not stick it out by a tree."

She had to agree. "You think there's nothing there? If that's the case, why would your *daet* send you a letter telling you to go look?"

"I think if there is something there, it wasn't originally meant for me at all," Isaiah replied.

And whatever meaning he was hoping to get, he wasn't going to find it. She could almost feel his heartbreak from where he sat, his expression stony and his grip on the reins too tight.

"It might be easier to forgive him than to excuse him," she said softly.

Isaiah didn't answer, and he slowed the horses as they came to a narrow, gravel road. She straightened, and he leaned forward, then steered the horses around a pothole that the wheels only narrowly missed.

She looked out over the fields to her right—the old Yoder place. She could see the roof of the barn far off, but the house wasn't visible. She hadn't been down this road before, never having had any reason to come this way. She'd only been on the Yoder farm for Service Sundays. She used to sit on the women's side of the service and Micah, Seth, and Isaiah would sit on the men's side, leaning together to share a joke or pass along some bit of wood or something one of them had picked up. The three friends . . .

And it wasn't that long ago, either, that everything was so much simpler, and her biggest problems seemed to be Mary Fisher's crush on her fiancé, and a talkative little sister who refused to keep her mouth shut about Bethany's engagement.

A large oak tree loomed up ahead, with gnarled branches spreading out over the field on one side and the road on the other. One of the branches had broken, a thick limb that hung awkwardly down to the ground, still connected at the trunk.

Isaiah reined in the horses and sat there, looking at the tree with pursed lips.

"I'm curious now," Bethany said, nudging his arm.

"Yah, I am, too," he admitted, and cast her an unfathomable look. "You want to help me look?"

"Sure."

Bethany moved over to Isaiah's side of the buggy so as not to step down into the ditch, and he reached up to help her hop down. He was strong, and she landed lightly beside him. There was no other traffic on the road behind them, and this little side road petered off and ended in patchy weeds about twenty yards ahead, so the only sound was that of some twittering birds and the rustle of the wind moving through the leaves of that mammoth tree.

His gaze caught hers and she sucked in a breath, and for a moment he just looked down at her as if trying to decide something. Then he dipped his head and put a finger under her chin to tip her face upward and covered her lips with his. His kiss was slow and warm, and he slid his hands around her waist, his fingers lingering over her belly in a way that made her heart speed up.

When he pulled back he gave her a melancholy smile. "I'm going to have to stop doing that."

She nodded. "I know."

And right now, in the middle of nowhere, with no one to see them, and no future possible between them, she should have been able to push him back. He would have listened—there was no question there. Instead, she reached out and touched his shirt and he moved closer again, his mouth hovering over hers. He smelled warm and musky, and she longed to slide into his arms and stay there.

"How am I going to do this?" he whispered.

"Do what?"

"Watch you, be your friend, and write to Micah and say that all is well?"

"But all will be well," she whispered back.

"Not for me . . ." He lowered his lips over hers again, and this time she strained up to meet him. His breath was hot against her face, and he slid his arms around her, holding her hard against his chest so that she could feel the powerful beating of his heart.

And she had to admit that seeing him on the street now, or in the shop . . . or sitting on the women's side during service and looking at him was going to be a whole lot different than it was before, because now she knew what his lips felt like, what his hands felt like, and exactly how weak-kneed he could make her with a single kiss.

Bethany pulled back and he released her.

"That isn't going to help matters," she said shakily.

"Probably not," he agreed, but his gaze was still locked on her. "I've been looking at you for years, watching you love Micah and wishing it could be me. I know I'm too late. I do. I'm just . . . I'm sorry. I'm not asking for more from you."

Bethany nodded. The problem was, she'd felt a fraction of this kind of attraction before, and she'd made a very poor choice. And now, with Isaiah, it was more powerful still, and she didn't dare trust this kind of feeling! It was misleading, it was dangerous, and she of all people should know to keep clear of it.

His kisses might leave her legs wobbly, but they weren't a promise of anything else. A moment of passion was just that—a moment. And it passed more quickly than she'd ever realized was possible.

"Come on, then," Isaiah said. He caught her hand, tugging her along with him into the shade of that tree.

She looked up, and the leaves rippled in the breeze, the foliage around the edges glowing golden in the sunlight. In the depth of the shade, the air was cooler, and she waited while Isaiah grabbed a limb and pulled himself up with one smooth movement. Once he'd gotten on top of the limb he looked around.

"Do you see anything down there?" he called. "Any holes dug, or anything like that?"

Bethany looked around under the canopy of branches; the earth looked undisturbed.

"I don't see anything," she said.

"I'm going to check something," he said, and he climbed over to another branch, and then another, then came closer to the massive trunk and stretched forward.

"There . . ." he said. "There's an old hole that used to be a squirrel's nest. . . ."

Bethany stood back, watching him as something thunked and rattled. Then he pulled it out—a tin box. He looked it over.

"I can't open it one-handed up here," he said. "Catch."

Isaiah lobbed down the box and she caught it before it hit the ground. It wasn't heavy, but something rolled around inside it. Isaiah jumped down from his perch, landing on the ground in a crouch. He brushed off his hands and she passed the box over.

"I was thinking he might have left a Bible out here or something, but this isn't a Bible," he said. He pried at the lid, but it looked like it had rusted a little bit, and it took some strength for him to finally get the lid free. When it came off he stared down into the box, his expression one of shock.

"What is it?" she asked, stepping closer, but she didn't need Isaiah to explain. Inside that tin box were two thick rolls of bills . . . and nothing else. Her heart hammered to a stop.

Money . . .

Chapter Seventeen

Isaiah picked up a roll of bills and it felt heavy. It was tightly wound; the bills on top that he could see were twenties. How much money was this? His brain seemed to slow to a crawl.

Where had this come from? And when had Abe left it, exactly? Who was this money for originally?

"This is the thing he left you?" Bethany asked slowly.

"I was expecting something a little more sentimental," he muttered.

He was bracing himself for emotional turmoil, memories from childhood, maybe even some guilt at his current distance from his father . . . not *cash*.

"How much is there?" she asked.

He flicked the edges of the rolled bills, then shook his head. "A few thousand?"

"Is that money from the fraud?" Bethany asked, her voice low.

"I don't know. . . ."

Bethany looked up at him, her breath shallow and her face pale. "It is."

He shook his head. "The police took all that money . . .

and the farm! It might not be anything to do with the fraud. It might be our money—money Daet hid away for some reason."

"No one sticks gainfully earned money in a tree, Isaiah!" she shot back. "Your *daet* would have put it in the bank, like everyone else!"

Bethany looked at him and he stared back. He wasn't really arguing with her, he was arguing with himself, because he agreed with her. That was the problem! This was dirty money—it had to be. But besides his paycheck, which was paltry next to these bundles of cash, this was his only hope of starting over, getting some space of his own for himself and his sisters.

"Bethany, I lost my inheritance," Isaiah said. "And it wasn't my fault! I had no idea what my *daet* was involved in, but I'm the one to lose. You'll inherit something—money, land, a business. I won't have a farm. I don't have a penny to my name except for what I earned from your *daet*. I'll never be able to afford a farm of my own—that kind of thing comes from a family, building something together. Whatever we built is gone. But this money—"

The words stuck in his throat. This money was a chance—maybe the only one he'd get. A job was a good thing, a job was necessary, but it wouldn't give him the jump he needed to get a proper start.

Bethany's gaze dropped to the rolls of bills again, and he could see the judgment shining in her clear gaze. She didn't see what he did—but she hadn't lost what he had either. She still had parents who could help her in her time of need.

"I'm not saying it's fair, Isaiah," she said. "But what your *daet* did hurt a lot of people. If they can be recompensed in some way, they should be."

But what about him? Should he be recompensed in some small way for everything his father took from him? What about his sisters? They had a farm to rely on a few months ago, and even if it wasn't fully paid off, it was a working farm they could live off of. Now what did they have? He wouldn't inherit from his uncle, even if he and Mel had managed to patch things up a little bit.

And this money could help him become the independent man he wanted to be . . .

Isaiah tucked the money back into the tin and started back toward the buggy. Bethany didn't move, though, and he stopped, looking back at her.

"That's wrong, Isaiah," she said.

"Everything is wrong right now!" he said. "Everything! I'm not saying that people shouldn't be paid back. They will be! But maybe this little bit of money is an answer to a prayer."

"You really think that?" she asked incredulously.

"I've been praying," he said. "We need a miracle."

"Yah, but miracles come from Gott. You have no idea where this came from!"

"Maybe this is an answer to *your* prayers," he said, closing the distance between them again in three brisk strides. "I don't know how much money is here, but I'm pretty sure it's enough to get my sister and me started in a new place, and to help you as well."

"How is that money going to help me?" she demanded. "I'm pregnant, Isaiah! That money isn't going to turn back time! It isn't going to change people's opinion of me if they find out!"

"It *might* help—"

"It won't!" She shook her head. "How could it? I made a mistake and I'm living with the consequences of that mistake. That money is from the con artists. I can't see it being anything else. And there is no blessing in stolen money."

"It might not be!" he said. Oh, how he hoped it wasn't . . .

"If it isn't, it's still supposed to go to the police. They confiscated all your *daet*'s goods to pay back his victims. That money there would be included in that. It isn't yours."

Was she getting some sort of pleasure out of pointing out just how destitute he was? Did she have any idea how embarrassing this was? He turned toward the buggy again, and this time she caught up with him, putting a hand on his arm.

"Isaiah—" she said.

"Bethany, I'm broke!" he snapped, turning toward her again. "I have nothing! Do you get that? I have exactly one paycheck from your *daet*. And I'm not going to inherit a single acre from my uncle! I've got the strength in my body to work and that's all I've got. My name is mud around here, and I don't have the family support my cousins do. I don't have a family business to lean back on, either . . . I've got nothing. Do you get that? Do you know what that's like?"

"I'm a woman," she said faintly. "I don't have a career of my own. I'm expected to marry, and I've all but ruined that for myself, so I have a small idea, yah."

"You've got a family," he said, lowering his voice. "You can work with your *daet*, if you have to. You have people who love you and want to protect you. They've been working their tails off to do just that ever since they found out about—" He licked his lips, not wanting to say it out loud. "Bethany, I'm a man. I'm supposed to be the one providing, and I've got two younger sisters who need me to step up and do just that, but it's not quite so easy as throwing your back into some hard work. The money comes slowly, and while I save for a place of our own, I've promised to pay my uncle so he doesn't have so much of a burden."

"He wouldn't take money from you . . ." she breathed.

"Oh, he will," Isaiah said curtly. "And I'm okay with that. I'm a man—I don't want to be coddled like a little child. But I won't have a chance to make something of myself like other men my age. I'll likely be paying for this for the rest of my life."

"People will forget," he said.

"No, they won't," he said bitterly. "Any more than they'll forget that your baby was born outside of wedlock. A community like ours remembers forever."

"So what are you going to do, then?" Bethany asked.

"I don't know."

And that was the truth of it. She saw this money as tainted, but he wasn't so sure! Daet was paying for what he did—financially, and with prison time. He was the one who got involved in this garbage. What was Isaiah supposed to do? Just bend his head and accept punishment for something that wasn't his fault?

Isaiah held out his hand to help Bethany up into the buggy, and she hesitated before taking it. What did she want from him—reassurance that he'd virtuously stay destitute to make everyone else feel like enough punishment had been extracted for his father's crime?

"I should get you home," he said.

Bethany put her fingers in his and he helped her up, then hoisted himself up onto the seat.

There was no perfect, virtuous path here. Too many things had already gone wrong! Abe's crime, Bethany's pregnancy, Micah's desertion, and the Yoder *kinners'* loss of any kind of start in life . . . None of it was fair. But this money could start to set a few things right again. Isaiah wasn't looking for wealth, just a start in life. He didn't want to benefit from his father's crime, but he didn't want to pay for it either! Isaiah wasn't a bad guy here, but looking at the way Bethany eyed him, it was hard to feel particularly good.

Isaiah put the tin on the seat between himself and Bethany, and she looked out the other side of the buggy, away from him.

What did she think of him now? She didn't approve— that much was clear. But he wanted to help her, too.

So maybe these rolls of bills were a gift from Gott. Maybe Gott was working with the same mess they were!

"Are you still going to help me with Micah?" Bethany asked quietly.

"Will you let me help you in other ways, too?" he asked.

"With that money?" she asked, then shook her head. "No. I'm not benefiting from that."

And yet Isaiah wanted to be the kind of Amish man who could be relied upon to do the right thing no matter what, even when it hurt. He wanted to be the kind of man who earned his neighbors' respect and trust because they knew his character.

He looked down at the tin between them.

"You aren't on your own, Beth," he said.

"I know. I have my family."

"You have me!" he retorted.

She looked over at him. "Do I? Because what I need right now is a way to keep my baby. That's what I need. I don't need romance. I don't need love. I need a reputation that will allow me to stay in this community and I need my baby." Tears welled in her eyes. "I know I've only made things worse with . . . whatever it is we're feeling for each other."

"You haven't made anything worse," he said, and he reached for her hand, but she didn't reach back.

"I'm being completely honest with you right now. I need to know if I can count on you to help me with Micah. Because if I can't, we need to come up with a new plan."

"Hey—I offered to help with this money, but that doesn't mean I'm backing out, okay? If I can help you, I will. You can count on me."

She nodded and leaned back in the seat. "Thank you. With all my heart, Isaiah. Thank you."

Bethany was going to be a mother, and whatever he was feeling for her, or she was feeling for him, it didn't matter a bit in comparison to her need for her child. If he wanted to give Bethany anything, he should give her the space she needed to start over. Isn't that what he needed, too? A fresh start?

Bethany watched as the scenery passed by at the steady pace of the plodding horses. That money sat between them like a boulder, and she leaned away from it. Did Isaiah really feel no guilt about benefiting from his neighbors' losses?

She'd been suspicious before that Isaiah might have been more involved in his father's fraud than he let on . . . and she couldn't help but wonder now. What was he going to do with that money? And what made him any different from his father if he was willing to start over on money stolen from his Amish brethren?

She stole a look at him and felt a squeeze around her heart. She'd wanted him to be better than this—to be the virtuous, good man he claimed to be.

But then, she was no better, was she? She was willing to live out a lie for the rest of her life in order to avoid the natural consequences of her own mistakes. So while she was judging Isaiah, she didn't really have a right.

Gott, I wish I were a better woman. . . .

It wasn't exactly a plea for forgiveness, because if she asked for forgiveness, she'd have to be willing to change her ways and put a stop to that lie, and she wasn't. She was willing to live a virtuous life here on in, to be dutiful and good to a husband she likely wouldn't be in love with, and to follow every rule with rare passion and energy . . . but this lie must go on.

Would all the good deeds in the world be enough to erase it?

The sun was setting as they turned into her drive and Bethany suddenly felt very tired.

When she got out of the buggy in front of her home she looked back to find Isaiah's eyes locked on her.

"I'll help you," he said quietly.

"Thank you." She felt her eyes mist. "Eventually, when we've both gotten through these hard times, we'll be able to be better people."

"You're already a good person," he said, looking slightly confused. "I know you."

"I'm a desperate person," she replied. "It's hard to be both good and desperate."

How many others had their secrets stashed deep beneath their outward morals and religiosity? She doubted they were alone in that.

The door to the stables opened and her *daet* came out. Beyond the stable, the sun glowed red along the horizon. She took a step back and cast her father a smile.

"Good night," Isaiah said, and she stepped farther away to give him space to turn the buggy around and head back up the drive, but her heart tugged toward him.

If things were different, if they were both a little less desperate and had a few more choices, she might have been able to let herself fall in love with him.

"Well?" Daet said, coming up next to her.

They both looked in the direction of Isaiah's receding buggy, then Bethany glanced up at her *daet*.

"He says he'll help me," Bethany said, a lump in her throat.

"So we can tell Micah, then," Daet said.

"Yah." She nodded. "We can tell him."

"Because he's inside. He . . . arrived just a few minutes ago and said he'd wait a while."

Bethany's mouth suddenly dried and she looked toward the house hesitantly. "I didn't see his buggy."

"It's under the shelter."

She followed her *daet*'s gaze and saw the second buggy then, next to their own, the horses in the corral beyond.

"I should talk to him, I suppose," Bethany said.

The last discussion had been completed around them,

mostly, but with Isaiah's promise to be the friend that Micah needed right now, she could carry on with her plans—go to Indiana and have her baby, then begin the lie that would give her a life.

"It's going to be okay, Bethany," Daet said quietly. "We'll figure this out. But with Isaiah's help, it will be better than okay. You'll come out of this and, Gott willing, you'll find a good husband who will see what a treasure you are."

Bethany swallowed and forced a smile. "Can Gott bless a lie?"

"Gott can forgive an awful lot," her father replied. "Let's leave that up to Him."

That was a hedging answer, but her father couldn't tell her that Gott would bless this. All they could do was hope that Gott would allow their plans. This child was coming, and it couldn't be Gott's will that a baby and a mother be separated, could it?

Bethany led the way into the house, and when she got into the kitchen Mamm and Lily were at the table with Micah. He had pie in front of him, but when she came inside he pushed back his chair and stood up immediately.

"We should talk," Bethany said.

"You go on and use the sitting room," Mamm said. "We'll give you some privacy there."

Lily stared at them both with open curiosity, and if it were possible to eavesdrop, Bethany knew that her sister would. Mamm put a restraining hand on Lily's shoulder, however, and nodded at Bethany.

"Shall we?" Bethany said, and she gestured down the hallway.

Micah pushed back his chair into place and gave Barbara a nod. "Thank you. The pie was great."

Mamm didn't answer, and Micah headed down the hall, his shoes squeaking against the hardwood floor. Bethany followed, and when they emerged into the sitting room she moved as far from the door as possible, casting a glance over her shoulder.

"You were out with Isaiah—" Micah crossed his arms over his chest. "Are you two . . . I mean, it looks—"

"I was asking him if he would be willing to hold up our deal—the one we talked about at your parents' home," Bethany said. "And he is. He'll be the one you can talk to, the one you can visit."

"If I'm not shunned," Micah said.

"You aren't baptized yet . . ." Bethany felt her heart clench. "You're free to come and go. It's me who's bound by the rules of the church."

She was the one who'd been baptized right after her Rumspringa, joyfully stepping into church life. And she was bound by those rules and expectations now.

"Do you love me still?" Micah asked hollowly.

Bethany blinked. "What?"

"Do you?" he pressed. "Do you love me enough to be my wife, and to raise this baby together?"

Her heart skipped a beat, and for a moment she thought she might throw up. Was he willing to marry her after all? Would this be her penance—marrying Micah?

"I—" She cleared her throat. "I'm not quite so naïve as I was before, so you can't expect me to feel quite the same way . . ."

"But do you love me?" Micah stepped closer, lowering his voice.

"Do *you* love *me*?" she countered.

"If you loved me enough to marry me, it might be

enough," he said. The words were like a slap. He wanted to know if she felt more than he did. . . .

"Are you willing to make a life here?" she asked. "Because that is the only way this will work."

She'd be a good wife—cooperative, patient, gentle. She might not love him, but she could choose to respect him, and do her best to make his life a good one.

"I'm asking once more if you could come with me. And we'd find our footing. Because I do love you . . . still . . . I mean, circumstances have changed, but we're still the same people, aren't we?" He looked at her helplessly. "Aren't we?"

There it was—he wanted her to be the savior of this relationship, the one to make up for his own deficits and go along with him into perdition.

"No, we aren't the same people now," she breathed. "I'm not the same person, at the very least. I don't love you enough to go English with you and make you feel like you're a good man after all this."

He winced and took a step back. "You're angry."

"I'm not, actually," she said. "I was before, and maybe I will be again, but right now? I'm just . . . tired. This baby has changed things, hasn't it? This isn't about us going off to start a life together because it's the only thing we've ever wanted. This is about two people who would have called off the wedding and not looked back if it weren't for a baby coming along. You don't love me, Micah."

"I don't think we have the luxury of thinking of that," he said.

"I'm not going English with you." That was what he was driving at, wasn't it?

He nodded, then sucked in a breath. "I'm sorry I'm not a good Amish husband, Bethany. I really am."

"This sounds like a goodbye," she said.

Micah nodded. "It is. I'm going to the bus station first thing in the morning; I'm going back to Pittsburgh. If I wait any longer, I'll lose my job."

"Won't you miss us?" she asked. "I mean . . . all of us: Bountiful, the community, the Amish way."

"Yah." He swallowed. "Yah, I will."

"And you'll still leave?" she asked.

"Just because something hurts in the leaving doesn't make it the wrong choice," he said quietly. "My *daet* told me that years ago, when I'd been dating an *Englisher* girl during my Rumspringa."

Somehow it still stung to hear Micah talk of other girls he'd dated. And she was no different than that *Englisher*, it seemed, swept into the past as a girl who wasn't quite the right fit.

"Micah, if you're going, you should go. If you aren't happy Amish, then I wish you only happiness with the English, if that's even possible. But don't tell me lies you think I want to hear. Now is the time for us to be honest with each other."

"Will you let me know when the baby is born?" he asked.

"Yah."

"And when I come to see Isaiah, you'll . . . come, too?" he confirmed.

"Yah, Micah. I'll stand by my word."

Was this what they'd come to, making cautious deals between them? But whatever they'd been before, it felt strangely far in the past. The Micah she had known before—the earnest, pious, determined young man—he never had been the real Micah. That was the man he'd wanted to be, but this was the real man—desperate to escape, excited about the unknown, and genuinely not in love with her.

"Should I use the same address?" Bethany asked.

"Yah, that will reach me."

Bethany dropped her gaze. "Okay, then."

Micah leaned down and bussed a kiss across her cheek, then he moved toward the door. She followed him out into the kitchen, and Micah gave her parents a solemn nod before heading for the door.

"Are you getting married, then?" Lily asked loudly.

The side door shut with a click and Micah's boots thunked down the stairs. He was gone, and she suddenly felt the urge to cry. Not because she loved Micah, and not because she'd miss him terribly, but because everything was changing, and everyone seemed to be slipping from the pedestals she'd had them on.

"No, Lily," Bethany said, wiping an errant tear from her cheek with the palm of her hand. "I'm not getting married."

"He's such an idiot!" Lily burst out.

"You will not speak about your elders that way!" Mamm said sharply.

"No, she's right," Daet said. "He's an idiot. But Lily, you aren't allowed to say so."

Mamm exchanged a look with Daet, and then she forced a smile. "I think that your heart will mend, Bethany, and I have an idea on how to help you get over the heartbreak. You and I are going to visit my aunt Dorcas in Indiana.

She needs help at her age, and I think it would make a good rest for you—help you feel better."

"Can I come?" Lily asked breathlessly. "I could help, too!"

"No, no, Lily," Mamm said. "Your *daet* will need your help in the shop and your sisters might need help with babysitting."

"True . . ." Lily seemed to accept this excuse at face value. "When are you going?"

"In a couple of days," Mamm said, sliding an arm around Lily's shoulders. "But don't worry, we'll be back soon. You can help take care of things while I'm away for a few days, can't you?"

And the scene was set—the trip to visit an aunt that would be extended for Bethany for approximately nine months.

At least there was a plan.

Chapter Eighteen

The next afternoon was Saturday, and Bethany sat on the side of her bed, folding her dresses one by one and laying them into her suitcase. Outside, wind whipped through the trees and the first drops of rain splattered against the window pane. A flash of lightning was followed by a distant peel of thunder. Bethany looked toward her hope chest, now halfway emptied. A matter of weeks ago she was joyfully filling it. Now she was filling a suitcase.

Micah's visit last night had been strangely freeing, and enlightening. Why had Micah proposed if he hadn't really loved her all that much? Or had he only realized that after he'd left and didn't miss her all that much? If she weren't in the position she was in, she'd think it was a blessing to find that out before irreversible vows were taken, but it didn't feel that way.

She'd been just as foolish, allowing herself to be seduced by a man she didn't really love half enough to marry either. Just because it was "that time" that everyone seemed to be settling down wasn't reason enough to bind oneself to a man for life. But she would be bound to Micah, not as his wife, but as the mother of his child. That wasn't going away.

"I wish I could come, too." Lily sighed from her seat by the window.

"Daet needs you at home," Bethany said. "You know that. Besides, we'll be back in a few days. You won't even miss us."

A lie. It felt heavy in her chest to lie like this, willingly telling untruths to benefit herself. A few months ago she would have been horrified at the thought of doing such a thing and now it came almost naturally. When would she have the luxury of complete honesty again . . . ever?

Lily leaned her elbows onto the window sill and looked outside mournfully. "Maybe if I went I'd meet a boy who'd want to court me one day."

"Oh, stop that," Bethany said with a chuckle. "You're nine. You have eight years before your Rumspringa, you know. Right now you're supposed to be a little girl—playing outside, helping in the kitchen, and not worrying about boys."

"Maybe you'll meet a man who will want to marry *you*," Lily said, and she stood up from her seat and headed over to the dresser, the top drawer open. She pulled out a *kapp* and looked at it thoughtfully.

"Do you want to try it on?" Bethany asked.

"Can I?" Lily asked hopefully.

Bethany rose to her feet and went to where her sister stood. She grabbed a brush and swiped it through Lily's sun-kissed locks before twisting up her hair into a bun at the back of her head and securing it with a few pins. Then she slid the *kapp* over the bun and pinned it in place, too, the strings hanging down over her shoulders.

"You look so grown up . . ." Bethany said quietly.

"I think I'm ready for *kapps* and aprons," Lily said primly.

"You'll have to convince Daet of that, not me," Bethany

replied. "Besides, *kapps* fall off if you run around too much, and aprons take some real work to get white again if you make them too dirty."

"I'd be quiet and clean," Lily said.

"Yah?" Bethany chuckled and Lily shrugged.

"Maybe not."

Bethany pulled the pins from the *kapp* and out of her sister's hair, letting her long, thick waves hang loose down her shoulders again.

"Don't grow up too fast," Bethany said. "You have no idea how many times you'll look back on these years and wish you could go back to when it was simple."

Back before she'd gotten pregnant, before she'd agreed to marry a man who would never quite love her enough, before she'd fallen for her fiancé's friend. Because Bethany had fallen for Isaiah, and while she was sad to be leaving her *mamm*, her *daet*, and her little sister, the thought of not seeing Isaiah for the better part of a year was aching in a strange, untouched place in her heart.

Lily headed back toward the window, and downstairs there was the clatter of pans. Mamm was making bread and she'd refused any help. When Mamm was stressed, she took it out on the dough, and Mamm had good reason to be stressed right now.

"Isaiah's here," Lily said.

"What?" Bethany went to the window and looked over her sister's shoulder. A buggy was just pulling up to the house, and while she couldn't see the driver at this vantage point, she did recognize the buggy.

"Isn't that him?" Lily asked. Isaiah got down from the buggy and headed for the side door.

"Yah, that's him. . . ." And seeing Isaiah wasn't going

to make this any easier. But she'd best go down and see what he needed. The way her heart sped up . . . that would take care of itself over the next few months. Her baby would come first—there was no competition there.

Bethany headed down the stairs just as Isaiah knocked, and Mamm looked up with a distracted smile.

"You'll get that?" Mamm asked.

"Yah."

Bethany went through the mudroom, and when she opened the door her heart gave a little squeeze at the sight of Isaiah standing there in the spitting rain. His hat was pulled down low over his forehead, and he cast her a rueful smile.

"Hi," he said quietly.

"Hi." She smiled, then glanced over her shoulder. She couldn't see her mother, but she could hear the thump of dough being flopped onto a countertop. "Are you here for my *daet* or—"

"For you." He licked his lips. "Can you talk?"

She nodded. "Let's go outside, though. Little ears and all that."

Bethany grabbed a shawl from a hook and held it over her head as they went back down the steps, the smell of earth and ozone swirling through the damp air. They headed across the grass toward the buggy shelter where Isaiah's horses were already standing out of the rain. She let her shawl drop when they got under the roof. The horses and the back of Isaiah's buggy blocked anyone's sight from the house, giving them some semblance of privacy.

Another flash of lightning lit up the sky, and then there

was a boom of thunder, this one much closer than the last, and the skies opened up in a downpour.

"I'm leaving Monday," Bethany said.

"Already?" Isaiah reached out and caught her hand, the gesture seeming to be a natural one between them now.

"I can't wait much longer," she confessed, running her free hand over her thickening waist, and his gaze dropped to her hand in his.

"Will you write to me?" he asked.

"I've been thinking about that," she said quietly. "If I do, I can't say anything about the baby. I don't dare put that into writing. So what would I tell you? About pies? About the weather?"

"I'd be happy to read about pies and the weather," he said, and he lifted his gaze to meet hers. "If that's all you could say, it would be something."

Would it be wise, though, to keep writing to him when she knew how she felt? Or would it only make their inevitable distance harder to bear later on?

"I came by to tell you that I handed that money over to the police this morning," Isaiah said.

"You did?" She smiled.

"I'm also broke," he said, then shrugged. "I know who I want to be, and I don't want any more lies or falsehoods pulling me down. That money isn't mine. If they decide I have any right to it, they can give it back."

"Is that what the police said?" she asked.

"Pretty much." He nodded. "I'll have to tell my *daet* what I did."

"You'll write to him?" she asked.

"I don't think I can put it off anymore," he said. "He'll probably be upset I handed it over, considering he was trying to help us in the only way he could from prison . . . But I'll do what everyone else is forced to do—I'll work for what I can get and live within my means."

"I'm glad you did that," she said, stepping closer as a whisk of rain-chilled wind wound around her. "It makes me feel better."

"About what?" he asked.

"About . . . everything we stand for," she said. "About the community, about our faith, about any of it mattering at all anymore. . . ."

Isaiah frowned slightly. "You're considering Micah's offer, I take it?"

"No!" That was what he thought? "He came by last night and gave me one last offer of taking me with him. I turned him down. We don't . . . love each other." She felt her cheeks heat. "I shouldn't even say that. I should keep up appearances and say he left me bereft and heartbroken."

"But you aren't," he said, a smile tickling his lips.

"No." She sighed. "I'm not. If it weren't for this baby, we'd have broken up and I'd have considered myself fortunate not to have married someone I didn't love enough. A baby changes things, but . . . not enough to have me go English with Micah."

"I'm going to miss you," he said, lifting his finger and running it down the side of her face.

"You should forget about me for a while," she said, sucking in a shaky breath. "When I get back you can tell Micah. But while I'm gone . . ."

"I'm not forgetting about you," he said gruffly.

"You have a life to put back together, Isaiah."

"Yah, I know that," he retorted. "And I'm supposed to just wish you well and forget everything between us?"

"Yah!" Tears misted Bethany's eyes. "That's what I'm going to try to do!"

Isaiah took a step back, as if he'd been slapped. "And you can do that?"

Could she? She'd certainly try. It was the only way to keep Micah at bay. It was the deal, wasn't it? They'd all promised that was how this would go, and in return she'd be able to raise her child with a somewhat tattered, but generally respectable reputation.

"You can pretend we aren't feeling this?" he demanded when she hadn't answered. "You're going to pretend this isn't love?"

Her heart stuttered to a stop as his flashing gaze locked onto hers.

As soon as the words came out, Isaiah knew he'd gone too far. Bethany was staring at him, looking mildly stunned, a tendril hanging limply down one side of her face. She was beautiful, even damp from the rain with a shawl pulled around her shoulders like it was some sort of shield. Her lips were parted, her brow furrowed, and he was tempted to crack that frozen look on her face by kissing her—but he wouldn't.

He'd never put his feelings for her into words before, but he knew that what he felt for Bethany he'd never felt for another woman. Ever.

Her cheeks pinked and she dropped her gaze. She didn't feel the same way, did she? The realization tumbled into his consciousness like a boulder. He was just another man in a lineup, falling in love with her with absolutely nothing to offer. No money, no security, no reputation, no good name . . . Just his bruised heart.

"Maybe this is one-sided—" Isaiah started, feeling heat rise in his neck. "Maybe for you, I'm just the lumbering idiot who was friends with Micah. But for me—" He licked his lips. "For me, you're the girl I pined for, the one who chose a better man, or so I thought. And I could have wished you both well, but when I got a chance to get to know you better, I realized that you were even more interesting, and kind, and sweet, and smart, than I'd imagined before. . . ." He looked away. "And I don't exactly have anything to offer . . . I know that. I'm not a complete fool. Forget I said it—"

The horses shuffled in their harnesses when a blast of wind brought a sheet of rain under the shelter, and Isaiah reached out, pulling Bethany farther toward the wall.

"You love me?" she whispered, and when he looked down at her, he found those dark eyes searching his face—for what, he wasn't sure.

"Yah . . ." he breathed. "I do."

When she hadn't moved away from him he bent down and kissed her lips lightly. Her eyes fluttered shut, and he covered her mouth with his and pulled her into his embrace. This was how he knew how to express his feelings—through his touch, through his kiss. She was the only one who'd ever stirred up this depth of feeling for him before, and as he kissed her, he felt a wave of longing that could have crumpled him where he stood.

A boom of thunder made the horses shift again uneasily. Isaiah released her, and she leaned her cheek against his shoulder, her breath warming his neck. Her voice was so low, he almost didn't catch it.

"Me too . . ."

His breath caught, and Isaiah leaned back so she'd be forced to look up at him. "Say that again?"

"I love you, too." Tears misted her eyes. "Although it doesn't matter, does it?"

"It matters," he said. "Of course it matters! If two people love each other—"

"I'm having Micah's baby!" she interrupted. "Your friendship is the only thing keeping Micah from exposing me and ruining any kind of reputation I might have! Besides, I'm not the kind of woman you need. You need someone who can give you some position in this community, someone who can be a preacher's wife—"

"I'm not preaching, am I?" he said irritably.

"Eventually you will. It's what you were born to," she said.

"Along that line of reasoning, I'll also end up turning to crime. I'm not the same man I was before this happened, Bethany."

"And I'm still not what you need!" she burst out. "And I can't be thinking about loving a man right now. . . . I have to prepare to be a mother! I'm going to have this baby and I don't know what I'm doing! I'm going to have to pretend this child isn't my own, and I'm going to have to let Mamm hold the baby in Service Sunday so it isn't too obvious that I'm the mother. I'm going to have to live the most painful lie possible, but at least I won't have to give my baby to a stranger and walk away! That's what I'm faced with, Isaiah! So can I have the luxury of falling in love? Can I think about kisses and rides in the moonlight and . . . any of it?"

"Maybe I can help you," he said.

"How?" Bethany demanded, looking around them as if the answer might be in the wooden wall of the stable or the misty downpour of rain.

Isaiah shook his head. "I don't know."

"There isn't anything you can do," she said. "I made my mistakes, and now I have to live with them. You can't rescue me, Isaiah."

"And loving me?" he asked miserably.

"Loving you just makes all of this harder," she said, her chin quivering. "Loving you *hurts*."

"It shouldn't," he whispered. "I'm not asking anything of you—"

"You keep saying that." She pulled away.

"What?" he asked helplessly. "What am I doing wrong?"

"Nothing!" she shot back. "You aren't doing anything wrong! But how do you expect this to work? What is your plan?"

"I don't have one!" he retorted. "But I love you!"

"Well, I need plans," she said, wiping a tear from her face. "And I need something solid that can give me a life with my child. That's what I *need*!"

"What if I married you?" he asked. "That would give you a life with your child. I wouldn't have much, but I could support you. I could love you. . . ."

"And Micah would come back and tell everyone that the baby is his," she said. "My family will be humiliated. My baby will be known as the illegitimate child of a man who went English, and people don't forget. You know that—you're living that now! Your father's shame is the cruelest, most undeserved punishment. But we'd do the very same thing to my child—load this baby down with the burden of his conception—and I'll be the mother who got pregnant before she was married. What a respectable family we'd make. . . ."

Her bitter words sank into his heart, deep enough to ache with the truth of them.

"Or . . ." she whispered. "We do it this way. We put our feelings for each other aside and move on. It's going to hurt, but it's possible to do. And this baby can grow up as an adopted child who is loved and forgiven for whatever an imagined, absent mother might have done . . . What is better for the baby?"

"You have to choose what's best," he whispered.

She nodded. "I already have."

And what about him? If he married the woman who was publicly known to be the one who had his best friend's baby . . . Yah, there would be gossip, and plenty of it. And his *kinner* would grow up with a shadow over them, too, with people who talked about them, who told and retold the story. His *kinner* would grow up with Bethany's child, and Micah would come to visit—the ever-present *Englisher* who would disrupt their lives . . .

If Isaiah wanted to start over, this wasn't the way to do it.

Just tell his heart that.

"I wish I'd asked you out first, all those years ago," he said helplessly.

"There is no changing history, Isaiah."

And there was no changing their community either, or the fallout from mistakes made in a moment.

The rain started to let up, and Bethany shook her head. "Let's not make this harder."

"I'm going to miss you," he said, and he reached out to catch her hand, but she slipped her fingers free and walked stoically out past the horses, past the buggy, and into the rain. Isaiah followed her as far as the edge of the shelter, watching her walk determinedly away from him, and his heart nearly cracked within his chest. He wanted to run after her, tell her she was wrong, that they could make this work, but he wouldn't do it.

He knew as well as she did that they had no hope of a proper Amish life together. And if she'd already given up an English life married to the father of her child, what made him think he could convince her to have a life of shame with him? They both needed the same thing—to be absorbed into a reputable family, where they could find some sort of balance again. Except neither of them were going to be able to be that Amish fresh start for the other.

Bethany's hair immediately was drenched as the rain pelted down and her *kapp* turned almost translucent, showing the twist of her hair beneath it. Bethany went up the steps to the house and paused at the door. She turned once, her gaze driving past the downpour and meeting his one last time, and then she pulled open the door and disappeared inside.

Isaiah hoisted himself up into the buggy and untied the reins.

Bethany knew what she needed, and he'd be true to his word and be the man he'd promised to be—honest, stalwart, and a good friend.

She'd never asked for his heart—only his help.

Chapter Nineteen

Sunday wasn't a service day, and Isaiah stayed at home with his uncle, aunt, cousins, and sister. Mel sat in the sitting room with the big family Bible open on his lap and read slowly and somberly as the family listened. Isaiah was the only one not sitting; he leaned against the wall, trying to keep his feelings hammered down deep enough that he wouldn't draw their attention.

Isaiah's mind wasn't on the Bible reading, though. It was on Bethany, and the fact that loving her couldn't ever be enough. He was thinking about his father, and the mess that they were trying to smooth over and fix if at all possible. An Amish life was supposed to be a simple one— pious, honest, hardworking . . . but there was nothing simple about the life Isaiah was trying to navigate.

Elizabeth sat on the couch next to Collette and Dawn. Seth perched on the arm of the couch, while Bart and Vernon sprawled on the floor. His aunt sat in the rocking chair across from Uncle Mel, who sat in the broad armchair, that heavy Bible balanced on his knees.

"'Agree with thine adversary quickly, whiles thou art in the way with him,'" Mel read slowly, his high German a little stilted. "'. . . lest at any time the adversary deliver thee to the judge, and the judge deliver thee to the officer, and thou be cast into prison. Verily I say unto thee, Thou shalt by no means come out thence, till thou hast paid the uttermost farthing . . .'"

The passage was from the book of Matthew, and Isaiah knew it well. The choice of scripture reading was ironic today, of course. Because Abe was in prison, and he wasn't getting out either, until he'd paid his time, and every last farthing to their name was going to repay the debt he owed to the victims. Was his uncle getting any bit of satisfaction out of the reading of this particular passage? he wondered.

Seth's gaze flickered up toward Isaiah where he stood, leaning against the wall, and Isaiah looked toward the window, avoiding his cousin's gaze.

His uncle's voice droned on, and Isaiah wondered how long it would be before he could get a place of his own. Elizabeth would be glad to get out of here—he knew that much. This wasn't their home—Mel wasn't their *daet*. This wasn't a long-term solution.

And yet he couldn't blame his unhappiness on his uncle. Isaiah straightened and eased toward the door. Mel's voice halted.

"Isaiah?" Mel said.

Isaiah didn't answer, and he headed out of the sitting room and down the hallway toward the stairs. Let them read the Bible, let them worship and think righteous thoughts. Isaiah's concerns were a little closer to earth today.

He headed up the stairs toward the bedroom he shared with his cousin. His heart had been through the wringer since yesterday, and he'd been holding off on writing to his *daet*, unsure that anything he had to say would even be helpful.

But now he no longer cared if he was being helpful or not. His *daet* wanted to hear from him, and Isaiah would give him an account of how he was doing after his father had torn away any hope he had of a future.

He found an envelope, a piece of paper, and a pen, and he sat down at the window, a book beneath the page to give him a lap desk of sorts, and started to write:

Dear Daet,

    I gave the money to the police. I'm telling you this straightaway because stolen money doesn't help me. I wanted to be like you—ever since I was a boy. I wanted to preach, to encourage our communities, and to have people look at me the same way they looked at you . . . because they respected you so much! I could see it in the way they talked to you—more politely than they talked to other people. Men would go to you for advice on their marriages, on their relationships with their extended families. You were the man I wanted to be when I grew up, Daet.

    And now, as unfair as it is, I'm inheriting your reputation in Bountiful. People do look at me the same way they'd look at you if you weren't in prison. They don't trust me because I'm your son. I'm supposed to forgive you and I can't.

    The farm is gone—I have no land. All our money is rightfully being distributed among the people you stole from, and I can't even get a place for Elizabeth and me to stay. We're with Mel—and it isn't easy.

And then there is Lovina—did Elizabeth tell you that she's run away? We worry about her constantly, but how do you find a legal adult who doesn't want to be found? She left a letter saying that she couldn't handle living with the shame of what you did anymore. So she's out there somewhere and I can't protect her!

Don't talk faith to me, Daet. Don't tell me about your faith, or what you hope will come of mine. I do still believe in Gott, and I do still believe in the Amish way of life, but that isn't because of you. It's because I still see what I want in life—men who can be counted on when times are hardest, women who pull together and make sure everyone is cared for. I see the kind of family I want—no one preaching or elevated, just honest people loving each other well.

So I've decided who I want to be, and I'm going to work toward that goal of being the kind of man who gives us Amish a good name after all. It hurts to stand by the right, even when it goes against everything I long for. But I'm doing it. I'm giving up the woman I love in order to stand by my word.

Don't ask me to forgive you. I'll manage it eventually, but not because you ask it of me. I'll forgive you because Gott requires it, and because that's what a good Amish man does.

For now, let me work through my pain. You work

*through yours. Maybe we'll both be better men at
the end of this.*

Isaiah

By the next day when Isaiah arrived at the book
bindery for his day of work, his heart didn't feel any
lighter, but he had made his peace with a few things. He'd
mailed off that letter to his father, for one, and when it
dropped into the cavernous depths of the mailbox, he didn't
feel any happier, but he did feel like it was the right step.

The work in the shop was slower that day, the main
orders having been completed. Isaiah's mind was still on
the letter he'd sent to his father. It wasn't going to be a
comfort to his father in prison, and he felt a pang of guilt
in that respect. But it would be honest, and maybe it was
time to sweep aside all the comforting religious blather
and get down to the heart of things.

The front door opened and the bell above tinkled more
cheerily than Isaiah felt. Nathaniel's back was to him as
he worked on some gold foil, and he raised his voice.

"Isaiah, would you get that?"

"Yah. Of course."

Isaiah recognized the *Englisher* couple—they'd come
into the shop before and bought a few little journals, and
this time they were carrying a lidded box, which they put
on the counter.

"Hello," Isaiah said. "How can I help you?"

"You do book binding, of course," the woman said.
"And we have a project . . . it's a bit of a personal one. My
grandmother kept journals all her life, and we recently
found a journal that my grandfather kept around the time

he met her. So we found the corresponding time in her journals, culminating in their wedding. And we wanted to bind both those journals together into a single volume."

"Can I see them?" Isaiah asked.

"They're right here." The woman opened the box, revealing two aged journals, both with cardboard covers. One was a little larger than the other, but when he opened it, he found that the writing area was actually similar.

"I believe we'd need to trim this one down to the same size—in fact, both would have to be trimmed," he said.

Nathaniel came up behind him and looked over his shoulder.

"Yah, both would need to be trimmed." Nathaniel reached over and picked up the smaller of the journals and flipped through it, sliding his hands along the binding and plucking at the threads with his thumbnail.

"It would need to start about halfway through," the woman said, taking back the journal. "Here, exactly. She was actually engaged to another man when she met my grandfather, and well . . . he's not really a part of the family story, now is he?"

The woman laughed at her own little joke, and Nathaniel nodded soberly, seemingly unmoved by the woman's humor.

"The journal would be pulled apart, then," Nathaniel clarified slowly. "Completely. We could return the pieces that aren't used, but there will be a few pages lost—just so you know. And it will cut right through the center of a folio, so that will make part of the binding weaker . . ."

Isaiah stood back, watching as Nathaniel worked through the details of rebinding two journals into one, and he picked up the second journal, flipping through the pages.

The handwriting was neat and small, and a few lines caught his eye:

> *She is extraordinary. She is worth anything I*
> *lose in marrying her. I hope my parents see what*
> *I see . . . to call her mine would be the greatest joy*
> *a man could know.*

Yah, that was a sentiment he understood well enough. He and the writer were generations and cultures apart, but there were some things that spanned all that—like love.

It took a few minutes for Nathaniel to go through all the details with the couple, and then he pulled out samples for binding, putting aside the ones that wouldn't work for their project, and showing them the options available.

As Isaiah watched the process—marking with little sticky papers the starting and ending points in each journal, the pages that would be included in the combined book, a thought began to germinate. There were other forces at work in the marriage between this woman's grandparents, but they were not binding for posterity a fully historical outline of all the people who came and went. . . . They were preserving a piece of the story—the part that mattered most.

"They only had two children," the woman's husband said, looking over at Isaiah. "And the youngest died in World War II, so that left only their daughter to carry on the family."

"And the man she almost married?" Isaiah asked with a small smile.

"History is written by the victors, isn't it?" the man said with a chuckle.

Isaiah smiled ruefully at that. Yah, perhaps history was written by the victors, but a legacy—that was written by Gott himself.

Maybe the problem that Isaiah was having was trying to be Amish instead of trying to be honest. Normally the two were the same, but in this situation, with Micah going English, with the pregnancy, and with Isaiah's promise to be the Amish man his father had failed to be . . . What if there was a solution here—one that took no shortcuts? What if he and Bethany were irrevocably, unapologetically honest . . . with the entire community?

Everyone would have an opinion, but a story could be lovingly bound for posterity, the extra, painful, unnecessary bits trimmed away.

Who was to say who he was? The community? Or Gott? Who was to say who they could be as a family?

When the *Englisher* couple left and Nathaniel gathered up the box with the two journals, Nathaniel's gaze landed on Isaiah and he paused.

"You look like you've had an epiphany," Nathaniel said.

"I might have," Isaiah replied. "This binding—what do you think of it? Is it false to cut out the other details?"

Nathaniel shrugged. "The making of a family, a marriage, is the closing of a circle. A good many things are pushed to the outside by necessity. That's what marriage is—two people turned toward each other. If that is the story that is bound for the family to remember, I can't think of a more beautiful analogy."

Isaiah swallowed, his heart beating hard. "I love her, Nathaniel."

The older man stood there, eyeing him expectantly. "My daughter, you mean."

"Yah . . . I know this must be a shock—"

"Not particularly," Nathaniel replied. "I have eyes, don't I? I've been your age before. I've fallen in love."

"If she agreed to marry me, would you give your blessing?" he asked.

Nathaniel looked up at the clock on the wall. "More pragmatically, the van is due to collect Bethany and Barbara in half an hour to bring them to the bus depot. If you have something to discuss with my daughter before she leaves, I'd get moving if I were you."

A grin spread over Isaiah's face. "I'll work late to make up the time."

Nathaniel paused, eyeing him skeptically for a moment, then he sighed. "We'll figure it out. Go."

And Isaiah tore off his apron and headed for the door. There was a way to make this work . . . if only Bethany would see it like he did. It would be a risk—it would be a scandal! But it would also be the most honest thing he'd ever done in his life.

Bethany closed a plastic zipper bag of cookies and put them into her bag. She was packing the food she and Mamm would have for the bus trip. They could eat at restaurants like everyone else on the way, but if they could save a little money, they should. An extended stay away from home would cost money—as would the delivery of the baby, and their family would have to pay for that out of pocket.

Bethany's chest felt constricted this morning. She'd spent much of the night crying—and she'd told herself it was because she'd miss her parents and Lily, but that wasn't all of it. She was crying because she already missed Isaiah. He'd quietly crept into her heart when she wasn't looking and she'd stupidly fallen in love with him.

She sucked in a breath, trying to stabilize herself, but Lily sat on a stool at the counter watching her pointedly.

"Are you going to miss me?" Bethany asked, attempting some cheer.

"For four days?" Lily asked. "I guess."

This wasn't a goodbye for the better part of a year—not that Lily knew of, at least. They were waiting on a taxi that would pick up all three of them, drop Lily off at the shop with Daet, and then carry on to drop off Mamm and Bethany at the bus depot.

"So, what will you do with yourself?" Bethany asked.

"I'll help Daet in the shop," Lily said, then her cheeks flushed.

"And?" Bethany prodded with a chuckle.

"Maybe I'll see my friends while I'm there."

"Any friends in particular?" Bethany asked, enjoying her little sister's uncomfortable squirming.

"Can I tell you something?" Lily asked, leaning forward.

"Yah, of course."

"Jeb Miller Junior told me that one day he's going to court me." Lily covered her mouth with her hands and beamed at Bethany.

Jeb Miller Junior was a distant relative of Johannes, Lovina's ex. Some family connections never seemed to die.

"Little Jeb . . ." Bethany frowned. "He's thirteen!"

"He likes me," Lily said.

"He's too old for you," Bethany said. "And you're too young for all that."

"It's a secret," Lily said, her smile fading. "And he's not courting me yet. He just said he would. One day."

Bethany turned back to packing the lunch, then shot her younger sister a glance.

"Can I give you a piece of advice, Lily?" Bethany asked quietly.

"Okay."

"Never do anything you wouldn't be proud to announce to Mamm and Daet at dinner," Bethany said. "It's a good rule of thumb. In fact, don't do anything that you don't want everyone in Bountiful discussing over their own dinners. If you always follow that rule, I won't have to hound you about Jeb Miller Junior or any other boy."

Lily shrugged. "I didn't do anything. . . ."

And Bethany knew that was true. Lily was a sweet girl and of course the boys would notice her. She was so full of personality and she was pretty in a wild sort of way. She wasn't really preaching at her sister—she was preaching at herself.

"I shouldn't have told you," Lily said. "I knew you ~~derstand.~~

~~thany~~ leaned down onto her elbows and ~~mile.~~ "As an Amish woman, your honesty ~~protection.~~ That starts now, you know.

You'll get a *kapp* and apron soon, and you'll start learning what's required of grown-up ladies."

"Do you think I'll get a *kapp* soon?" Lily asked hopefully.

"I was a little older than you when I got mine, but . . . yah. Soon you will."

Bethany straightened and headed to another cupboard to grab some napkins. When she came back to the counter Lily had a thoughtful look on her face.

"If you never do anything that you'd have to lie about, then you're safe, I think," Lily said.

"That's very true," Bethany said.

How long had it been since Bethany had been able to pray? Days? She used to pray constantly, lifting up her heart to Gott in happiness or even boredom. But she wasn't praying now, was she? Every time she tried, it felt hollow, and lonely.

Mamm came downstairs with her own small suitcase at her side. She put it down by the door and smiled over at Lily.

"The taxi will be here soon, dear girl," Mamm said, wrapping her arms around the girl. "I'm going to miss you!"

"It's only a few days," Lily said, leaning her head against Mamm's shoulder.

"I'm still going to miss you."

"Can I have a *kapp*?"

"What . . . now?" Mamm looked down at her. "You're not that old yet."

"Bethany said she was only a little older than me," Lily

pleaded. "I'm ready! I'll be clean and I'll be very ladylike. I will!"

"I am in no rush for you to grow up," Mamm said, then she looked down at Lily for a beat and sighed. "We'll discuss it when I get back."

Lily shrieked in delight, disproving any of her previous claims to being ladylike, and Mamm rolled her eyes, casting Bethany a smile.

"Are you ready, Beth?" Mamm asked.

Bethany looked around the kitchen, her heart heavy. This was a goodbye in more than one way. She was letting go of her ideals in this trip. She was embracing a lie and doing what she must to have a life after this baby was born.

She *deserved* a life. Micah would have one, and he'd been just as big a part of this pregnancy as she was. Didn't she deserve another chance to just be a normal woman in this community? It was a logical argument, but it fell flat in her own heart.

Bethany licked her lips. "What if I stayed, Mamm?"

"What?" Mamm said, then shook her head. "My aunt needs help. We're doing a good deed, here." Then she gave Bethany a warning look and pinched her lips shut.

"I'm serious," Bethany said quietly. "What if I stayed?"

Her mother marched to the door, hauled it open, and said brightly, "Lily, go out and wait for the taxi, will you?"

Lily went to the door and looked out. "It isn't here yet, Mamm."

"Out—" Mamm gave the girl's back a gentle shove, and Lily cast a quizzical look over her shoulder before she disappeared outside and Mamm slammed the door unceremoniously behind her.

"Stayed?" Mamm asked incredulously.

"I'm going to be a liar, Mamm. I'm never going to be able to go to Gott again, knowing my conscience isn't clear, because I'll be living in a perpetual lie!"

"You'd rather let all of Bountiful know?" Mamm asked, tears welling in her eyes. "You won't get married. People will talk! Your baby will grow up with a *mamm* who has a spoiled reputation, and you won't even be invited to quilting circles anymore. You'll be . . . on the outside. I've seen it happen, my girl. It's heartbreaking and it's a lifetime of punishment."

"Or I lie, and I have friends and community, and I stop praying."

"Why stop?" Mamm said. "You will always have Gott!"

"Because I can't pray *now*," Bethany whispered, her voice choking with emotion. "And I miss that. . . . I miss being able to stand outside on a dewy morning and pray. . . . I miss walking down the street and talking to Gott in my heart. I miss feeling Gott near me, and I feel like I've lost that. If I have to choose between talking to Gott and a quilting circle—I'd have to choose Gott!"

Bethany met her mother's gaze and felt tears welling. She blinked, but one escaped, and Bethany wiped it off her cheek. Mamm came closer and grabbed Bethany's hand in a strong grip.

"Your belly is going to start showing very soon," Mamm said. "And once that happens you will no longer have any choices left if you stay here. We have to be practical right now, and you will have plenty of time to sort through your feelings about this later. But if you wait, you won't be able to change your mind! Now, I have everyone expecting us to go help my aunt. Am I supposed to tell them that my elderly aunt suddenly doesn't need help?"

Another lie. Lie after lie to cover the original one.

"Go to Indiana," her mother said gently. "Have the baby, and if you choose to tell everyone the truth when you get back, I will support you."

"Will you?" Bethany asked tearily.

"I love you, Bethany," Mamm said. "You're my beautiful girl. I'd do anything for you."

"Will Daet support me if I tell the truth?" Bethany asked.

"No." Mamm shook her head. "He wants you to have a future! He wants you to have the life we had, with marriage and love and *kinner*. . . . He wants you to have the community that means so much to us. He wants only good things for you, Bethany. And you won't have many of those if you don't follow the plan!"

Bethany wanted to live an honest life, but did she want to give up everything that made life sweet? Did she want to become a walking warning to every other girl in the community? Did she want her child growing up in the shadow of her mistake?

She'd already messed up. Maybe this was simply part of the consequences of that mistake. . . .

The door opened and Lily stuck her head inside. "The taxi's here!"

"Just give me a minute," Bethany said to Mamm. "I'll be out soon. I promise."

Mamm nodded and picked up her suitcase and headed for the door. When Bethany was alone once more she rubbed her hands over her face. There was a hope chest upstairs engraved with the words *worth more than rubies*, and it had always represented her father's love to her. But Gott was her Father, in a deeper and broader way than her earthly *daet*. And to Gott, she was worth more than rubies, too.

"Gott, I don't know what to do . . ." she whispered, but her stomach sank at the lie. There was no use lying to Gott. He already knew the worst. "I do know what to do. I have to live honestly—I have to stop lying, and I have to take the next right step—one at a time. I just need the strength to do it, because it is going to break my parents' hearts."

She felt stronger somehow, and for the first time in a long time she felt the warmth of Gott's presence. If Gott would sustain her, she'd have to trust her own future and her baby's to His hands, because she couldn't control any of this if she followed her conscience.

Chapter Twenty

Isaiah's heart was lodged in his throat as he urged the horses to trot faster down the road. Gott willing, he wouldn't miss her, because if he had to wait nine months to see her again, it was going to be the most exquisite agony a man could go through.

But he'd wait if he had to. Or he'd get his own ticket and head to Indiana. . . .

It was no use thinking up his worst-case scenarios, and as the horses trotted toward the gravel drive that led to the Glicks' home, his heart sent up a prayer with every beat.

When their drive came into sight he couldn't help leaning forward, and he could see the yellow cab parked in the drive when he guided the buggy onto the Glicks' property. He wasn't too late after all. . . .

Barbara was handing suitcases to the cab driver, and Lily sat on the step tying her shoes. Bethany wasn't in sight, though. Barbara looked up when she heard the horses.

"Oh, hello, Isaiah," she called. "Did Nathaniel send you to pick up Lily?"

Isaiah guided the horses toward the stables where his buggy wouldn't be in the way of the cab, and as he passed

Barbara, he said, "No, I'm here to see Bethany. Is she around?"

He reined in the horses, and when he looked toward the house the door was just opening and Bethany came outside. She stood in the doorway looking wan and tired, but when her gaze landed on him, her cheeks suddenly flushed pink.

"We don't have much time—" Barbara said. "Where is your bag, Bethany?"

Bethany didn't answer her mother, but she came down the steps, moving around her sister and heading toward his buggy. Isaiah jumped down and had to stop himself from pulling her into his arms and kissing her right there in front of her mother, her sister, and the *Englisher* cab driver.

"What are you doing here?" she asked softly.

"I—" He smiled hesitantly. "I already missed you."

She smiled at that, and he noticed that her eyes were red-rimmed. She'd been crying recently.

"Are you okay?" he asked, tugging her farther away from the others.

"Not entirely," she said with a shaky smile. "I'm about to do something stupid."

"How stupid?" he asked with a frown.

"I'm going to tell people the truth about my pregnancy," she said, and she met his gaze with an uncertain look. "I'm going to be honest and I'm going to face it."

Isaiah blew out a breath. "Really?"

She nodded. "I can't live my life lying, Isaiah. I have to be honest—about my mistakes, about all of it. And I'm not going to let Micah dictate how I live either! I'm going to find a way. And I know it's going to be hard for my parents, and I know I'll probably never get married—"

He couldn't hold himself back any longer, and Isaiah dipped down his head and caught her lips with his. She was startled, and then her eyes fluttered shut and she leaned into his arms. When she pulled back Isaiah saw Barbara staring at him in dismay.

"What are you talking about, you'll never get married?" he said. "Marry me!"

Bethany stared at him. "What?"

"I'm serious!" he said. "I know I've been trying to sort things out, but I was working with your *daet* this morning and it all suddenly came together for me. It's all about the framing. Every family has a story, and there are some parts that get trimmed from the telling because it's not part of their family. Bethany, I know people will talk, but they'll talk anyway."

"Micah won't stay away, though," Bethany said. "He'd be . . . in our life. He'll be this child's father—"

"Yah, I know, that," Isaiah replied. "I promised him I'd be his friend—I'd take care of you if he was gone. And he's made his choice—and, more importantly, you made *yours*! Bethany, I want to take care of you. I want to be a *daet* to your baby, and I'll deal with Micah in the picture. I can handle that. Tell everyone the truth—all of it. I'll still marry you proudly. I'll be the *daet* your baby knows best—I'll be the man who shows this child just how loved you are."

"We'd be a scandal," she whispered.

"For a while." He smiled slowly. "Maybe for a very long while. But we'd also be a family, Bethany. And we'd be living our life together with integrity. I think Gott could bless that."

"You make this sound possible," she breathed.

"It is! If you love me like I love you?" he asked hopefully.

"You know I love you . . ." She smiled mistily. "More than anything . . . but are you sure you won't regret this? I don't think my heart could handle calling off another wedding."

She was afraid he'd change his mind? That wasn't even a possibility! He'd marry her tomorrow if the bishop would arrange it. A chance to be Bethany's husband wasn't something he'd toy with.

"Are you really afraid I'd back out on you?" he asked, his voice dropping. "I'm the choice you can count on. I'm the one who is going to go on loving you for every day I'm alive. I'm asking you to marry me, and I'm not going to change my mind about that. I know exactly how hard it will be, and I also think every risk is completely worth it, just to be yours. I'm willing to face scandal . . . if you are."

Bethany nodded.

"You'll marry me?" he whispered.

"Yah!"

He pulled her into his arms and kissed her again, and while he knew that everyone was staring, he didn't even care. She'd agreed to marry him! He lifted her off the ground and spun her in a circle. As he pulled back from the kiss, she laughed as her feet touched the ground again.

"Mamm?" she said, turning around to face her livid mother. "I'm not going to Indiana."

"No?" her mother asked faintly.

"I'm going to marry Isaiah."

Barbara threw her hands in the air and turned toward the driver. "Can I get those suitcases back, please? I don't think we're going to be taking our trip after all."

"What's happening?" Lily demanded. "Is Bethany getting married?"

"Are you okay with that?" Isaiah asked with a grin.

"I think you'll do nicely," Lily said with a nod.

Isaiah was getting a family—a big, sprawling, loving extended family—and while not many people knew the secret yet, he was also going to be a stepfather. He was choosing both Bethany and her baby, and he was going to love them with every ounce of strength in his body. This was the man he wanted to be—an adoring husband, an eager father, and Amish to the core.

Let Bountiful talk . . .

Epilogue

Isaiah and Bethany got married the first week of July in the bishop's backyard with only a few family members present to witness the event. Bethany had begun to show in her pregnancy, and she'd stopped trying to hide it, too. Word of exactly what had happened had whipped through Bountiful faster than a flu, and Bethany and Isaiah got their share of stares and whispers behind their backs, but the Glicks stood loyally behind their daughter and her new husband.

There were no invitations for Isaiah and Bethany. No one knew quite what to think. Then Tessa and Daniel invited them to dinner, followed by the bishop and his wife, but on Service Sundays people still stared.

For the start, the new couple stayed with Bethany's parents while Isaiah saved up to rent their first home. And by the time Bethany was large with child, Isaiah had a little house rented just outside the town of Bountiful—complete with a stable, some pasture, and a chicken coop.

Moses Levi Yoder was born by C-section in a local hospital in mid-February, and when Isaiah got Bethany back to their little house Elizabeth was already there, ready to lend a hand with housework and anything else to help Bethany through her recovery. For Elizabeth, it was a welcome change from living with her aunt and uncle.

That first evening in their home, Bethany was propped up in bed with the tiny Moses in her arms. She'd just finished feeding him, and the baby's eyes had drifted shut. Isaiah sank onto the edge of the bed, looking at that tiny face, the fingers, the tuft of brown hair . . . This wasn't his child—not biologically—but tell his heart that, because looking at the baby boy, he felt a wave of love so strong that it nearly shook him.

"Do you want to hold him, Isaiah?" Bethany asked.

"Yah . . ." Isaiah reached for the baby, and as he pulled him into his arms, Moses squirmed and whimpered until Isaiah had him tucked against his chest and properly covered up again. Outside the window, snow was coming down in lazy spirals.

"He looks like you," Isaiah said, his voice choked with emotion.

"Maybe our next child will look like you," Bethany said hopefully.

"No—" Isaiah turned and reached for her hand. "Don't do that, Bethany. He's beautiful, just like his mother. And I'm going to love him just as fiercely as I'll love all our *kinner*. I promise you that. Gott gave us a boy—and I've never been more grateful in my life. I've already made my peace with this."

Isaiah looked down at the baby again, and he ran a finger over the downy head.

"I'm your *daet*," he whispered. "And this is our home."

He'd have to write to Micah—and he wouldn't put that

off. He'd tell Micah all the details: the baby's name, his weight, his length, the very moment he was born . . . and the fact that this was very likely the most beautiful baby ever born.

Tomorrow would be a busy day. The grandparents from both sides—the Glicks and the Weibes—would come to see the baby, and there would be gifts and food to last them for the weeks to come.

When Isaiah looked over at Bethany again her head was resting on the pillow and her eyes had drifted shut. Her cheeks were pink and her hair was spread out over the white pillowcase in chestnut waves. She'd been through a lot in the last couple of days, and he knew that rest was vitally important for a new *mamm*.

Isaiah leaned over and bussed a kiss across her forehead, looking lovingly down at his wife.

The bedroom door was open, and he heard a shuffle in the doorway. He looked up to see his sister standing there with a dish towel over her shoulder, a wistful smile on her face.

"Do you want to hold him?" Isaiah whispered.

"Yah . . ." Elizabeth smiled mistily, and it took them a moment to transfer the baby and his blanket into her arms. "He's beautiful, Isaiah. I don't care how he came along—he's wonderful." Then she looked up at Isaiah. "The bishop just came by—"

"He's here?" Isaiah asked.

"No, no . . . He left about ten minutes ago, but he didn't want me to disturb you three." She angled her head out of the room, and Isaiah followed her into the hallway, closing the bedroom door softly behind him.

"He was delivering a message from Bridget Lantz. Bridget's daughter has to go to Indiana because her daughter is due to give birth to triplets in a couple of weeks. So Bridget will be on her own for a while, and she wanted to know if I could go help her in her daughter's absence."

"Oh . . ." Isaiah nodded. "That's really nice that she thought of you."

"I'm rather surprised she did, quite frankly," Elizabeth said. "And I told the bishop that I wasn't sure because I'm supposed to be helping Bethany right now, and with the C-section—"

"I'm sure her *mamm* won't mind coming over to help her out," Isaiah said. "And Barbara will probably have to wrestle Tessa to keep her away if she knows that Bethany needs a hand." He shot his sister a grin. "It's up to you, Elizabeth. Do you want to do it?"

A smile tickled the corners of Elizabeth's lips. "I do, actually. It would be a nice change of pace for a bit. You and Bethany wouldn't need me for long, and I really don't want to go back to Mel right away. . . . So, if you don't mind, I'd like to accept."

"I don't mind a bit," Isaiah said.

"Just as long as I can come back to visit this little guy," Elizabeth said, looking down at the sleeping Moses. "He's just so sweet. . . ."

The Yoders were still an infamous family—Isaiah suspected they would be for quite some time. His father was in prison still, and Lovina was out there living her English life, but Isaiah felt deep in his heart that Gott wasn't finished with any of them yet. They might have drama enough to fuel the community gossip for years, but Isaiah didn't care. They might be infamous, but this family was growing . . . and so was his heart.

"Here," Isaiah said, reaching for his son. "Let me hold him again."

He was already missing the little guy, he realized, looking down at that little squished face and the tiny, clenched fists. Isaiah wanted to hold him for a few more minutes, memorize his face and the new baby smell of him, before Isaiah did his duty and sat down to write that letter:

Dear Micah,

   The baby has arrived—and we all love him more than life. . . .

Connect with U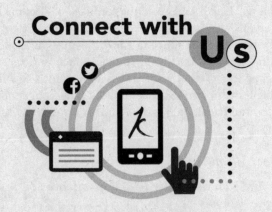s

Visit us online at
KensingtonBooks.com
to read more from your favorite authors, see books
by series, view reading group guides, and more.

 Join us on social media

for sneak peeks, chances to win books and prize packs,
and to share your thoughts with other readers.

facebook.com/kensingtonpublishing
twitter.com/kensingtonbooks

Tell us what you think!

To share your thoughts, submit a review,
or sign up for our eNewsletters, please visit:
KensingtonBooks.com/TellUs.